TOYLAND

THE LEGACY OF WALLACE NOEL

TONY BERTAUSKI

Copyright © 2022 by Tony Bertauski

All rights reserved.

No part of this book may be reproduced in any form or by any electronic or mechanical means, including information storage and retrieval systems, without written permission from the author, except for the use of brief quotations in a book review.

THE CLAUS UNIVERSE

The Claus Universe is a collection of standalone novels.
Jump in anywhere you like.

BERTAUSKI.COM/CLAUS

PANDO'S SONG

I*f you want to play, and stay out all day, I know the place we can do it.*

PROLOGUE

A funeral isn't a fun way to start. But this isn't your usual Christmas story.

Great-aunt Annie was a hundred and thirty-six years old. You read that right. That's not how long people live, but you heard what I said about this story.

We didn't call her Great-aunt Annie. We just called her Awnty Awnie because she wasn't great. I mean, she was great. Just didn't seem old. Eternally young. But, like I said, this story starts with a funeral.

By the way, no one ever called her Aunt Annie. It was Awnty Awnie, one word. *Awntyawnie*.

What I remember most about her, besides the infectious high-pitched laugh and her doughy hugs, was that she was a wonderful storyteller. Probably the best ever. That's where Piper gets it.

When Awnty Awnie started a yarn, everyone listened. Neighbors, pastors, little kids, dogs. You knew a story was coming when she patted her knees.

"There was this time..."

They were all Christmas stories about reindeer and snowmen,

elven and Santa Claus. Stories you never heard before. She believed them. And so did we.

Then one day forgot them.

Before she passed, she forgot our names. Even Pip. There was one story left, though. One she never told.

It began after the funeral.

Everyone was in their dress-ups. Pip wore what four-year-olds wear: frilly dress and sparkly red shoes that tapped the floor. Tin had just started driving a car, whatever age that is. She wore a dress, too. Not sparkly shoes, though.

Awnty Awnie's house was as old as she was. The paint was peeling and the foundation cracked by a giant oak tree. Awnty Awnie didn't care. Once upon a time her house looked like a greenhouse.

She loved nature.

Pip's mom was planning to auction off the house with all the stuff in it. Her collections were in piles, boxes and cabinets, under beds and behind couches. There were newspapers, magazines, yarn, hats, and stuffed animals everywhere.

She loved her stuffed animals, too.

Pip and I climbed the steep stairs to an old, stuffy attic, where she played with Awnty Awnie's stuffed toys. Pip would've told stories till it was time to go home if her mom didn't start crying.

We went back downstairs when Oscar called. He took care of paperwork for Pip's mom. Stepdad stuff. I don't know why stepparents are always the bad guys. Tin and Pip had different dads. Tin's dad wasn't a bad guy, just sort of not around. Pip's dad was bad-bad. Their mom left him before they got married. Then she met Oscar.

He was a keeper.

He came over to help, but still he couldn't understand why Pip's mom was crying. A walnut was just a walnut, not the thing she'd carried home from school when a bunch of girls teased her and Awnty Awnie chased them off with a broom.

"Just let the auctioneer have it all," she said.

She had a box full of memories to keep her crying for a month. Tin didn't want to let the memories go like that. She didn't have as many memories as her mom did. If she didn't keep going, Awnty Awnie's last story would've have been lost forever.

Tin found the footlocker.

It was metal and dented, with leather straps and rivets along the seams. It contained a heap of random stuff—wooden shoes from Holland, leather bolo ties, pan flute CDs—along with plastic binders of black-and-white photos. The pictures weren't that interesting, really, just trees and flowers, hills and buildings and things.

"I didn't know she travelled," Tin said.

"Neither did I," her mom added.

There was a lot they didn't know. Mom found an old leather-bound journal with newspaper clippings glued to the pages.

"Who's Wallace?" Pip said.

She read the journal's cover. Pip was only four, but she was precocious. She even knew what *precocious* meant.

"Look." Tin held up a photo.

It was grainy, but they could make out what looked like a very tall treehouse. Oscar was the one who called it a fire lookout used by foresters. The man in the photo didn't look like a forester.

He had a very round belly and a thick gray beard. He was wearing a white T-shirt with suspenders. But, oddly, he was wearing a floppy hat. The photo was black and white, but it didn't look like a Santa hat. It had a little bell and looked more like something an elf would wear.

He was hugging a giant stuffed panda bear. It stood nearly as tall as he did. Mom flipped the photo over. Awnty Awnie's handwriting was in blue ink. *Wallace and Pando, 1908.*

"That's a Noel Bear," Oscar said.

I knew what a Noel Bear was. Of course I did. I didn't know who Wallace Noel was.

All those stories that Awnty Awnie told had, in one way or another, come from a beat-up metal footlocker, a journal and a collection of black-and-white photos. But her last story is this one.

If you ask me, it's her best.

PART I

MISSOULA, Montana – Parker Stevenson, 51, a long-haul trucker, left Christmas Eve.

"It was about two minutes after midnight," Stevenson said. "The roads were empty. And all of a sudden, I see what looks like a man on the side of the road. Only he ain't hitchhiking. He's just walking on the snow."

Stevenson claims to have pulled over out of concern. The man didn't appear to be wearing a coat on a night when the temperature was well below zero. According to Stevenson, the man was about five feet tall with a full beard and vivid green eyes. He was wearing a T-shirt with suspenders. But that wasn't the strangest part.

"He was barefoot."

The man got in the truck but didn't appear to be cold, according to Stevenson. They rode for a couple of hours. At a truck stop outside Missoula, Montana, the man disappeared. There isn't much known about the stranger who, Stevenson reports, never told him his name.

"He was looking for someone who lost a hat."

Any information regarding someone who knows of someone matching this description, contact the local authorities.

1

Tin's head was cold.

The rest of her was toasty. Pip had crawled into her sleeping bag sometime in the night. Tin didn't mind the kicking so much. The body heat was welcome.

Monkeybrain's lanky arms were around Pip's neck. The purple monkey was bald where Pip rubbed the fur between her fingers. Tin had done the same thing when she was Pip's age and Monkeybrain slept with her. She'd traded in her toys for boys a long time ago, but Monkeybrain was staring at her like he remembered her.

It was chilly. Cobwebs waved near an odd-shaped heating vent. It was a triangle. The tepid air smelled like hot coils. It masked the smell of mouse droppings.

Tin pulled her phone out. Her lockscreen was her favorite pic, one she would use as a profile pic if she did social media. It was her in full gear with a lacrosse stick yoked across her shoulders. It wasn't so much the pic she adored as it was the memory it carried.

Her last game.

That depended on her knee. *Tin knee,* her teammates said. *Hard to be a thug with tin knees.* Tinsley wasn't a thug off the field. Only when she needed to be.

She slid out of the sleeping bag and put her feet in open boots. She found her stocking cap on the floor. It had slid down a metal slide that led to a round door. It looked like a bank vault from a bad movie.

This place is so weird.

The floor and ceiling slanted toward a rectangular window sliced into a short wall. Tin had to crawl on her hands and knees to peer through it. The glass was algae-crusted; the morning light was dull. Vines and branches grew against it like twisted fingers. She rubbed off a spot of grime.

The fire tower.

According to the photos in Awnty Awnie's locker, there used to be a field of wildflowers out there. Now it was trees. But the fire tower looked exactly the same. It stood alone, untouched, overlooking thousands of acres belonging to Awnty Awnie.

And now Mom.

It was nearly impossible to find. The will identified the place with coordinates. There was no address, no street signs. When they looked it up on Google Earth, there was nothing but trees.

Mom doubted the place was there anymore.

Monkeybrain peered out of the sleeping bag. Tin grabbed her backpack and slid down the slide, her boots thudding on the iron door, and turned the wheel. The hinges squealed.

There was a railing outside the bedroom. Below, a fire was roaring in a wide fireplace. The front room resembled a lobby in an M. C. Escher painting—all the strange angles and random walls, the jigsaw-puzzle windows and sloping floors.

The bedroom was somewhere between the first and second floor. So, floor one and a half. Nothing in this place seemed to line up. The stairs leading to the first floor went up then down then back up again before she climbed down an aluminum ladder.

A Victorian couch was in front of the fireplace. A fresh log was throwing red tracers against the black grate. Tin put her hands out.

"What is this place?" Corey was buried under a pile of blankets.

An upside-down staircase was attached to the far wall. It led to a door in the top corner of the room. If gravity ever reversed, someone could take the stairs. Otherwise, they were decoration.

"You sleep out here?" she asked.

"The rats kicked me out of my room."

There were framed photos on the wall. They were crooked and misplaced. Maybe that was on purpose, it was hard to tell. The sepia photos were from back in the day, similar to the ones Awnty Awnie had in her footlocker.

It was mostly shots of stuffed animals. They were on an elaborate wooden playground, lined up and posed to jump, some watching from swings. There was another one of an amphitheater between the trees, with dolls on stage and brown teddy bears in the crowd.

The one with Pando raised the hairs on her neck. It was the giant panda bear on a porch swing, all alone. Strands of Christmas lights, the old-fashioned kind with big bulbs, were hanging from the eave. A wooden sign was post above the door.

Toyland.

"Was your uncle Willie Wonka?" Corey said.

"He's not my uncle."

"Then why we here?"

The property had been bequeathed to Awnty Awnie almost fifty years ago. She'd never said anything about it. Mom found the papers in a lockbox at the bank. Maybe Awnty Awnie forgot.

But she had pictures.

It was her mom's idea to come here for Christmas. She and Oscar had checked the place out in August. They had a hard time finding it. It was country dark, the kind of dark where you couldn't see your hand without a light. They were going to camp in the trees when the house just popped out of the dark.

They camped in the backyard, and then she thought they could spend the holidays there. Pip thought it sounded fun. Corey was there because Oscar was married to their mom.

One big happy family.

"You could've stayed with your mom," Tin said.

"That's what I said, but this is Dad's Christmas. And your mom really wanted me to come because she hates me."

"You're not funny. Are you texting under there?"

"No, why? Are you getting service?"

He popped his head out. His glasses were crooked, but his hair was a perfect mullet. *Mullets never go out of style.* He was only fifteen. Tin didn't argue. A mullet fit him.

"I got service on the entry road."

"Oh, so, like, just walk through the snow a quarter mile and there's service?"

"Just read a book."

"*You* read a book."

There were hundreds of old hardbacks in the lobby. They were stacked at angles or leaning on sloping shelves. They looked published right about the time the printing press was invented.

She reached in her backpack and dug out the leather journal from Awnty Awnie's locker. She'd read all the stories. Twice. Pip read them, too, sort of. She mostly pretend-read.

"You'll like it," she said. "It's urban-legend stuff."

"About your uncle? I'll wait for the movie."

"He's not my uncle."

But he had a point. No one knew why Awnty Awnie had inherited this place. If they were just friends, she wouldn't own this place.

He went back to his phone and Tin crossed the crooked room, passing a ghostly couch hiding beneath a white sheet against a wall (another Victorian couch, she'd peeked) and through a doorway, down two steps then back up one giant step.

Her mom was on the far side of another giant room, this one with a walnut table long enough to host two football teams. Oscar was at a stove that wasn't much bigger than the one at their house; he had to stoop to avoid banging his head on dusty pots and pans. He was wearing a blue bandana and an apron that said *Man of the Kitchen*.

"It all still works." Mom was unloading boxes into a walk-in pantry. "The stove, the fridge. Amazing, right?"

Her pants were frozen around the cuffs. Snow was melting on her legs. Her nose and cheeks were rosy. It was the first time Tin had heard her humming in months.

She'd cut her hair after Awnty Awnie died, and stopped dying it. Now it was mostly gray and framed her face. She rarely seemed to blink, either. It was sort of a Zen laser beam whenever she was awake. But now there was softness on her cheeks.

"Want some light?" Tin reached for a string.

"Bulb's burned out. I got something for you and Corey though." She tossed an empty box into the dark end of the pantry. "Go find a tree; bring it into the lobby. Pip's nervous Santa won't know we're here. We can decorate it with popcorn and pine cones."

"Just go cut one down?"

"We own a million of them now." She smiled brightly. "There's a workshop somewhere on the west end. I'll draw you a map. I'm sure there's a saw in there. Find a scrawny tree, too. You know how Pip likes them."

Her little sister (technically half-sister, but Tin never thought of it that way) felt sorry for the ugly trees. They were the last ones on the lot that no one wanted. She liked to make them feel special, dress them up with ornaments.

"This is strange, coming out here for Christmas," Tin said.

Mom wiped her hands and Zen-stared. This was the thing she always did when she took life's inventory. *It goes so fast,* she would say.

"I never had a family tradition. My parents divorced when I was younger than Pip, and then your father and I didn't work out... and then Pip's father didn't work out... I think you see a pattern. I just, I don't know, just always wanted you to have something that made Christmas special, something you would remember. You know, like a big table filled with uncles and aunts and cousins passing turkey and opening presents."

She looked around and shrugged. At least there was a big table.

"When your aunt died, I just thought maybe it was a sign that we could start something new. You know, this place was supposed to be some sort of resort, I think. It was built, and then at the last second Wallace just closed the road, and no one saw him again."

She heard herself describing a very sad ending to a place where she wanted to start a family tradition. Tin wondered if she'd read the entire journal. The newspaper clippings sounded like urban legends, but there was one thread of truth holding them together.

Wallace wasn't normal.

And this place was proof. It was a twenty-thousand-square-foot architectural sculpture. *And if it was supposed to be a resort, why is the kitchen so small? And the table so big?*

"And there's heat." Mom smiled. "A Christmas miracle."

She hugged her. It wasn't the stiff *I-hug-because-I'm-your-mother* hug. It was warm and soft. She was good at that. She was short and stocky but soft at the same time. Sort of like Tin, only grayer. Pip was skinny like her dad, but if they ever found photos of Tin, Mom and Awnty Awnie at the same age, it would be proof of genetics.

Oscar slid an egg and bacon sandwich on the counter. Tin hugged him, too. He was bony and sharp at the elbows, not as soft as Mom or as strong. If those two ever arm-wrestled, Tin would bet on her mom. She ate while her mom unloaded the last box into the dark pantry. She was humming Christmas songs. So was Oscar. They were well on their way to a family tradition.

One like no other.

Mom's map led Tin and Corey down a wide, curving hallway that ended at a blank wall. They went down another hallway so narrow that they turned sideways to get through it. A steep ramp took them to a set of crooked double doors.

They opened with a squeal.

Paint chips fluttered from the edges. They turned on their phone lights. Cobwebs looked like silky blankets. The floor had a gray blanket of dust. Mouse turds were scattered.

"Your uncle was really into toys," Corey said.

If the photos next to the fireplace didn't tell the story, the workshop did. It was an enormous den of benches and shelves, with little drawers and pegboards holding old tools with wooden handles. There were jars of glass eyes, netted bags of plastic baby arms, furry pelts and other things.

"Look over there." She pointed at a cluttered corner.

"For what, a telegram machine?"

"An ax or a saw."

Tin wandered over to what looked like the main work space. There were old sketches pinned to the wall, the paper yellow and torn on the edges. The faded graphite lines showed a fat furry panda bear, the arms and legs out like DaVinci's *Vitruvian Man*. Small drawers were filled with spools of thread and tiny clothing; wooden figurines were mounted on sticks.

A dusty sheet was draped in the corner. It looked like there were arms beneath it. It was just a sewing machine. Storage boxes were under the bench, organized and tightly put into place. There was a small gap. She pointed the phone light.

Something was on the wall.

It was a rusty hinge mounted above a small flap of wood. There wasn't a draft coming through the seams, so it probably didn't lead outside. She slid the boxes in front of it.

Just in case it's a doggy door. Or something else.

"Think this will work?" Corey held up a tiny plastic ax.

Tin's heart was beating too hard to laugh. The sewing machine freaked her out. So did the door.

There were fine-toothed saws and rusty carving knives on the workbench but nothing that would cut down a tree. In the opposite corner of the room, wooden handles were poking out of a barrel like baseball bats. She swung the phone light, and shadows moved eerily.

"Look over there," she said.

"Nope. That's a nest of vipers."

"Where do you think we are?"

"We're in nature, Tin. Don't you get it? We're in the food chain now."

"We're in a workshop."

She went deeper into the room, where the shadows were darker, but the tools were bigger. The shelves were deep and the boxes filled with blocks of wood, bags of sand, stacks of spoked gears and other components.

"People think nature is all butterflies and hummingbirds," Corey continued, "but it's also cockroaches and rats and pit vipers."

There was a bundle of wood scraps about eye level. And there, slim and curved, was a long wooden handle. She stood on her toes. A few of the boards fell from her fingertips and revealed the rusty head of an ax.

A real one.

She strained on her toes and brushed the cold steel when the shelf gave way. The brackets broke from the wall, and an avalanche of heavy jagged stuff came crashing down in a dusty explosion. It barely missed her feet.

"Now you did it," Corey said. "You destroyed three dollars' worth of wood."

She brushed herself off. The ax was buried in the debris. She stepped carefully. It came free with a tug, and more items broke loose. Something was exposed. A sheet had been pulled off the corner. It was behind a box of mechanical parts. It wasn't very distinct, just an old metal corner, dented and scuffed.

Just like the one in Awnty Awnie's closet.

"Help me," she said.

"Yeah, no."

"There's no vipers, Corey."

He held her outstretched hand as she climbed over the wreckage. She had to dig it out. Corey stood back while she moved each piece, one by one, and took it out to the hallway. It looked more like a buried treasure than a box of doll heads. A padlock hung from the latch. They stared at it.

"He's dead, so..." Corey picked up the ax. "I don't think he'll mind."

"Still feels weird."

"This place is weird."

It only took one swing. She felt a little less guilty that it wasn't her idea, but technically this place and everything in it belonged to her mom. Not that her mom wanted them to be chopping locks off antiques.

Tin pried the lid open. It was old clothes—folded trousers with suspenders, thick wool sweaters and worn leather boots. They smelled surprisingly fresh, like clean snow.

"Well, this sucks." Corey dug through them. "No bullion."

"Bullion?"

"Yeah, you know, treasure. Maps. Gold. What are we going to do with old pants? We could say they're from the Civil War." He held a pair up. "Probably get a hundy on eBay."

He stacked piles on the floor until the footlocker was empty. They were definitely old and smelled more like a worn boot now that they were out. The last item was different than the rest.

A floppy green hat.

It was the kind you'd see someone wearing at the mall. It was old like the trousers and made of thick felty material with a fuzzy hem that was probably white at one time. A tiny bell rang on the end.

"That's not from the Civil War," Corey said.

"Pip will like it."

"Dibs on the rest."

She'd stop him from selling it, but not from taking it back to the lobby. He barely fit down the narrow hallway with all the stuff. The bell on the green hat rang in her back pocket. She liked the way it sounded. She assumed she'd found an elf hat, but, later that night, she would put it on and learn the truth.

The hat found her.

2

"Is that too heavy?" Tin asked.

"We've only passed a thousand crappy trees." Corey was dragging the ax. "I'm tired."

Pip would've loved any one of them. They were all sad. Tin just wanted to look around. They'd exited somewhere on the north side of the building and crossed a rotting deck she'd seen in one of the pictures, the one with Pando propped on a swing.

The strands of old-fashioned Christmas lights were hanging from the eave. Some of the bulbs were broken, the wires dangling. The porch swing was still there, but hanging from one chain.

No Pando.

But the sign was still there. Toyland was carved into a shingle of wood and hammered in place with twenty nails, half of them bent.

She followed what looked like a narrow path through the trees. Seemed strange, a path like that. Maybe it was from deer. A structure was at the end.

The amphitheater.

That was also in one of the photos, one with a group of dolls on stage and stuffed bears in the audience. A tree had collapsed part of it and bent the struts. Saplings had sprouted between the benches.

"How about this one?" Corey picked up a fallen limb. "It's pretty crappy."

The narrow trail forked. One path went deeper into the forest. The other wandered toward an opening and ended at the edge of a clearing. It was a perfect circle of frozen earth.

The fire tower was in the middle.

"Feel that?" She tapped her teeth.

There was humming in her chest, too, like she was holding a tuning fork, or a speaker bellowing a long baritone note.

"No," Corey said.

She shaded her eyes. A small cabin was at the top of the fire tower with a slanted roof and a single door. A giant lightning rod was attached to the roof's peak.

"Why isn't anything growing here?" she said.

"Nuclear waste, probably. That's probably a reactor up there. Which would explain why there's electricity in the fun house your uncle abandoned. Also would explain why it looks like a black hole is about to open up."

The atmosphere around the lightning rod was warped like heat on summer asphalt. Toyland, however, was covered with jigsaw-shaped solar panels, and three wind turbines were out front. No need for a nuclear reactor.

Tin watched her stepbrother plod over the frozen soil. There were no steps to climb to the top. Branches were stacked underneath it. Corey stared up.

"Man, I can feel it now." He put his hand on his chest. "Luke, I am your father. Hear that?"

There were shallow tracks where the branches had been dragged before winter froze the soil. They were small branches, mostly twigs, but they were sort of organized in a way that, at one time, formed a chimney.

"This is a bad idea." Her eyes were itching. *Are they vibrating?*

"Why?"

"I don't know, cancer?"

"You're paranoid."

"How are you afraid of imaginary vipers but not cancer?"

"Cancer don't have fangs, ding-dong."

It looked like there were steps that came all the way down at one time, but they were broken off about thirty feet above the ground. She shaded her eyes.

"Look."

The struts where the steps ended were twisted. Large chucks had been hacked like they'd been ripped off. A large tangle of steel was piled at the far edge of the circle. It was remnants of steps.

Corey kicked the branches. "And someone tried to burn it down."

Ashes puffed up. The pile had been lit on fire at one time. The metal footings were blackened. It was going to take more than a campfire to bring it down.

The steps had been removed and there wasn't a ladder. But the tower legs were scaffolding. *Why wouldn't they just climb that?*

"Ironic, right? Fire. Fire tower." He pointed down then up. "Get it?"

"Hilarious."

"Tell your face." He walked back to where he'd dropped the ax. A few minutes later, she heard chopping. He would leave a perfectly crappy tree for her to drag back, and not bother to take the ax with him.

Tin kicked at the branches.

Something was snagged in the center of it. She pulled the branches off one at a time. It was white and puffy, but it wasn't snow. It was cotton.

Like stuffing.

THE TREE WAS in an iron kettle.

Mom had propped it up with boards and nails. It leaned to the side. The twisted branches were heavily hung with ribbon-tied pine cones.

It looked like they were boiling it.

Pip danced around it and sang songs until Oscar brought the popcorn out. They began stringing it with needles and thread, eating half of it before getting the first one done. Mom and Pip had collected berries from the woods, bright red and hard. Tin held Pip up to put a paper star on top.

"Monkeybrain's in the bedroom," Pip said. "Can you go with me?"

"Let me help Mom first," Tin said.

Corey and Oscar had gone to stock up on firewood. Tin went out to the car with her mom. The sky was filled with stars. She craned her neck and blew icy clouds into the night. It was beautiful, but strange. The stars seemed to vibrate in waves, like a dial tuning them in and out of focus.

"Think Pip's having fun?" Mom asked.

"She could have fun anywhere. As long as Santa finds us."

"I have just the thing."

She handed Tin the stockings then dug a box of presents out of the trunk. They left some in the car to put out on Christmas morning.

"Did you see that?" Tin nodded at the amphitheater. The moon was catching the bent scaffolding.

"I saw it. Oscar and I were talking about what it would take to clean this place up. Can you imagine? People would love this experience. I mean, it's a strange building in the middle of nowhere. We bill it as an eclectic experience. I don't know why Wallace kept it all to himself."

The million-dollar question.

"There's something strange about the fire tower, Mom. It looks like someone tried to burn it down. And nothing grows around it."

Mom climbed out of the car. "We'll have to do something about that. Can't have Pip climbing it. You know how she is."

"Someone took care of that. They took the ladder down."

"Good." She piled one more box on Tin's load. "What's this?"

"Oh. A hat for Pip. I found it in the workshop."

Mom pulled it from Tin's pocket. The little bell rang. All at once, things in the forest moved.

"That was creepy." Her mom laughed and stuffed the hat back in her pocket. "Let's go inside."

They ducked under the dead strands of Christmas lights. The rectangular front door slid on cast-iron rails. The fireplace was throwing shadows across the lobby. The sad tree was flickering.

"Presents!" Pip yelled.

They piled them around the tree. Pip read the names and separated them into groups. Mom ignored the needle and thread and just ate the popcorn. Oscar pinned the stockings on the mantel. Corey played on his phone.

"I hear something!" Tin shushed everyone. "Listen, listen."

"I think it might be Santa," Mom whispered. "He's making a practice run."

"Shhhh." Pip stood absolutely still.

Tin wiggled her hips again and the little bell rang. She pulled the green hat out of her pocket. It was too big for her sister. The soft trim would have fallen over her nose. But it was so soft and warm that she would love it anyway. Tin danced around the tree, the little bell playing a jolly melody.

Pip raised her arms. "Where did you get it?"

"Santa left it." Tin started to put it on. "One of his elves must have—"

Snow.

Snow was everywhere.

Up to Tin's knees. Bitter wind spit against her arms and cheeks like pellets. She wasn't breathing. The cold shocked her breath. Tears spilled down her cheeks. There was no fireplace, no walls or ceiling. No tree.

"Mom?" Her voice sounded watery. "Pip?"

Her ears ached. The landscape blurred. Her skin hurt. She took a step and fell. The snow burned her hands. She crawled to her feet.

Something was out there.

It was hunched over and trundling toward her. She started for it too quickly, falling twice before getting close enough to see it was a man. He was bundled in furs and carried a large pack. He fell face-first and didn't move.

Tin dropped next to him.

Her chin was beginning to tremble. She tried to roll him over. It wasn't that he was too heavy or not cooperating. It was just he didn't budge, like he was solid ice. A frozen carving she couldn't move.

He groaned. Looked up.

His face was a beard of icicles, and the tip of his nose discolored. There were two moles above his right eyebrow, side by side. He'd been out there too long. Frostbite was going to leave a permanent mark if he didn't get help soon.

Where am I? *she thought.*

A little bell rang. The hat. She reached for it—

Pip was clapping.

The sad little tree was back. The fireplace and lobby, too. The staircase on the ceiling and the crooked pictures. Tin could feel her fingers, and her ears didn't hurt, and her eyes weren't watering. She was motionless, mouth open, hat in her hand. Pip grabbed it and Tin yanked it away.

"Tin?" Mom said. "Hey, what are you doing?"

"I... something's wrong with the, uh, the hat."

"You sure it's the hat?" Corey mumbled.

"Let me just... I'll be right back."

There was a bathroom down a hallway that tilted to the left. It was the size of a small closet with a sink and mirror. She threw the hat on the floor and splashed her face. There was no redness on her cheeks. Her hair was black, no flakes of snow or ice.

What was that?

She grabbed the bell to keep it from ringing. The hat had a warm, thick feel to it, an authentic feel that would actually keep her head warm. She put her hand inside it and felt around.

The little bell was ice cold.

She stuffed the hat in her back pocket so Pip wouldn't see it. She pulled her hair into a ponytail and tried to walk normal up the slanted hallway. Corey was at the fireplace.

"Where is everyone?" Tin said.

"Something rumbled and your mom thought there might be

something wrong with the boiler room. I don't really know what a boiler room is, but if it goes out, she said we're going home. Keep your fingers crossed."

"Home?"

"Like in the morning. Seriously, cross your fingers."

"No, I mean..." She swallowed. "When did it rumble?"

"Um, what?"

"When I was in the bathroom?"

"No, weirdo. When you were dancing with the hat. Did you pass out?"

She went up the short ladder and up and down the stairs and through the portal doorway to the bedroom. The cobwebs were waving across the vent.

The furnace was working just fine.

She tried not to pace so the floor wouldn't creak, but she couldn't stand still. It was the only way she could stay ahead of her thoughts. An avalanche was about to bury her.

"Okay," she whispered, "let's trace this. I went to get the presents, came back to the tree, danced with Pip, and put the hat on, and then I had a dream. That was it. A dream that lasted a second. A dream I could feel and hear and—"

"You need a doctor?" Corey peeked in the room.

Tin shoved him up the slide. He was a late-blooming fifteen-year-old she could push around. Puberty had only just arrived and one day he might be stronger than her. But not now. Count the adrenaline fueling her mood and he didn't stand a chance.

"Don't tell anyone." She pushed him on the bed. "What I'm about to say, don't tell Mom and never, ever tell Pip. You hear me?"

He looked scared. Their parents had only been married a year. That wasn't long enough to know what a stepsister was capable of doing. She began pacing again, all the way to where the room narrowed and then back to the slide. She told him the whole thing—the snow, the wind, the man with the icicle beard and frostbitten nose. The two moles above his right eyebrow, side by side.

"Put it on."

"What?"

"I just want to see what happens." She put the hat in his hand. "I'll yank it off as soon as you do. Just put it on."

He wasn't moving. She had been in the Arctic for what seemed like forever, but it was probably only fifteen minutes. But when she took the hat off, it was like no time had passed at all. Pip was still clapping and Mom was on the couch.

Not even a second.

"Seriously. Put it on."

It wasn't fair. But she didn't want to be the only one freaking out. She shoved it on his head, pulling it all the way down to his eyebrows. He grimaced and slapped at her. The little bell rang. He looked up from beneath the fuzzy trim.

"I feel stupid."

She jiggled the bell. "Maybe it was the tower. You were right, the radiation. I feel weird inside."

"I was there too, ding-dong. And radiation doesn't make you hallucinate when you put on an elf hat. Or maybe it does. Doesn't matter, it's just a hat."

She fell on the other bed. The adrenaline spike was waning. She was weak and tired. And something else.

"I'm starving," she said.

"That's what haunted hats do." He threw it at her. "They give you the munchies."

"Tin?" Pip opened the door. "You all right?"

Tin hid the hat. "I'm okay, Piper. I think I ate something funny, that's all."

"Can we sleep downstairs with Corey tonight?"

"Yeah. That's a good idea."

Tin forced herself to stand, careful not to wobble. She was drained. Pip climbed the slide and grabbed her hand, and they dragged their sleeping bags off the beds. Corey carried their pillows.

"Where's Monkeybrain?" Pip searched her sleeping bag.

"You sure you left him up here?" Tin asked.

"I'm sure."

"Well, go down with Corey and ask Mom. I'll be down in a second."

Pip took Corey's hand and they started down the slide. Corey let out a *weeeee* that lasted half a second. Tin shoved the hat in her pocket to make sure the bell didn't ring. She waited until they were halfway down the steps.

She'd seen a purple arm.

It was a little closet with a low doorframe. She had to duck to look inside. Monkeybrain had hands that would lock together. Pip would latch them around her neck and carry him like a momma holding her baby. And sometimes that hand would catch on things.

Like the closet doorframe.

"What are you doing in here?" Tin said.

Her legs turned a degree colder. There was a little door built into the baseboard, just like the one in the workshop. It had a hinge on top so it could swing open.

It definitely didn't lead outside.

She shoved her duffel bag against it. Whatever that was for, she wasn't letting it in or out. Or letting Pip sleep up there again. She clutched Monkeybrain against her chin as she slid to the door. Something else wasn't right.

He was warm.

3

Tin launched out of deep sleep to the crackle of embers and found herself on a musty couch. The hat was in her pocket. She'd gone to sleep wearing jeans and a sweatshirt.

"Another visit to the North Pole?" Corey was thumbing his iPad.

There were two other couches around the fireplace, with empty sleeping bags and dented pillows.

She flopped back on the couch and stared through dusty beams of midmorning sunlight. There was a door in the ceiling, like the one she'd seen under the workbench and in the closet. There was nothing leading up to it, no upside-down staircase or swinging rope. It was just a door in the middle of the ceiling.

And it seemed normal.

The scent of biscuits and gravy called from the kitchen. She found a cold batch waiting on the stove and ate three bowls. Mom was outside with Oscar and Pip. They were playing in the snow. Mom came into the kitchen with snow-dusted hair.

"Good morning," she said. "Feeling better?"

"I'm... fine. Why, is something wrong?"

"No." She stole a biscuit. "Not like you to sleep late. Hey, when you're ready, we're thinking about taking a hike this morning. There's a trail that goes into the woods. Corey's going, too. Aren't you, Corey?"

"Is the furnace all right?" Tin asked.

"Furnace?"

"Yeah, you know. Last night, there was a sound. Corey said you went to the boiler room or something."

"Oh, yeah. It's fine. Maybe it was the house settling. Go on, get a shower if you want. I'll clean up."

Corey was still camped on the couch. A new log was catching fire. He wasn't exactly warming up for a hike.

"Want to know about your uncle Wallace?" he said.

"No." She climbed the ladder one creaky rung at a time.

The bedroom vault was cracked open. She stopped and listened. She swore she'd closed it. *This is how paranoia starts. Simple things like snow become suspicious.*

She peeked inside. The duffel bag was exactly where she'd put it. The little creepy door hadn't been pushed open, and nothing was out of place. There was a bathroom down a narrow ledge with a tall railing. She showered until her bones were warm.

Corey's couch was empty when she came downstairs. She found everyone in the backyard.

"It's snowing!" Pip threw up her hands.

It was, in fact, snowing. It started almost exactly when she walked outside. A snowman was slumped at the bottom of the steps. He was half as tall as Pip and staring at the ground. Broken twigs were stuck in his middle section.

Mom gathered everyone and, with a backpack full of snacks, they started down the path. Pip held Mom's hand until they reached the amphitheater. Animal tracks dotted the stage, and a few of the benches had been cleared. Tin didn't want to feed paranoia by asking if they'd been out there while she was in the shower.

Maybe animals put on a play.

Corey came up behind her. The others had already taken the path that went into the forest. The fire tower was the other way. Even from that distance, the top looked like a boiling cauldron.

"Was that like that before?" Tin said.

"Probably about to blow." Corey lifted his phone and filmed several seconds.

"Don't get lost!" Mom called.

Their bright winter coats bobbed between the trees, and Pip skipped behind them. Oscar said the path was from deer and elk and other large animals. Tin preferred that answer to all the ones her paranoia was giving her.

"He was a Lithuanian immigrant," Corey said.

"What?"

He held his phone up. It was Wallace Noel's Wikipedia page.

"You getting service?" she said.

"I walked down the road this morning, caught a bar about a quarter mile out. Want to hear it?"

"No."

"He came over on a boat with his mom in 1851. He had a brother, too, but he got sick on the way and he, uh, well, he died. Wallace fought in the Civil War and then, uh..." He scrolled down the page. "Dude, people are really into your uncle."

"He's not my uncle."

"There's, like, whole conspiracy websites dedicated to him. Like rabbit hole city, you know? Listen to this. He and his mom went to Chicago after they immigrated. He went to school for a while, fought for the Union in the Civil War—there's a creepy picture of him—then he got back and spent the next couple of decades on ships until he finally joined an expedition to the North Pole in 1881.

"The trip got all sorts of attention, but then it supposedly shipwrecked, and no one was supposed to survive. Then a group of them found their way back, and he was one of them. Says here that he got separated from the group for days, and they thought he was a goner, but then he just showed up, still alive. Oh, man. He's your uncle for sure. Ugly as a camel."

Tin shoved him into a tree and snow fluttered down.

"So it gets weirder. He basically disappears from public, probably moved out here to build the Willie Wonka factory. Next thing you know, he introduces Noel toys to the world. *The World's Best Friends,* he said. And everybody loved it. Guy made millions and no one really knows why everyone loved them so much.

"And then all of a sudden he was, like—gone. Production stopped. One theory is that the toys had a marble in them that made them special. But when some of them fell out through, like, rips and stuff, they were choking hazards for little kids. That's where the saying comes from, don't lose your marbles."

"No, it doesn't."

"I'm just reading. Anyway, these other companies basically ripped him off and started making the exact same things—bears and pigs and every other animal on Noah's ark—but no one cared about them like Noel's because of the marbles, I guess."

"Let me see." He showed her a photo of the marble. It looked more like a metal ball bearing. "No, the picture of Wallace."

He flipped back a few pages. Tin snatched the phone. The photo was from their return from the expedition. His face was gaunt. Dark circles around icy blue eyes and sunken cheeks beneath protruding cheekbones. Two moles, side by side, above his eyebrow.

The nose was discolored.

There was scarring. It was disfigured like winter had taken a bite. The phone slipped from her glove and disappeared in the snow.

"It's him," she said.

"Uncle Wallace, yeah. I just said that."

"No, no, idiot. From last night, when I put the hat on. The-the... the dream," she whispered.

"Oh," he whispered back. "I didn't realize he had toys on the North Pole."

"What? No, the frostbite on the nose. The moles." She dotted her eyebrow. "That was him."

"Look, he's not the only one who came back with frostbite. Or has moles. And you were staring at photos on the walls before your *dream.*" He air-quoted. "I put the hat on and nothing happened to me. Your uncle Wallace was weird and so are you. And your mom's calling."

Tin lost sight of them.

The path went through rocky terrain that turned sharply. They were huffing before they were halfway there. Tin dug a granola bar out of her pocket. She was hungry again.

She couldn't remember if the black-and-white photo they found at Awnty Awnie's house—the one with him and Pando—showed his nose. It was too far away. And he was really fat with suspenders and a bushy beard, not emaciated or gaunt. Maybe he got the nose fixed. He had the money, not that plastic surgery was much of anything in the early 1900s.

Still.

Everyone was waiting where the trail ended. It teed and went in opposite directions. The paths curved in very smooth arcs, not wandering at all like wildlife trails. Oscar was looking through binoculars and pointing. Mom held them up for Pip. They didn't see the little patch of color half-buried in the snow not too far in front of them.

It was fuzzy.

"Want a look?" Mom asked.

Tin took the binoculars and looked at the elk grazing for lichen. Mom pulled out snacks, passed a bottle of water around, and decided to head back since they weren't sure where the paths went. Oscar was giving Pip a piggyback ride.

"You and Corey can keep going," Mom said.

Corey was already leading the way back.

"That's all right." Tin held up the binoculars. "I'm just going to look a bit more and catch up."

The fuzzy orange color was in the trees, as if someone went straight instead of turning down one of the paths. As soon as she stepped off the path, she felt a strange shiver. It was only for a moment, but it washed through her like a cold wave and left a wake of gooseflesh beneath her coat. She looked closely at what was buried beneath the snow.

A stuffed orangutan.

It was half-buried in the leaves and snow. He was matted and torn. He'd been out there awhile. And that wasn't all. There was a stuffed raccoon a few more steps away, in the same sad shape, and a stuffed pig.

The pig didn't look too bad.

The glassy eyes hadn't turned milky with age, and the fabric was still intact and somewhat clean. She picked her up—for some reason the pig felt like a *her* and not a *him*—and squeezed. There it was.

Don't lose your marbles.

THE PHOTO WAS GRAINY.

Tin zoomed on the face. Corey had downloaded it on his trip down the driveway. It was proof there was a man who looked like Wallace Noel. This photo was taken in 1932 by the owner of a diner who found the guy interesting, and made its way into urban legend.

Tin had read the leather-bound journal Awnty Awnie hid in her footlocker. It was full of clippings and sightings and theories about Wallace Noel. And this was before the internet.

Why did she never mention him?

This photo from the diner, however, didn't look exactly like the man she thought of as Wallace Noel, but he had a gray-peppered beard. The angle didn't reveal whether there were two moles above his eyebrow or not.

He called himself Mr. Doe.

"I don't know." Tin zoomed in till the photo was a blurry mix of grays. "Maybe."

"Maybe?" Corey said. "Who else would it be?"

"Anybody."

"He said his first name was Pan." He waited for her to get it. "Pan Doe?"

"It doesn't say he said his first name."

"What else would it be?"

He scrolled through the stories of witnesses who came out to Toyland to conduct business. They said that every stuffed animal that left the factory came out to Toyland before going to the stores. *An incredible waste of time and money,* a former employee said. *We couldn't talk him out of it.*

He'd be sitting on the porch with stuffed animals, or around a campfire or in the living room, always with toys, just like the photos that were mounted next to the fireplace. *He was lonely,* another employee stated. *They were his only friends.*

Eventually, he cut off all meetings with his company. Toys were delivered to the end of the driveway, but the driver wasn't allowed to get any closer. He unloaded the delivery and left it on the ground. When he got back, the delivery was gone and another one was waiting to be picked up and taken to the stores. No one asked questions.

As long as Noel toys were popular.

"And then one day, it disappeared," Corey read. "He was gone."

"It?"

"It, he, same thing. The deliveries started to pile up until someone went to check on him. The house was unlocked. No note, no nothing. It wasn't long after that the word about a man who called himself Pan Doe was seen on roadsides or hiking trails or farmers markets."

"Mr. Doe."

"Whatever."

She looked at the photo. "He's not supposed to have a nose, remember? Lost it to frostbite."

"How do you know he lost it? Maybe he got it fixed."

"In 1932?"

"Pan. Doe. He disappeared; the records are there. There are people all over Canada who met Pan Doe out there, said he was looking for someone or something. Some journalist wrote a whole piece about him in *Life* magazine."

"You mean started an urban legend."

"Facts are facts, Tin. Why are you arguing?"

"Just because it's written down doesn't make it fact. I mean, look, the lady at the diner said he had green eyes, right? But the guy I saw on the North Pole had blue eyes."

"You mean the guy you dreamed about on the North Pole."

"Whatever. Those pictures downstairs, blue eyes. Guy in the diner, green."

"Maybe he wore contacts."

"To change eye color?"

"He couldn't see or she was half blind, I don't know. This is, like, super obvious to me."

Tin shook her head. She wanted to agree with him. Those little details weren't adding up. Something was missing.

"Why don't you see?" he said.

"What?"

"Put the hat on like last night, go back to the North Pole, and ask the dude if he's Wallace or Pan Doe."

Stairs were creaking. Not even the ghost of Wallace Noel could sneak up on them in Toyland. A shadow fell through the cracked doorway of the bedroom, and a little face squeezed through it, purple and fuzzy.

"Will you tell me a story?" Pip said in Monkeybrain's gruff voice. "Please?"

"I'll be down in a minute, okay?"

"Who's that?" Monkeybrain nodded at the bed.

Tin was afraid Pip saw the hat. The piggy from the woods was propped on the pillow. Her arms were out and ready for a hug.

"That's Piggy," Tin said.

"I thought you escaped."

"What?"

Pip pushed through the door. "Popcorn is ready," Monkeybrain said. "I love popcorn. I'm going to—"

"Don't."

Tin said it too seriously. It was the way Pip was doing Monkeybrain's voice, the way his big eyes were staring at her that freaked her out just a little.

"Sorry, sorry." Tin ran to the door before Pip sulked off. "I didn't mean it. I just... what did you mean that she escaped?"

"You hurt his feelings."

Tin stroked Monkeybrain's fuzzy back and plumped out her lower lip. She remembered doing the Monkeybrain voice when she was little, too. It sounded a lot like Pip's version. *How did she know?*

"I'm sorry, Mr. Monkeybrain. I know you love popcorn. I was just... never mind. I'll be down to tell a story after I help Corey with something. Okay?"

"Does he have a girlfriend?" She turned Monkeybrain's head and barely moved her lips. Pip was better at it than Tin ever was.

"No," Corey said.

Tin put her finger to her lips and nodded. Pip giggled. She raced down the steps. Tin told her to slow down. There were no railings in some places, and there was a ladder at the end. Monkeybrain stared over her shoulder, hands latched around her neck.

"What was that all about?" he said.

"Did you hear what she said about the pig? *I thought you escaped?* I found this in the woods." She picked up the pig. "Weird, right?"

"Um, it was weird you said I had a girlfriend."

"That's what you got out of that?"

"You're the one who doesn't believe all these stories about Pan Doe and Uncle Wally and then you just make up something about Brenda being my girlfriend. So you tell me what's weird."

"I didn't say Brenda." She put Piggy in the corner and pulled the hat out from beneath the covers, careful to keep the bell from ringing. Pip seemed to have forgotten about it. Last thing Tin wanted to happen was her little sister warping her brain on the North Pole.

Dream or not.

"One more time?" She offered the hat. "Just to make sure I'm not crazy."

"You're crazy."

"Humor me." She dumped the hat into his hands. "I'll text Brenda for you, tell her you're a stud."

He held it by the bell then stared inside it, feeling the seams with his fingers, turning it inside out. With a shrug, he pulled it on his head. Immediately, his eyes went wide. Tin didn't know what to do. Time went so fast when she had done it. He folded his arms.

"Oompa-loompa, doom a dee do."

He threw the hat at her and started dancing more like a robot than an elf. Although, to be honest, she didn't know what an elf danced like. It wasn't that.

"Nothing happened?"

"No. Nothing."

She looked at the hat like a rabbit was hiding inside it. It was warmer than when she gave it to him. And he only had it on a few seconds.

"So you going to text Brenda?" he said.

She was rubbing the hat between her finger and thumb. Her scalp tingled. She wanted to put it on. *It wants me to.* That was a crazy thought. *It feels true.*

"I'm going to put this on," she said.

"Good for you."

"I want you to count off one second then take it off. Got it?"

"How about you count a second and take it off. It's not that hard."

"Say it. Say you'll take it off my head in one second."

"Really?" he said. "I'm getting hungry."

She took a deep breath. Her chest fluttered. It was the way her scalp tightened as she lifted it up; the way her belly twisted. Corey made a stupid face. It was just a hat.

"Hold out your hand," she said. "Like that, be ready."

She grabbed his arm and propped it next to her head. She felt better if he was right in front of her. He was the safety net. And if nothing happened, then she'd put the hat in Pip's stocking.

"As soon as—"

"It's on your head," he said. "Got it."

She took another breath. Downstairs, Pip and Mom began singing "Jingle Bells." Tin held her breath like she was diving into the deep end and did what she did the first time she stepped off the high dive.

Pip was singing, "Oh what fun it is—"

Mosquitoes.

They buzzed in her ears, hovering high-pitched in the muggy, humid air. Green was everywhere. The walls and ceiling were branches and tree trunks. Diffuse sunshine filtered through the forest canopy.

She was standing in a soft bed of ferns and matted foliage.

A loud cry of a small engine broke the melody of birdsong. It was followed by a series of cracks that grew progressively louder. There was an explosion. Branches crashed to the ground. A giant was coming.

"Timber!"

There was a rush of wind and a cascade of debris. She looked up from a bed of ferns. The sky peeked through a hole in the forest. A beam of sunlight fell like a spotlight.

She remained still.

Sweat stung her eyes. A red line had scratched her forearm. A stream of blood had reached her elbow. She reached for her head, where a little bell jingled.

Footsteps crunched through the leaves.

The smell of smoke preceded a shadow over a mossy log. An old leather boot stomped the rotten bark. She watched a stout man with suspenders nearly put his boot on her stomach. A cigar caught between his teeth, he stopped a few feet from where she lay and took the wide-brimmed hat off and wiped the sweat from his balding forehead.

There were two moles above his eyebrow.

A woman followed. She was much younger than him. He was weathered with gray in his beard. She was maybe twenty years younger or more, her complexion smooth beneath the shade of a wide-brimmed hat.

Awnty Awnie!

She wore a flannel shirt rolled up to her elbows and cargo pants tucked into boots. It was Wallace with the cigar, the icy blue eyes darting around the forest. He tugged the yellow ribbon on a scroll of stiff paper and unrolled it.

He muttered to Awnty Awnie around clouds of smoke. Even when Tin stood up, they didn't turn or address her. They only stared at the paper.

Off in the distance, an old structure was mounted above the canopies. It was square and roofed, perched on four legs of scaffolding. There were figures up there, pulling materials up with winches and ropes.

The fire tower.

Wallace surveyed the space around him, consulting the plan with Awnty Awnie. She offered advice, tracing her finger across the page—a fingernail that was unpainted and chewed down to the cuticle. Just like Awnty Awnie always did. The roar of a chainsaw called from the trees again, this time going to work on the fallen giant.

Tin moved around them, her eyes on Wallace's face. They didn't notice her. His beard was thick, dark brown with streaks of gray. His icy blue eyes were tucked beneath bushy eyebrows. The moles were unmistakable.

The nose was scarred.

The tip was bulbous and wide with raised bands of scar tissue. He grunted and sort of laughed at something Awnty Awnie said. She put her arms around his belly. He looked strong, not overweight.

Tin caught a glimpse of the paper. It was an architectural drawing.

He rolled it up and marched forward. She reached for it, but the paper was like sheets of concrete, not fluttering or wrinkling beneath her touch. His arm was immovable, the sleeve not giving when she brushed it. He ducked beneath branches, and Awnty Awnie was right behind him.

Tin was in their wake.

"In a one-horse open sleigh," Pip sang.

The walls and ceiling were back. The moldy smell. Corey had his hand out, fingers apart. Tin's legs were cold rubber. She fell on the bed. All her strength had drained like a plug had been pulled. She drew a tentative breath.

"Uuuuh, you all right?" he said.

"You were supposed to grab the hat."

"I didn't even say, like, one before it, uh, did that." He picked the hat up like a dirty diaper.

"Did what?"

"Just flew off. And your hair, it was like all electricity. I thought maybe you were goofing on me."

Her thoughts were a shaken snow globe. The smell of popcorn was in the room. She began salivating. *I'm starving.*

Oscar called to come downstairs. Corey responded he would be there in a minute. She almost drooled. His dad called again.

"What's going on down there?" she asked.

"The house, it, uh, did that thing again."

"What thing?"

"Like before." He shrugged, wide-eyed. "The noise."

The house had shuddered when she put the hat on, just like the first time. Her mom thought it might've been the boiler room. Corey ignored his dad while Tin stood up. There wasn't a cut on her arm.

Still shaky, she explained what had happened. The forest, the falling tree. Wallace.

"Awntie Awnie was with him."

"Your aunt? Like with him with him?"

"His nose was fixed."

She could argue that it didn't mean it was Wallace, but the moles. *It was him.* He looked healthy and those eyes were the same icy blue.

The fire tower was there.

It was probably always there. Wallace built the place next to it. There were workers up there doing something, adding onto it. Changing it.

"What did it say?" he said. "The plan? He was looking at plans, right?"

"It was Toyland."

She'd barely had time to glimpse it. She'd seen something on it that was interesting, but the memory was fading. She closed her eyes to concentrate. *What was it?*

"Tin?"

Pip climbed up the slide and crawled onto her lap. Monkeybrain was around her neck.

"Hey, Pied Piper. I'm coming. Corey will take you. I'll get my jammies on so we can sleep down there again, okay?"

Pip sucked her thumb and didn't move when Corey reached for her. Tin kissed her forehead.

"Race you," he said.

She bolted in a fit of giggles. Corey peeked back into the doorway.

"Told you," he said. "*Uncle* Wallace."

The stairs sounded like they were about to crash into pieces. Tin was tired and weak and couldn't understand what had happened. Or what any of this meant. Maybe he was her uncle and they had secretly married. That would explain why Awnty Awnie inherited the property.

Why did she ignore it?

She closed her eyes again and concentrated. She reimagined the whole thing, starting with when the tree fell and she watched him unroll the plan. She'd gotten up and looked. There were words all over it, but two of them stood out.

Toy Room.

4

Popcorn.

Crunchy, buttery popcorn danced in her dreams. It wasn't sugar plums or fanciful wishes or Christmas presents stacked to the ceiling. It was white puffy kernels of popcorn all in a line, marching one by one into her mouth, over her tongue and down into her stomach. And they were all dancing to a familiar song.

Where have I heard that song?

Tin opened her eyes and stared at the little door in the ceiling.

"Hungry?" Mom was folding sheets on the other couch.

"What time is it?"

"I was about to wake you up." She sort of smiled. "Can't sleep through our haunted vacation."

Tin rubbed her face. She could smell the popcorn on the sad little tree, strings of it sagging on the branches. The thought of it made her hungry.

"Where is everyone?" Tin said.

"Pip is outside. Corey is helping his father." She started rolling sleeping bags.

"Something wrong?"

"That sound last night has got me a little concerned, that's all."

"Was it the boiler room?"

"Maybe, I don't know. This whole place is a little strange, in case you haven't noticed. The way the solar panels and wind turbines work is a little over my head. And it's not really a boiler room. I don't know what it is. It's more complicated than anything Oscar and I have seen."

She took Tin's pillow. That was what she did when she was nervous. Fold stuff and put it away.

"I don't know, maybe I rushed us up here. It might not be safe, the power system, I mean. I've been thinking maybe we should go back before Christmas and send someone up to check things out."

Mom looked at her. She was checking Tin's mood, seeing how she felt about leaving.

"Anyway, you hungry?"

"Starving."

Her mom led the way to the kitchen. She was wearing three sweatshirts and a pair of gloves. Despite being heavyset, Mom was always on the cold-blooded side. Tin was barefoot with a T-shirt that was slightly damp. She'd been sweating all night.

Scrambled eggs were on a plate. Tin pulled up a stool and dug in. They were slightly cold and crispy on the edges. The cheese was stiff and gooey. Tin barely chewed.

"You feeling all right?" Her mom's hand was cold on her forehead. "You're a little warm."

"I'm good. Do you have any more?"

The cold air was making her hungry. This must be what bears felt like after hibernating. Tin found a tub of cold eggs in the refrigerator and didn't bother dumping them on her plate. She drowned them in ketchup.

"Slow down," her mom said.

Tin made an effort, counting to three before each bite. Her mom finally stopped staring. There was nothing left to fold, so she started wiping down the counters.

"How did Awnty Awnie know Wallace?" Tin asked.

"I don't know. She never said anything about him. She was always single. I don't even remember her dating."

She wrung the sponge in the sink.

"Then again," she continued, "I thought she hardly ever left her house."

"What do you mean?"

Her mom told her about those pictures in the footlocker while she washed the last of the dishes. Most of them were vintage 35mm slides that if you held them up to the light, you could make out the image. Mom had found a projector and went through them. They were from all over the world—remote mountaintops and desolate islands, crowded cities and foreign lands. Sunsets in lush valleys and sunrises on sandy beaches. Awnty Awnie was a world traveler before she was a homebody.

"I had no idea," her mom said.

"Were there photos of her?"

"Some, yeah. One of her walking on a beach." Her mom smiled. "Her bathing suit looked like a nightgown."

Someone had to take the picture. "Did she ever go to the North Pole?"

Her mom took the empty container from Tin. She had been licking the ketchup from the inside. She could eat another tub full if it were in front of her.

"The pictures were from all over the world, so maybe."

"Were there any photos in the snow?"

"Why are you so curious?"

"You inherited this place from a man you never heard of. Aren't you?"

The legal papers had been pored over months ago. Awnty Awnie was the rightful owner of ten thousand acres of undeveloped mountains in the middle of nowhere. It had been signed over to her by Wallace Noel with no explanations, and Awnty Awnie had never said a word about it. There was no one to ask, either. The how and why it happened seemed to be inconsequential.

"Did you know Wallace became an urban legend after his business closed?" Tin said.

"Who told you that?"

"There were all those stories in the leather journal. Didn't you read them?"

She chuckled. "Your aunt used to read a lot of gossip mags."

"Corey found some stuff on the internet."

Her mom dried the last plate and began unpacking a cardboard box. That was her standard reply to something ridiculous.

"Look what we found." Mom pulled a large package out of the box. It was a kit for an elaborate three-story gingerbread house that looked more like a mansion. "There are twenty of these in the back of the pantry. I guess Wallace liked gingerbread."

"Wallace has a Wikipedia page, did you know that?"

Mom sighed. She wanted to move on and get back to their haunted Christmas without focusing on the haunted part.

"Corey got reception down the driveway. There are tons of sightings of a man who calls himself Mr. Doe. Corey thinks his first name is Pan."

"Did it also talk about aliens and elves living in the North Pole?"

"*In* the North Pole? What do you mean *in*?"

"That's what Awnty Awnie used to say, but it doesn't matter. Websites like that go down deep rabbit holes. Better to stay aboveground where the sun is."

"Wallace travelled to the North Pole, did you know that?" Tin said. "He went on an expedition that was shipwrecked. Almost everyone died. You can look that up. That's not in a rabbit hole."

"Look, don't get wrapped up in Wallace Noel. He was an eccentric businessman. A lot of successful ones are. This place is old and spooky, I get it. But if you start looking for ghosts, you're going to see ghosts."

She kissed Tin's forehead.

"We're going to make gingerbread."

A door closed somewhere. Boots squeaked down a long hallway. Pip tracked bits of snow into the kitchen. Her cheeks were pink and her nose snotty. Monkeybrain was latched around her neck, with snow clinging to his fur.

"Mom, Mom, Mom, the snowman is gone. Corey knocked him down."

"Boots, please," Mom said.

Pip wiped her nose and began stripping off her winter gear. Her mom made her stand in the corner. Pip handed Monkeybrain to Tin and latched his arms over her head. Despite the wet snow clinging to his fur, he was warm.

"He-he took the sticks and the carrot," Pip continued, "and didn't leave anything. And Monkeybrain is nervous."

"We can make another one. Want to help with the gingerbread house?"

Pip leaped up and down with her socks dangling off her feet. Snowman forgotten. She climbed onto a stool and pulled the gingerbread house kit out of the box. Tin snuck a few errant crumbs to eat while she and Monkeybrain watched them unpack. Mom pulled a floppy red hat out of the box.

"Look at this."

She put it on Pip's head. Tin involuntarily flinched. The white furry trim fell over her sister's eyes. Pip pushed the hat back. A tag was attached to the seam. It was from the store.

There's no tag on the green hat.

"I don't see directions," Mom said. "Can you check another box?"

Tin went to the pantry and tugged the string. The lightbulb was burned out, so she lit up her phone. It was a deep pantry. The shelves were empty except for the boxes of food they'd brought with them. Something crunched underfoot.

"Ahhh," she cried. "Look."

It was pieces of gingerbread, hardened and crushed. The remnants of the body had been pulverized. The head was barely intact.

"He must've fallen out of the box," Mom said.

"Can we make him back?" Pip asked.

"Of course. And maybe we can make him a friend." Mom pulled

the Santa hat over Pip's eyes and turned to Tin. "Hey, where's that elf hat you found—"

"Ah!" Tin threw Monkeybrain across the kitchen.

He thudded on the refrigerator, lanky arms and legs swinging wildly into a heap. Pip jump off her stool and swept her purple companion off the floor, squeezing him tightly.

"Sorry, sorry. I didn't mean to..." Tin turned to her mom. "There was a spider on my neck and I just... I'm sorry, Pip. Is he all right?"

"It's all right," she whispered to him. "She said she's sorry."

Tin kept her distance. Monkeybrain's head fell over Pip's shoulder, big eyes fixed on her. It was a spider on her neck, that was what she kept telling herself. A bug or something.

His fingers didn't move.

Pip hooked his hands around her neck and went back to the counter, where she explained to her purple friend what gingerbread was and how he was going to like the icing. Mom whispered to Tin, "She's all right. Go on."

Tin, with her hand still on her neck, stopped in the doorway.

"Hey, Pip?" she said. "What did you mean when you said Monkeybrain was nervous?"

Pip was singing a song and making a gingerbread wall dance. It was familiar, but she couldn't remember the words.

"Piggy is gone," Pip said.

"Piggy?" Tin looked at her mom then remembered the pig she'd found in the woods. "The one in the bedroom?"

Pip shrugged. "That's what he said."

"Said what?"

She nibbled on a gingerbread wall and offered Monkeybrain a bite. Mom had to ask her to answer.

"He's nervous," she said, crumbs falling, "because Piggy might get lost."

❄

TIN WRAPPED a towel around her damp hair. Steam was wafting. The hot water heater worked just fine. Her pendant necklace stuck to her chest. It was oval and metal, a necklace Awnty Awnie always wore, and the one item Mom wanted Tin to have.

She grabbed a pair of jeans. The button pinched against her belly. The jeans were old with ripped knees. They used to be comfortable. She hurried back to the bedroom and pulled on sweatpants instead. A few minutes later, Corey came up.

She looked down at the lobby. A fire was roaring with empty couches. She quietly latched the door and climbed up the slide.

"Have you seen Piggy?" Tin looked under the beds for the tenth time. "I left her right there, remember?"

"Your sister probably has him, or her. How do you know it's a girl?"

"Do you know what she said? She said Monkeybrain was worried because she might get lost."

"Sounds legit." He flopped on the bed. "I wouldn't mind doing the same, as in getting lost from this place."

"Don't you get it?"

"Yeah. I heard you. Then I said, *I wouldn't mind—*"

"Do you remember where I found Piggy? In the woods."

"Is this a test?"

"It's weird, right? All the stuffed animals out in the woods and my sister saying Piggy might get lost *again*." She grabbed handfuls of his sweatshirt. "Right?"

"Yes." He nodded mechanically. "It is weird."

She shoved him down and stood in front of the empty closet. She rubbed her neck. She'd scrubbed with shampoo until it was raw. That sensation she'd felt when Monkeybrain was holding on to her still lingered. It wasn't delicate spider legs crawling up her back. She'd lied about that.

It was felty fingers.

"Did you see this?" She pointed in the closet.

"Is it a pig?"

"Just... look."

He slowly, reluctantly, peeked at the small door. He pushed it with a finger. The hinge squeaked.

"Maybe Uncle Wally had a wiener dog."

"There's one in the workshop, too."

"A wiener dog?"

"A door, idiot."

"I'm afraid to ask." He stood up. "What do you think they're for?"

She started to say it then stopped herself. Mouth open, her thoughts folded themselves into an unrecognizable origami that fluttered down to her stomach. He'd check out if she told him she thought Monkeybrain grabbed her. He already didn't believe her about the hat.

"Looook," Corey said slowly, "I don't want to say I'm the voice of reason here, but—"

"I don't know," she blurted. "I don't know what the doors are for. I just know I found stuffed animals in the woods and-and-and there's a weird little door in the closet and Piggy is gone and I don't know."

He looked a little panicked. She was breathing a little too fast and she was about to say maybe, you know, Piggy went through the door. Everyone was too calm about this place. But then everyone didn't put on an elf hat and transport to the North Pole.

What's happening to me?

When she looked up, he was wearing the floppy green hat with a kind grin. He put his hands out like it was nothing, just like before. There was no noise in the house, no visions.

"You think I'm lying," she said, "don't you."

"I mean—"

"Mom wants to go home, you know. Because of the noises."

"Yeah, they're a little, you know, not right. But compared to bedroom chutes and ladders, they're normal."

"Do you want to leave?"

"Haunted Toyland? I'm going to say yeah."

She snatched the hat off his head and fell on the bed. It was nothing like that Santa hat her mom found in the kitchen. This was just so authentic, so warm. A tingling sensation tugged inside her belly. Her legs were still a little jelly from putting it on the night before.

"Awnty Awnie was there," she muttered.

"Where?"

"When I put the hat on. And it wasn't a dream, Corey. I was there. I could feel the leaves and trees. I was scratched and bleeding. I wasn't able to move anything, you know. Like it was a memory or something I couldn't change. It happened and I went back to see it."

"But you touched the ground," he said. "You were scratched by a branch. So something's touching you. It doesn't make sense, you know that, right?"

She was shaking her head because he was right, it didn't make sense. But what did? Nothing about this house—the fire tower, the fact that there was heat and a refrigerator and lights—made any sense. *Least of all, an elf hat.*

"I think it's trying to tell me something," she said.

"Like it, uh, it's talking to you?"

"The visions. I think something happened here, and somehow this knows." The little bell rang. "It's showing me."

"Like a movie. Cool, cool, cool." He backed up. "I'm not going anywhere, no need to worry. Just maybe, you know, I'll take a walk down the road, catch a bar of reception, Google *psychotic breaks and elf hats.*" He deadpanned, "You got a problem, stepsis."

She shoved past him and walked down the slide. The iron door clanged behind her and echoed in the lobby. She was almost to the rope ladder.

"Where you going?" he said.

He was right, she had a problem. And it started with the hat. There had to be answers. She was going to start where they found it.

5

"You destroyed this place," Corey said.

The workshop doors were askew, but not in the normal *M. C. Escher meets Willie Wonka* askew. One door wouldn't budge. The other one took some effort.

The center table was buried. Tin had knocked down a shelf when they found the hat. The entire wall had fallen since then. Every tool, every box was turned over. Plastic doll parts, brassy screws and rusty bolts were scattered.

Their phones cut dusty beams. She stepped over shards of mason jars that once held miscellaneous fasteners. The schematic of Pando was still pinned above the workbench.

"Uh, Tin?"

Corey was pointing his light into the back corner. A rope ladder had unfurled against the wall. Tin added her beam and slowly made her way across the room.

It was more than a rope ladder. It had been engineered like steps supported by thick ropes, something that could be pulled into the wall. It reminded her of the steep stairwell at Awnty Awnie's house.

All these mystery doors have access. It's just figuring it out.

She tested the bottom step. The ropes creaked and swayed.

"You're going up?" he said.

She put all her weight on the second step. "Get closer and light my way."

He was still standing at the entrance. She pulled herself up a step at a time and held the ropes in case a tread snapped. There were fifteen of them, each made of rough-hewn cypress and each one more untrustworthy than the one below it.

She was near the top when the outline of a door as black as the wall was visible. It hadn't been behind the shelves. They just didn't see it the first time. *But the ladder wasn't here.* Her hands ached. It would be a long and dangerous fall onto a heap of pointy things.

"Closer."

She waited patiently. Each step Corey took required another chiding to take the next. Her grip was trembling by the time he was near the bottom step. Her heart thumped once as she reached for an inset T-shaped doorknob. The well-oiled latch clicked and the door swung inward.

"What is it?" Corey called.

It felt humid and smelled green. She pulled herself up. There was a floor just past the last wooden tread. Carefully, she put her weight forward and reached for her phone.

"There's another door." She waved the light.

It was a short tunnel maybe three steps long. The floor was as black as everything else. The dust had been disturbed. Something had come through there. No telling how long this had been closed up. Maybe those footsteps had been there for fifty years or more.

She tested each step and reached out for another T-shaped doorknob. Yellowish light knifed out as she threw it open. Scents of a forest flooded the short tunnel.

"Tell me it's gold," Corey shouted. "Is it gold?"

Tin's thoughts and words were stolen by the sight of it. She stepped through the second doorway and let the wonder wash over her, humid and alive. A massive tree was growing through the floor, its trunk gnarly and knotted, the branches stretching and brushing the algae-stained windowpanes of an arching greenhouse ceiling. Vines hung like ropey tendrils.

The vines dangled over cluttered shelves, stacks of boxes, and leaning towers of rubbish. Narrow aisles wandered between towering walls of junk.

She took a step and caught herself on what looked like a streetlight post. The aisle was slippery. Not wet or cold, but icy. She took two careful steps and looked like a tourist in a foreign land—the sepia sunlight, the fallen leaves, the endless array of stuff.

This was going back in time.

The tree and vines hadn't grown through a break in the floor. They were anchored in oversize planters, the walls splitting along the sides, roots spreading like anacondas.

There was tapping behind her. Corey was testing the black tunnel. But when he saw what she saw—the tree, the stuff—he forgot where he was going. And she forgot to tell him.

His first step went flying.

He grabbed her sweatshirt with one hand and a coat rack with the other. A clatter of metal pans and an old set of antlers rattled on the floor. A fur pelt smothered their faces. It tickled her cheeks, musty and old. Corey threw it off with a groan. They lay there staring at ribs of the yellow panes of greenhouse glass, a translucent roof that was shaped in a half hemisphere connected to the wall.

"Is that," he said, pointing, "what I think it is?"

She hadn't noticed the life-sized mobile hanging above them. There were nine of them, two by two, each pair in front of the other with legs outstretched. Their antlers arching out. But one of them was in front, a massive animal with a set of antlers that dwarfed the others. The only thing missing was the sleigh.

Ronin, she thought. *The one in front is Ronin.*

She didn't know how she knew his name. He wasn't a reindeer anyone sang about. But he was the one who led the sleigh, the one who protected the herd. *Did Awnty Awnie tell that story?*

"Did he, uh, did he stuff them?" Corey said.

"They're not real." She carefully rolled onto her side. "Careful."

They helped each other stand. She stood the coat rack up and hung the fur. She'd seen that fur before. The man who was wearing it was lost on the North Pole with frostbite on his nose.

"Wallace," she whispered.

She took baby steps to her right, holding onto solid objects where she could find them—a book rack made of walnut with hand-carved faces, a sculpture carved from white marble of an elf with oversized feet, an ornate cabinet with a slate inlay and a mirror that made her look distant and warped.

Her slippery route wound past a bookshelf against the wall. It reached all the way to the glass ceiling. A ladder was bolted to rails so it could be pushed side to side to access all the hand-sewn covers, hardback and faded. She pulled one off the shelf, signed by the author.

Charles Dickens.

Just past a bamboo bird cage (the door open) and a rack of feathered spears, the space opened up to a chemistry lab, complete with glass tubes and flasks and long-melted puddles of candle wax. This space was somewhat orderly, a hardbacked chair pushed in, all the test tubes in their racks.

A journal was left open.

It was squared to the edge of the counter, the pages thick and brittle. The handwriting was beautiful. She couldn't understand a thing, all of it symbols and equations—chemistry far beyond what she'd studied in high school—along with sketches that seemed more like fantasy daydreams.

The aisle continued through a maze of items—wooden skis, a wall of plaster masks, a collection of paper lamps—that led to the apex on the other side of the tree. The branches hung over an arching dais.

Someone was watching her.

She took wide steps up to the platform, thankfully not slippery, where a desk faced the glass wall. Once upon a time, she imagined, this was where Wallace sat with an unimpeded view.

Now it was Pando.

The famous life-sized panda bear was seated in a leather-padded chair. The arms and legs were thick and stiff. The fur was dense and in the familiar black and white patterns with two big green buttons for eyes. The chair was turned toward her like someone who was expecting her arrival, but it was only the button-eyed panda with a grin stitched beneath his shiny nose.

The desk was wider than usual and, unlike the laboratory, cluttered with useless things beneath fallen leaves and brittle twigs. Shelves were positioned next to it and loaded with office items. A rack of scrolls next to it. Several books were set upright, leaning as if some were missing.

A zebra was in the middle of the desk.

It was a normal-sized toy, one a child could wrap her arms around. The black and white striped legs were splayed outward, the fur dusted with pollen and debris. The head was bowing as if it was looking at the center of the desk. It had been there for some time.

Tin pushed the chair to the side. Pando fell forward. He was warm from the sun. She pushed him upright. He was heavy and firmly packed. She reached for one of the slender leather-bound books.

It was a journal.

The cover was soft and scratched where it had been continuously handled. The font was recessed and gilded with gold letters. She smelled its oldness. Her chest fluttered with anticipation.

Just like Awnty Awnie's journal.

Awnty Awnie had filled her book with newspaper clippings. Tin turned a page in hopes of finding explanations. Perhaps there were such musings at one time. But no longer.

The pages had been ripped out.

Threads hung from the binding. The inside of the cover was dated. It was about the time the urban legends began. Only the corner of a page remained. It clung to the bottom of the binding, a triangle of hope in black ink.

... a way out, it read.

"Tin," Corey called, "you've got to see this."

The route to the other side of the room was circuitous and slow. Twice she almost went down. He was staring at the brick wall. There were no shelves or books like she'd seen on the other side.

It was photographs.

They were black and white, framed and squared on the wall. They were scenic shots of jungles and mountains, rivers and volcanoes, oceans, snow, deserts and wetlands. All the things her mom had described in the slides she'd found in Awnty Awnie's footlocker.

Corey was staring at one.

The woman was wearing a flannel shirt with the sleeves rolled up. The man wore suspenders, with a wide-brimmed hat shading his face and a cigar between his teeth.

"It's them..." She shook her finger at it. "I was there."

"They looked like that?"

Chills clamped down like a cold iron vise. Her scalp was shrink-wrapped. She grabbed onto an armoire. That was how they were dressed in the dream, when the tree fell, when they looked at the plans.

"Exactly."

There were progressive shots of the construction of Toyland—the skeletal scaffolding, the walls and roof, and windows. The fire tower stood in the background. Toyland was finished in the last photo, with someone in it.

It was Wallace.

He was wearing a white T-shirt with suspenders and a generous belly. Awnty Awnie was leaning on him. They were smiling.

"Notice anything missing?" Corey said.

She looked back down the line. "No toys."

He was right. There were toys in every photo in the lobby—at play, swinging, posing.

"Is that what I think it is?" Corey said.

Wallace and Awnty Awnie were shoulder to shoulder, checkered shade falling through his mesh hat. One beefy hand was over her shoulder. His other was behind his back. There was nothing unusual about it. The way they were leaning forward looked natural. Corey noticed the roll of paper peeking out from behind his sleeve.

He's holding the plans.

Tin looked around the room. She'd seen a thousand items since entering, and she'd only been down one of the aisles.

"It's here."

Tin traced her steps back to the entrance, fingers crawling over animal skulls and dusty oil paintings, tipping over tripods and wicker chairs and brittle wreaths. Corey followed like an eighty-year-old man afraid of snapping a hip. She was never much of a skater, but here she glided down the aisles, holding large objects along the way.

She shoved toward the tree and bounced her way toward the front of the room, items rattling an obstacle course for Corey to step over and pick up. She took the steps up to the desk. *The rack of scrolls.* Most were yellow with age, some blueprinted. She reached for one in the center.

The yellow ribbon.

She threw it on the desk. The scroll was tightly wound and took some effort to lay flat. The smell of old paper crept over her.

"This is it," she muttered.

Corey shuffled around the bend and stepped onto the non-slick treads. "Thank you," he panted. "Who puts ice on a floor—hey, is that Pando?"

The plan crackled. She was afraid it would explode into dust. It freshened the memory of when she was in the forest. The lines were sharper then, and the plan was cleaner. Now there were hand-scrawled notes and arrows and question marks, areas on the house circled, and interconnecting lines. Most of it was illegible, but she read the one label she remembered. It was in big block letters in the lobby. Only it didn't say lobby.

Toy Room.

"Look." She dropped her finger on the arc-shaped room. It was penciled in. "This is where we are right now."

"Looks like it wasn't part of the original plan."

He was right. The lines were sketchy. It didn't go with the rest of the architecture, either. It looked more like a loft thrown against the building.

"What's up with the walls?"

He traced lines throughout the building. They were double lines with a gap between them. But not all the walls were like that. She'd heard Mom talk about load-bearing walls when they were remodeling. Tin didn't know what that meant; she just assumed load-bearing meant thicker. These double-lined walls were something else. They traversed Toyland.

"What do you think this is?"

He slid his finger to the outside of the plan and tapped a circle that went around the entire building. She couldn't remember if it was there in the forest. It wasn't exactly centered on the plan, either.

"Property line?" she said.

"That's not ten thousand acres."

They weren't seeing something. She felt her back pocket. The fabric was warm again. When she had put the hat on, she didn't just see things. She went there. The bell rang when she pulled the hat out of her pocket.

Pando tipped over.

"Ho." Corey jumped back. "I almost had a heart attack."

The panda bear crumpled forward. It was wedged between the ornate armrests, the green button eyes staring at the floor. It startled Tin, too. She pushed the big bear upright. The fur was soft. It didn't look anything like the zebra, no leaves or debris or spiderwebs.

"What happened here?" she mused.

"Are you asking the bear?"

The answers were right in front of them. They just couldn't see them. There were too many pieces from too long ago. *If only Awnty Awnie were here to ask.*

"Put it on," Corey said.

"Huh?"

"The hat. Put it on."

The hat had been telling her what happened. Was that a good thing? Mom wanted a normal Christmas. This wasn't it so far. Maybe it would have been normal if she never found the hat. But they did find it, she did put it on, and now they were in a secret room with a map.

"I can't," she said. "The noise."

"Noise?"

"Both times I put it on, there was a noise. My mom said we were going home if it happened again."

"Put it on. Now."

She smacked his hands. "We need to find out what happened."

"Why? I thought we were here to open presents and then go home, not solve urban legends." He slapped the hat's bell. "Put it on and get this over with."

"That's why you want me to put it on, so we can go home?"

"Hey, you get what you want; I get what I want. We're all winners."

Tin studied the hat. The answers were in her hand. There had to be a way of getting to them without scaring Mom. She went down the steps and somewhat gracefully slid down the aisle. She was going to get the answers.

Just not here.

PART II

CALGARY, Alberta, Canada – Patricia Shephard, 37, owner of Patty's Diner, reported an incident that occurred the morning of Christmas Eve.

"He really, really liked fish," Shephard said. "Ate everything I had in storage."

The stranger, who introduced himself as Mr. Doe, arrived on foot when Shephard opened in the morning. She was a little concerned at first, given his disheveled appearance. Given the long and bushy beard and the fact that he wasn't wearing a coat would give anyone concern. But he looked hungry.

"He wasn't skinny," Shephard said. "He had these wild green eyes that I couldn't say no to."

They spent an hour in a conversation about Christmas. Mr. Doe appeared to be quite knowledgeable about the history and mythos surrounding the holiday and insisted he knew it firsthand.

She grew concerned for his mental health when he insisted Santa Claus lived with elven on the North Pole. When asked why no one has ever seen them, he said they lived inside the ice and had technology that kept them invisible.

Shephard called the authorities to check on his safety when he left on foot. He left Shepard with a Christmas present before suddenly leaving. "He fixed the coffee machine," Shephard said. "So he knew something."

Any information regarding someone who knows of someone matching this description, contact the local authorities.

6

Tin and Corey were in the kitchen, coats on. Mom's cheeks were smudged with flour. She licked icing off her thumb.

"You two all right?"

"Um." Corey pointed. "Is that…"

"Oh." Mom laughed. "Yeah, we were just going to make a gingerbread house, but there were more boxes in the pantry. We just couldn't stop. Like it?"

They didn't know what to say. It was like the world champion of gingerbread houses—three stories tall and spread across the long dinner table. Pip was on a stool, icing shutters on a wall. Monkeybrain hung on her back and looked over her left shoulder.

"Your dad needs help," Mom said to Corey. "He's out back."

Tin studied all sides of the gingerbread monstrosity. It had odd angles that went in several directions with blackened squares on parts of the roof.

"It's Toyland," Tin said.

Mom pasted a wall in place. "What?"

"Toyland. You guys just built a model of this building, Mom."

She stepped back and tipped her head. It hadn't occurred to her. "It does sort of look like it."

"Sort of?"

"Come on, it's not hard. Just glue a bunch of weird angles and it looks like it," Mom said. "Where have you been?"

"We thought, um, we would hike down the driveway and pick up a bar of reception, check email, you know."

"Oh, don't do that. We're camping, hon."

"I promised Corey I'd text someone for him. It's just a short hike, Mom."

"All right. Want to help while you wait for him to come back?"

Pip was singing to herself, tongue between her teeth with one eye closed. The Santa hat kept sliding over her eyes. Tin peered into the open gingerbread rooms where the floors were checkered with colorful squares of candy.

"You're not supposed to be up there," Pip said.

"Where?"

Pip just shrugged. Monkeybrain's head nodded on her left shoulder. She was hyper-focused on getting a section of the roof just right. The gingerbread man was leaning against the front door. His body was more icing than gingerbread. It looked like Pip had mixed icing with shattered crumbs to mold him back together. The head was pasted on top, the eyes round, the mouth a flat line. Tin reached for him.

"Put him down!" Pip shouted.

"Pip," Mom said. "No, ma'am."

"Gingerman didn't say she could pick him up."

"Tin's just looking, hon. You need to apologize."

"It's all right," Tin said. "I'm still sorry for throwing Monkeybrain. So we're even."

Tin put her arm around her little sister. Pip put the gingerbread man in a large room where the roof was off. Candy canes were used as posts on the front porch, which meant the room was the lobby. She had used red gumdrops for the fireplace.

"Cool name," Tin said. "Gingerman."

"He said he's OG."

"Original gangster?" Tin laughed.

"Original gingerbread," she snapped.

"Watch your tone, young lady." Mom shook her head. "Someone might need a nap."

Pip didn't look tired. She was focused on another panel of roofing, tongue out and eye closed. Monkeybrain was staring over her right shoulder.

"Imagination is working overtime," Mom said, then whispered, "Just do what she says."

Pip stood on the stool. Tin held her while she leaned over to slide a wall in place. Pip hummed that familiar song as she glued the seams. Monkeybrain was pressed between them. Tin tried not to look him in the eye.

"Got to pee." Pip climbed off the stool.

Tin stood back while Mom prepared more gingerbread. They'd been at it all day.

"Do you realize how amazing this is?" Tin said.

"She became obsessed, our creative little monster. You should've heard her earlier, giving me instructions on how to put this section together then that one."

"How *is* she doing it?"

She stood back and shrugged. "I don't want to stop her. She's been making up songs and telling stories about Gingerman and Gingerann, where they were going to live happily ever after."

"Gingerann?"

"His girlfriend, I guess. Pip said she doesn't live here anymore."

Gingerman looked like he'd been run over by Santa's reindeer a dozen times. Tin put him back in the lobby before Pip caught her. Mom moved him against one of the walls.

"She's particular about where he goes," Mom said.

She started wiping the table. Flour dusted the floors, and globs of icing needed to be scraped off. There were still more boxes of gingerbread in the pantry, Mom told her.

Pip skipped into the kitchen and counted her steps in singsong cadence then climbed on a stool to finish the wall. Monkeybrain was still looped around her neck.

"If you want to play, and stay out all day, I know the place we can do it..." And then she hummed, bobbing her head. *"La-la-la-lal-lahlala."*

Tin had heard that song before. Those were the words.

"She's in a flow state," Mom whispered. "Be back before it gets dark, all right? We're going to eat dinner in the front room and tell Christmas stories. You have to make up your own story and tell it in front of the fire, so be thinking."

Tin washed her hands. "I'll tell one about Gingerman and Gingerann."

Mom wiped the end of Tin's nose. "You'd better not."

"Finished," Pip announced.

Tin helped her down. She stroked Monkeybrain, relieved he didn't feel warm or squirm. He wasn't even looking at her. Mom said it was time to start cleaning up, and Pip didn't argue. Tin kissed her on the Santa hat and wagged the white fuzzy ball.

"See you at dinner," she told her.

Pip was already singing. Tin was on her way out.

"Oh, hey," Mom called, "where's the hat?"

"Hat?"

"Yeah, the one you were going to give to, uh…"

She secretly pointed at Pip. Tin had taken it out of her back pocket and put it in her backpack before they came into the kitchen. She thought her mom had forgotten about it.

"I don't know. Why?"

Mom pointed again. Pip, standing on a stool at the sink, stopped her song and spoke without turning.

"Monkeybrain wants to know."

7

"It's like one degree out here," Corey said.

Tin had paced a rut across the front porch. Corey was wearing every bit of winter gear—coveralls, coat, ski mask and fat padded gloves. Tin was overheating.

She started down the road.

The car had been half-buried in a drift that Corey and Oscar dug out. The tracks of their arrival had been scrubbed and filled by snow.

"What's the hurry?" he said.

"Let's get to the end, come on."

"The end? That's like a mile."

"Not all the way. Just come on."

"Oh, hey. Let's catch a bar."

He had his phone out. If he was going to lag, she was going alone. The driveway was level and made for an easy pace. By the time she reached the fourth turn, he was nowhere in sight. The sky was already dusky. She would have to jog back to be in time for dinner. She unzipped her backpack. The green hat was warm.

This won't take long.

The trees were dense. A narrow path went into the forest on the right side of the driveway. It arched into the dim shade. The path continued on the other side of the road. It looked a lot like where they had hiked the day before when she found the pig.

"We're close." A patch of Corey's bright red coat plodded around the bend. "You can send that text, too. To Brenda, remember?"

She put her hand over his phone. His nose was bright red. She told him about how Pip was the one who built the gingerbread replica of Toyland and there weren't any directions. And then Mom had asked about the hat.

"You know what she said?" Tin shook the green hat. The bell rang. "Monkeybrain wanted to know where it was."

"She always says that."

"No, but this time it was different."

"No, it's not."

"Monkeybrain told her how to build Toyland. A four-year-old can't do that, Corey. Nobody can."

"Can we just do the... the thing?" He doodled at the hat and lifted his phone. "And then send a text."

The cold was beginning to seep through her sweatshirt, but her hand was toasty inside the hat. That was why they came out there, to put the hat on, not talk about gingerbread houses and precocious four-year-olds. Or staring monkeys. *And Pip always says Monkeybrain wants to know. Corey's right. Just that it feels different this time.*

"Okay," she said.

The hat couldn't be making the noises in the house, but once was coincidence and twice was suspicious. If it happened three times, Mom was going home. Tin wanted to come outside to try it.

Just in case.

"Hey, is that a pig?"

Corey nodded past her. Just beyond where the trail entered the trees was something pink. Tin put the hat in her backpack. She stepped onto the trail and felt a cold chill on her hand as she reached for it. The pig was in the trees again, like the last time.

Monkeybrain is worried.

"Before you go all conspiracy, just know that there's got to be more than one pig," Corey said. "Like thousands. And Wallace took pictures with all of them."

She squeezed the pig. She was just sitting there, out in the open. She looked down the trail. There weren't any more stuffed animals like last time.

Corey stumbled over to look at the pig. He yanked his hand back. "What was that?"

"What?"

"Really?" He gently waved his hand like searching for threads of a spiderweb. "Felt like I hit my funny bone. I thought maybe I touched a live wire or—"

He did it again. This time he threw his glove off and shook his hand like he'd put it in a beehive.

"Oh man, oh man," he said. "You didn't feel that?"

Tin stepped closer to where he had been reaching. There was nothing there. No wires, no spiderwebs. She reached out, slowly, and felt a tingle.

"I feel something," she said.

"Something?"

"I mean, it's a little cold. Do it again."

"You do it." He put his glove on.

She moved her hand back and forth and felt the sensation crawl up her arm. She went down the trail. The sensation was consistent. There were no large trees growing along the path. A few saplings but nothing more than a few years of growth. It continued in a long, relatively smooth arc.

Somebody cut the trail.

Trails tended to follow the terrain, meandering in a path of least resistance. This was straight as far as she could see. But that wasn't what was curious about it. No matter how far she went, she could feel the same cold energy just off the path.

"Look. You see that?" She knifed her hand at the trail. "It's sort of straight, but bending, right? Sound familiar?"

"I mean, it, uh…" He closed one eye. "I got nothing."

She drew a big imaginary circle. He nodded along and then, wide-eyed and slack-jawed, drew his own circle.

"Wallace wasn't just doodling on the map," she said. "He was drawing a path around the palace."

"And made it electric."

"Yeah. Maybe." She tapped her chin. "Try it again."

"Nope."

She put her hand out. It was still strangely chilly. There were invisible fences for pets, but it wouldn't generate a cold force field five feet off the ground.

"What are you doing out here?" Tin held the pig out.

"What'd she say?"

She shoved the pig in her coat. "It's getting dark."

"She said that?"

There wasn't time to put on the hat, but suddenly she had other questions. She wanted another look at that map. If only she would've looked back toward Toyland.

After she stepped through the force field.

8

Oscar and Mom were cuddled beneath a blanket on one of the couches. Pip was reading from a book propped on her lap. Tin looked down then went inside the bedroom.

"Be careful," she said.

Corey had his arm between the bed and wall. Paper crinkled like wrapping paper. He pulled the plan from the hiding place.

"How much you think it's worth?" he said.

She took it from him and unrolled it on the bed. A corner had been ripped off, and deep creases ran through the middle of it.

"If we post that on eBay, we're talking, like, thousands, I bet. Wait, what am I thinking? This is Wallace freaking Noel. It's got to be worth—"

"We're not selling anything."

She didn't know why they were hiding the plan, or why she didn't tell her mom about it. She knew why she was hiding the hat, though. Corey looked over her shoulder as she ran her finger across the title block. There was a scale in the corner. She put her thumb on it to measure distance.

"That's not right," she said. "We hiked, like, half a mile down the driveway before we got there." She tapped the circle.

"More like a mile."

"You felt it, so did I. This means something." She lightly traced the circle. "It's out there."

They both stared at it.

"It's a fence, I think," she said. "Like for pets."

"To keep us from escaping."

"What? No."

"That's what they're for, Tin, keeping pets from escaping. So maybe Uncle Wallace had a pack of hunting dogs he didn't want roaming the hillside and just forgot to turn it off before he checked out."

She thought a moment. He might be onto something.

"Or maybe it's keeping something out," she said.

"Okay. Maybe. You're freaking me out a little but all right. But you walked through it and nothing happened to you. And I could've gone through it, too. I just didn't want to."

Tin ran her finger from the palace down where she imagined the path cut through the forest. There were several trails, including the driveway, and none of them were like the circle. There was something different about that path, like something had been pacing around the property. Around and around.

Like animals inside a cage.

"Monkeybrain was worried about Piggy," she said.

"He was?"

"That's what Pip said. He was worried about her."

"You're sticking with Piggy's a girl?"

"And then we found her out there again. Maybe something was trying to get her. She's valuable or something."

"You mean like maybe she's stuffed with money. Or diamonds. What if Wallace was mobbed up and—"

"No. Just... let me think a second." She rubbed her face. "Let's just start with how Piggy got out there."

"I'm sure he made more than one stuffed pig."

That was the logical conclusion. There had to be thousands of stuffed pigs just like this one. But why did she feel familiar?

"She was on the other side of that invisible fence." She traced an imaginary path. "Like she was dropped."

"Great. So basically you're saying someone else is here and they're after stuffed animals. That's great, Tin. I mean, I already felt safe after you put the hat on and had the crazy dreams, but now I think it's obvious we're all going to die now. I think, right now, it'd be a good idea if we—"

"Stop. I'm just thinking out loud. There's a good explanation; we just don't know it yet. And we can't tell my mom or your dad because they'll want to go home."

"You're missing the point I'm making."

"Something's going on here, Corey. It wants us to know."

"No, it doesn't. Maybe it wants to eat us."

"It would've done that already. No, it's something else."

She leaned the plan against the wall so she could look at it while she paced. Corey peeked down on the lobby. Pip was still telling her story. There was something off about the circle. It wasn't centered on the plan.

That's it.

It was slightly to the left and toward the top. She put her finger in what would be the center. There was nothing on the plan, but she knew what was there.

"The tower," she said. "It's coming from the tower."

"What is?"

"That's what the tower is doing; it's emitting some sort of energy field. Think about how strange it looks, like the atmosphere is warped, right? You thought it was a nuclear reactor, but maybe it's just sending out, like, an electromagnetic field."

"A force field, right. Makes total sense. Uncle Wallace built a force field generator in 1920. Why didn't I think of that?"

She leaned on the bed. "And remember how the steps had been taken down? The wood someone stacked under it like they were trying to set it on fire? He was keeping someone from turning it off."

She didn't tell him about the fuzzy stuffing that was in the firewood. He was already worked up.

"And you don't want to tell our parents because..."

She took a deep breath. Keeping it a secret wasn't a good idea. *But maybe just a little longer.*

"Think they'll believe us?" she said.

"If we take them out there and they put their arm through the electric wall? Yeah, they'll believe. I mean, I don't know about your dream hat, but when the wall zaps their arms, they'll be true believers."

"We'll ruin Christmas."

"You know what else will ruin it? A toy monster that—"

Tin clamped her hand over his mouth. His eyes were getting bigger. She put her finger to her lips and gently let go.

"There's no toy monster," she said.

"Are you kidding me?" he whispered loudly. "You just said all of that and you think this is a safe merry place? What if it thinks we're toys?"

"We're not toys."

"I know that. But what if it—"

"Shhhh. Think of all the money we won't make if we leave right now. All that treasure in the loft selling on eBay. You'll buy everything you ever wanted. Just calm down. Pull it together. There's something strange about this place, but there are no toy monsters. Okay?"

He nodded abruptly, closing his eyes. "Okay. All right."

Tin studied the map again. The balance of the circle had been solved. It was coming from the tower. But there was something else bothering her. The handwritten notes on the plan were barely legible. She tapped the lobby.

"He labelled this one *toy room*. Pip said that was Gingerman's room."

"Who's Gingerman?"

"That was her name for the gingerbread man. She was real intense about putting him in there, said it was his room."

"Pip says a lot of things."

"She also built a replica of Toyland."

"I built the *Millennium Falcon* out of Legos when I was six." He tapped his head. "From memory."

"She's four. And no, you didn't."

"Yeah. I did."

"You're missing the point. She insisted that was *his* toy room." She tapped her chin and stared. Why was that bugging her? *It was the way she said it.*

There was a knock on the door.

Corey jumped. Mom peeked inside. Tin's heart leaped. The plan was on display, but her mom just smiled and said it was story time. Maybe Corey was in the way and she couldn't see it. Or maybe she didn't think anything of it.

It was story time.

❄

CANDLES CASTED flickering shadows over the stockings. Each of their names was outlined in gold glitter on the fuzzy hems.

Tubs of popcorn were on the couches. Mom and Oscar were digging from one of them. Pip was snuggled between them, her head above the sleeping bag. Her laughter bubbling.

Tin was looking at the tiny door on the ceiling.

She was on her back, the scuffed hardwood against the head, feet propped up. No socks, her soles warming at the fire as she told the famous Mr. and Mrs. Big Toe story and their eight little toes.

Pip's favorite.

There was a hole in Mr. Toe's sock. He was on the right foot. He was cold at night when he poked out. Mrs. Toe told him he needed to get his nail cut. There were arguments and jokes, whining from the little toes.

It ended and Mom went to warm up hot chocolate. Oscar told Corey to put away his phone. Pip went off to the side with Monkeybrain to prepare her story. She liked to practice, but it sounded more like a conversation. She talked to Monkeybrain all the time, but there was something different about this. There were pauses.

She's listening.

"My favorite part," Corey said, "was when Mr. Big Toe told Mrs. Big Toe that little toe was a giant wart."

"Shut up."

She turned her head, a satellite homing in on an imaginary conversation that was beginning to sound like a disagreement.

"Pip?" Tin said. "You all right?"

"Is Momma back?"

Mom and Oscar came from the kitchen with trays of hot chocolate with melted marshmallows. The musty smell of the lobby turned buttery and chocolatey. Corey put away his phone before his dad saw it. Oscar threw fresh logs on the fire. The smell of chocolate and smoke invaded the lobby, the pop of dry wood sending glowing embers against the screen.

"Momma?" Pip whispered.

"Oh, yes." Mom cleared her throat. "Good evening, ladies and gentlemen. Please welcome to the stage a very special Christmas story. Put your hands together for our own Piper!"

They clapped. Pip whispered something to Mom.

"Oh, and Monkeybrain!"

Pip took her place in front of the fireplace, her face bathed in shadows. She curtsied to more applause. Monkeybrain's lanky arms were snugly around her neck, his purple face pressed against her ear.

Pip bowed her head and took a deep breath. Dramatic tension filled the lobby.

"This is going to be good," Corey whispered. "Not as good as the toes—"

"Shh."

Several more seconds of quiet were filled with crunching popcorn and sips of cocoa. Pip looked up with her hands at her sides.

"It was a very cold Christmas Eve in the port town. The snow was as deep as it had ever been. And colder than anyone could remember. The sky was so clear that you could read a book by moonlight. That Christmas Eve, Gingerann was working at the hospital.

"She didn't have children or a family, so she worked on Christmas

Eve so the other nurses could be at home to wake up with their children. Even though she didn't have a family, she hoped to have children someday. The doctors told her it wasn't possible, but miracles happened every day.

"She wore a floppy red hat and curly green shoes, and candy canes were always in her pocket. She loved Christmas, but she really loved this one. The sailors were coming home."

She bowed her head to gather her thoughts.

"That was oddly specific," Corey whispered.

"They came back from a long journey to the North Pole, where they had gotten lost and forgotten. It was a Christmas miracle they returned at all. Sick and hungry, they filled the empty beds. The doctors and nurses tended to their wounds. They smelled worse than they looked. But Gingerann took one look at them and announced, 'No one will be lost this Christmas!'"

Pip's voice echoed.

No one was munching popcorn anymore.

"You sure she's four?" Corey whispered.

"Gingerann tended their wounds," Pip continued. "She dressed them with ointment, medicine and spooned warm soup. She sat by each one and told them Merry Christmas, tucking a candy cane into their pockets. The healthier ones ate it right there.

"The last one was in the worst shape of all of them. He smelled sour and of something rotten. His hands were wrapped in grimy bandages. His eyes peeked between bands of gauze. She feared he might have lost parts to the cold, but all worry fell away when he looked at her. It was those eyes that captured her heart. They were the blue of a deep ocean, the blue of an endless sky and solid ice.

"She sat by his side and never left. All through the night, she held his hand. Sunlight crossed the room. That was when the real Christmas miracle occurred. When Gingerman showed his face."

"This is about gingerbread?" Corey whispered.

Tin barely heard him. Pip lifted her face upward as if gazing on morning light. She smiled like she was remembering.

"His eyes crinkled as he began to unwrap the gauze. She probably should've stopped him, but one by one he slowly revealed a smile. There were scars, but, miraculously, he looked better than his shipmates. It was truly a Christmas miracle. He squeezed her hand and whispered his secret. He said, 'I am the toymaker.'"

Toymaker? Chills shrank the flesh of Tin's neck.

Corey dug out his phone and showed it to his dad, quietly whispering as Pip fell silent. Oscar nodded.

"They left the hospital on Christmas Day, Gingerann and Gingerman, hand in hand. She never came back. They moved to the country and built a house where every day was Christmas. Gingerann wanted a family, but the doctors were right. No miracles there. So Gingerman made her one. And their hearts swelled with joy."

"Made her a family?" Corey whispered. Tin elbowed him.

"But as time went on, the Gingerman grew fatter but not jollier. His Christmas spirit wore thin and leaked from him like a balloon old and fading. He grew troubled and dark. She understood what was happening, and her heart was broken. She didn't know who he had become, but she knew what made him that way.

"Gingerann never returned to the man she loved. The only Christmas miracle left was that she somehow forgot about him. There were no memories, only pictures of someone she used to know."

Pip faced the fireplace. Her back was to the audience, Monkeybrain firmly attached.

"*If you want to play, and stay out all day,*" she began singing, "*I know the place we can do it...*"

A second wave of chills swept over Tin. Pip continued humming, watching the fire. Mom looked at Tin then shrugged. This was stranger than the gingerbread replica in the kitchen. Oscar and Mom whispered. They began clapping.

"That was, um, that was... amazing," Mom said.

"Did you get that?" Oscar asked Corey. "All of it?"

"Yeah," Corey said. "A little dark."

Mom hugged Pip, and Oscar knelt down next to her. They were slightly confused and maybe a little nervous. She was smart for her age and good at a lot of things. But this was uncanny. Unnatural. Four-year-olds didn't tell stories like that.

Or build gingerbread house replicas.

Mom and Oscar went to the kitchen. Tin could hear them muttering. It was likely a discussion on how to raise gifted children. Corey went to the bathroom. It was just Tin on the couch now. Pip was still looking into the fire. She held Monkeybrain against her chest. The fuzzy purple hands were around her neck.

"Pip?" Tin said. "Where did you hear that story?"

Pip was humming the song, swaying back and forth. Then she stopped and spoke without turning. Her voice was calm and in the same tone as the story.

"Their story's not over, Tin."

That sent a quiver down her spine. The shock, though, was delivered when Monkeybrain slowly pulled himself up. His head over her shoulder, he looked right at her with those big eyes.

Tin stepped back, wondering if Pip was playing a trick, lifting him up and pretending he was real. Then he did something that was utterly impossible.

He smiled.

9

Tin opened her eyes to blackened logs. She blinked heavily, her eyelids slowly falling. The blankets were on the floor. So were her sweatshirt and sweatpants she had shed sometime in the night.

She listened to the embers pop and the haunted groans of a crooked old roof and leaning walls. Pip had slept with her mom on the opposite couch. It was empty.

She shuffled into the kitchen. Everyone was at the stove with plates and forks. Corey was pouring a pool of syrup on a stack of French toast.

The gingerbread monstrosity was still unfinished. Walls were stacked and waiting to be assembled. Gingerman was in the toy room, right where Pip said he belonged. She was licking her fingers, singing a song, but not the one from last night.

"Tiiiiin!" Pip shouted. "It snowed last night."

She sounded like her four-year-old self again. The calm and unsettling storyteller tone was replaced with giddy excitement. She hopped back to the stove. Mom put a piece of French toast on her plate.

"Good morning," Mom said. "Get yourself a plate—aren't you cold, hon?"

Tin was wearing boxers and a T-shirt. Everyone else was bundled in sweatshirts and stocking caps. Their breath escaped in a wispy clouds.

"Where's Monkeybrain?"

Pip ran her tongue over her sticky lips as Oscar glugged a river of syrup on her plate. She followed him out of the kitchen. They were going to eat in the sunroom, where they had a view of the woods.

"She's full of beans this morning," Mom said.

"Do you know where her monkey is?" Tin said.

"She put him upstairs with the pig, said they were telling secrets. Her imagination is running on high octane."

It's not her imagination, Mom.

"Get something to eat, hon. We're going to make another snowman, one Corey won't tear down." She poked his ribs. He looked confused. "Maybe a snowball fight later, boys against girls."

Despite Tin's reluctance, anxiety and the need to talk this out, she was hungrier than all of them combined. Mom went to join Pip and Oscar. Tin didn't bother with a plate, folding a piece of French toast and putting it down like a hotdog-eating contest. The second one she drizzled with syrup.

"We need to talk," she said.

"You need to eat like a human," Corey said.

"By the fireplace."

She took three pieces of French toast with her. She paced and chewed, looking at the photos on the wall—the animals posed like family. Piggy on stage. She hadn't noticed that before. That could be a different one than the one upstairs with Monkeybrain. *Telling secrets.*

"Did anyone say something?" she said.

"About what?"

"About what? What do you think?"

He chewed loudly while listening to her recap the story Pip told.

"That was Wallace and Awnty Awnie," she finally said.

"I got that. Didn't know your aunt was a nurse."

She wasn't a nurse, but she worked for the Red Cross when she was young. Tin remembered the black-and-white photos of her wearing the white hat with the plus sign.

"Your sister's smart." He pointed the fork. "Like scary."

"No, she's not smart. I mean, she is but not like that. That was like a professional storyteller, you saw it. You filmed it. It was like she was..."

"She was what?"

Tin didn't want to say it. *She was someone else.*

He licked his thumb and swiped his phone. The video from last night began. Pip's voice had an edge to it. It was the way she was speaking, the words she was using. Tin watched it over his shoulder. It ended when she began singing.

"Weird." He dropped the phone and shrugged.

Her sister was precocious. She was eccentric. What she wasn't was that.

"You weren't there," she said.

"I'm pretty sure I was."

"No, I mean, you left the room when she was still singing and..." She pinched her lower lip. There were a lot of things that had happened. But she was about to cross an outlandish line. She stopped and stared while he smacked his lips.

She told him.

Corey nodded along, cutting up the last piece into small bites. When she finished, she waited. He pointed the fork.

"What did she mean the story isn't over?"

"What? That's not—no, I mean, the part about Monkeybrain. His mouth moved. He smiled, Corey. I saw it."

"You sure she didn't just..." He moved his hand like a puppet.

"No. No, she didn't."

"She was facing the fire, right? She could've just pushed him up and made it look real. Super easy trick, you know that, right?"

"And made him smile?"

He shrugged. "I don't know."

"I do!"

"I mean, the firelight, the creepy story."

She was grateful he was finished eating and put the plate on the couch because she was about to smack it across the room and grab his baggy sweatshirt and shake him back onto her team. How could he not believe her? After what they'd seen.

Unless he doesn't believe me.

She snatched the phone and played the video again. Monkeybrain was wrapped tightly around her back, his face pressed against her ear, his purple fur sticking up like a cute little monkey from outer space. It was dark, but his lips weren't moving. But that didn't explain the tone of her voice. And where did she get all of those details?

Maybe they're not accurate. She just made it all up.

"Where you going?" he said.

She took the ladder two rungs at a time, the planks cracking like they were about to cave. The bedroom vault door was closed. Her heart was thumping when she pushed it open, cold and hard.

Monkeybrain and Piggy were on the bed.

They were propped against a pillow and looking at her. That didn't mean anything. Pip was always careful about positioning her toys when she put them to bed.

There was nothing else in the room. The little door in the closet was still blocked by her luggage. She sat on the bed and waited for them to say something, to blink or smile or nod.

"What's happening?" she whispered. "Tell me."

They sat there like toys, both of them. They didn't say a word or bat an eye. *Because they're toys.*

Tin backed out of the room. Monkeybrain and Piggy watched with inanimate stares. She closed the vault, feeling a bit more normal. Because it was dark last night. That was why she saw what she saw. And she was tired.

"Okay," Corey called. "This is... not right."

He was staring at his phone. The video had reached the part where Pip was singing the song, the same song she'd been singing when she was building Gingerman's house.

"Look." He pointed the phone at her.

The first thing she recognized was Pando the giant panda bear with green button eyes, the same stuffed panda in all the photos, the one that was in the loft. The words below it looked like lyrics. She squinted to read the small print. The first couple of lines didn't make sense. But the middle part did.

If you want to play, and stay out all day, I know the place we can do it...

"She was singing that," Tin muttered.

"Yeah," Corey said. "That's on the page I downloaded the other day. It's a radio commercial for Noel Toys. Look closer, when it was written."

"1932."

"Yeah, right. Right?" He ran his fingers through his hair. "It's impossible, right?"

"I don't know. I mean... she said..." Tin looked at him. "She said Monkeybrain was singing it."

"Oh, man." He slid back his sleeve. "I just got the chills. Did you?"

She'd had them since waking up. Pragmatic Corey had left the room and Corey *are-there-vipers-in-the-room* was back. He believed her. The song was proof.

"She thinks Monkeybrain is talking to her," he muttered.

"Thinks?"

"Yeah." He stopped pacing. "What?"

"You said *thinks* he's talking to her."

So maybe they weren't step for step. One thing she could clear up. She dug through the clothing she'd shed in the middle of the night.

"We're going on a hike," she said. "If the map is correct, the trail should circle the property, right? We go out and test it. If the wall is the same all the way around, we tell my mom and your dad everything. But not before we do this one more time."

She shook the green hat at him.

If she was imagining this, the hat wouldn't work and none of this was real, it was all her mind playing tricks, and everything was just a coincidence and the result of an old creepy building and urban legends.

I want to put on the hat.

❄

IT WAS SNOWING.

The snowflakes were fat and drifting, piling onto the already fresh foot of snow. Pip was flinging it like confetti. Mom and Oscar were on their knees, packing it around a smooth snow boulder.

"Where you going?" Mom asked.

"Hiking." Tin pulled the backpack over her shoulders.

"You're not going to help?" Pip said.

"When we get back."

Mom dusted her gloves. She straightened Tin's coat and zipped it up then squinted; it was filled with suspicion.

"What's out there?"

"Fresh air, beautiful day. You're always trying to get me to exercise, so."

"Okay. All right." She pulled a wooly cap over Tin's head. "Just don't stay out long. Oscar said there's a lot more snow on the way. I don't want you getting lost."

"We're staying on the trail, like last time."

"Don't wreck this snowman, Corey," Pip said. "This one is supposed to guard the door."

"What?" he said.

Tin hopped down the steps before her mom's X-ray vision saw exactly what she was planning to do. The trail was slightly dented from earlier hikes. She stopped near the dilapidated stage. Snow crested on the caved-in platform. No footsteps from wildlife.

"You running a marathon?" Corey huffed.

She took a right.

"Hey, uh, I didn't knock down the snowman," he called. "Just saying."

She ignored him. None of that was important. Not school or social media or a stupid snowman. She marched all the way to the circular patch of frozen ground where the snow seemed to evaporate.

The sky above the tower was warped.

It was a watery veil that waved like the surface of the ocean or heat waves on a sand dune. Corey stood next to her, slightly winded, breath steaming through his scarf.

"It's more than a fence." She stepped onto the frozen earth. The vibrations were in her chest, subtle and deep. "All he had to do was bury a wire if he wanted to keep something out. Or in."

"Not if it's a monster or—"

"Vipers, yeah. It's just, that's a lot." She pointed at the towering structure. "And modern, too. I mean, even for now. He was doing something to it back then. How?"

His eyes were watery in the slit between his cap and scarf. "You asking me?"

Tin followed the circle around. A narrow path was on the opposite side, wandering into the dense forest.

"Watch for toys," she said.

Corey was too far behind to hear, which was fine. He wasn't going to see anything besides his boots. She kept up her pace until he was out of sight. The path was narrower than the other ones, the ground rockier and sloping upward. The snow found its way through the trees.

The path ended at the circle.

It arched in both directions just like she expected. She didn't need the map to guess what it was going to do. If they walked far enough, they would cross the entry drive and eventually end up right where they started. They didn't have time to go that far, not with more snow coming.

She waited for Corey on an outcropping of craggy stone. She could see the house. The pitch of the roof peeked through a gap in the evergreen trees. Snow had settled around the black solar panels.

"You tired?" Corey dropped his backpack. "I'm tired."

Tin unzipped her coat while he tore open a granola bar. Sweat tracked her cheeks and dampened her sweatshirt. She dug into her backpack. A fuzzy tingle was on her fingertips. Corey squatted on the ground and watched her hold up the hat.

"Where you from?" she muttered. "What's happening?"

She hoped asking out loud would give her some answers. The visions were so random.

"Are you talking to the hat?"

She pulled Corey up and squared him on the path. The palace was just over his shoulder. She put the hat in his hands.

"Put it on me," she said. "Don't count this time. Just take it off as soon as you put it on."

The hat was so ordinary that she doubted anything would happen this time. He practiced sweeping the hat off, tossing it from one hand to the other.

"Get serious," she said.

As much as she wanted another vision, there was no explanation for how the hat worked. Corey was there if something went wrong. Maybe she should tell her mom, put it on in the house.

"Ready?" He held up the hat.

She took a deep breath and let it out slowly. "Make it fast."

She straightened her back. The tingle of the invisible wall ran across her shoulders. She was standing too close to the edge of the path and started lifting her hand to stop him, to give her a little room—

A light bulb.

It hung naked from a wire, swaying in a narrow hallway. Stark shadows danced along the walls and disappeared in the dark. Something scuffed the floor.

Wallace was behind her.

He was bent over at a door. The color was more cherry than scarlet but was faded and eerie in the harsh light. Wallace's T-shirt was stained. The suspenders clung to the outside of his bare shoulders. He hadn't showered. She could smell him.

Grunting, he prodded the doorknob. Metal tumblers turned in the lock. She was surprised when he stood up, wondering if he was in a hole. He was shorter than the last time she'd seen him. Maybe it wasn't him after all.

When he turned around—his hair as white as his T-shirt and wildly electric, a bearded bush hiding the lower half of his face—she didn't recognize the eyes.

They were bright green.

He was muttering, nothing she could understand. The distant gaze suggested he wasn't talking to anyone or anything, just a nervous string of syllables. His cheeks were damp and the whites pinkish around the green irises. He blew his cherub nose like a tuba into a handkerchief.

His belly protruded from the lower half of his shirt, the buckles on his suspenders buried beneath an avalanche of blubber. His fingers disappeared in the thickets of whiskers like an itch he just couldn't scratch.

He shuffled past her.

His feet were bare and swollen. They looked more like paddles. Or snowshoes. The soles scratched the floor. A sharp shadow cast over the door and shortened as he neared the only light source. Behind him, there was a soft thumping.

It was coming from the door.

Tin moved to the side. He brushed against her, squeezing her against the wall. Her breath came out in thick clouds as white as his whiskers.

The scuffing footsteps receded.

"Hello?" She put her ear against the door. "Hey—"

The naked light bulb blinded her. She threw up her arm. Wallace was staring at it. There was something red above his head, like the door had moved.

The walls had vanished.

The wind suddenly numbed her face. The light bulb wasn't swaying.

It was the sun.

They were outside. The lawn was crisp and frozen and stretched up a slope to a tree line. The fire tower was in the middle of the field, in the middle of a barren circle of dirt. Wallace was alone. A red balloon waggled over his head, a thin string taut in his hands.

The frigid wind filled her eyes with tears. He was tying something to the string. He held it against his stomach, short fingers ruddy and fat and struggling to work a knot.

It was a key.

An oversized bronze one. The kind with a big loop at the end and large simple teeth. He secured a knot to it three times before lifting it up. When he let it go, the balloon initially dipped from the weight then caught the wind and soared up and up. He stood there, craning his neck until it reached the trees. When it was a red dot in the gray sky, he looked back at Toyland.

Then he followed the balloon.

"Hey," Tin said. "Stop!"

One wide foot in front of the other, the frozen grass crunched beneath his wide soles. Tin looked back. There were no trees blocking her view. She saw the half-domed loft with the glass bubble roof cantilevered from the wall. In the frosted windows, a dark form was standing, watching Wallace recede.

He was nearly to the trees when she turned around.

"Come back!"

Tin took a step and the world tilted oddly. She wasn't falling forward. The ground was tipping away from her. She was falling backwards. There was the sky.

Then a bright light.

A chilly vibration rode through her jaws and down her neck. It filled her body. Abstract images crisscrossed a white background of static, straight lines, geometric. A voice bubbled through the haze, a sound muffled in layers of fabric.

Trees, she thought. *Those are tree branches.*

She was looking through limbs barren and heavy. Cold specks spotted her cheeks. A snowflake landed on her nose.

"Oh man, oh man, oh man." Corey's voice was suddenly clear. "Are you dead? Say you're not dead."

She felt his hand on her forehead. The back of her head throbbed. She moved her arms, heavy and rubbery, and pushed herself up. A headache greeted her.

"You just went down," he said. "Faster than before. I mean, I just grazed your head with the hat and you fell backwards and... Tin? You there?" He clapped in her face. "Hello?"

She pushed his hands aside. Sounds were so loud. The claps were like explosions. Fallen foliage wrinkled beneath her, little bits stuck to her cheek. She spit them out.

"The hat barely touched you," he said. "It was like—"

"I'm fine."

She put up her hand. It took several seconds to recall what had happened. They had walked the path all the way to the circle. The fence was on her shoulders. She told him to wait.

"He locked them in," she said.

"What?"

"Wallace. He locked a red door. He was shorter." She looked up, recalling the light bulb, the narrow hallway. "His eyes were green."

"I told you! Wait, who'd he lock in?"

She shook her head. There were so many things about him that felt different. *Why were his eyes green?*

"They were knocking on the other side. It was a-a-a..." It was just a hall and a light and a door. "And then he left."

"Where?"

"Wallace, he locked them inside a room, somewhere in Toyland, I think. And then he just walked off."

She tried to stand. He grabbed her before she fell over. Someone had been watching Wallace from the loft. Unless that was where he locked them. *But there was a red door.*

"Hang on," Corey said. "He was shorter?"

She wasn't imagining it. He was at least a foot shorter than her, like the fatter he got, the shorter he got. And he was just in a T-shirt with no shoes or socks. He walked into the forest. Tin could barely feel her face it was so cold.

"Where's the hat?" she said.

"I, uh..." He looked around. "I must've dropped it, but, uh... huh."

He raked the leaves on all fours.

"You started falling," he said, "and I dropped it when you stumbled back. I mean, I tried to grab you. I swear. I, uh, I went through the fence even. It stung, like full body."

She held onto a sapling as the head rush settled. Corey pushed all the leaves to the side. He yelped when his fingers touched the fence. She could see it now, the way the fence was warping the details of the trees beyond it.

Where's the path?

It was just trees. No footsteps in the snow, no indication of the path they took to get there. And something else was missing. There was a gap in the trees where she'd been looking before he put the hat on her.

"We've got to go back through." Corey got up and started huffing up courage.

"Corey."

"Like a Band-Aid."

"Corey."

"You want to go first? Good idea. Maybe it will weaken it, you know. Like take the sting out. I'll go right after you."

"I know what the tower is doing."

Tin pointed at the gap in the trees. He looked around, a little worried. She had the look of someone seeing a ghost. But he followed her gaze and saw nothing.

Nothing but trees.

"You going or not?" he said.

He wasn't seeing it and that was the point. There was no path. No hat. She let go of the tree and reached out until the fence tingled her fingertips. Just beyond it, the ground was undisturbed, the snow white and perfect. She kept her eyes cast down as she stepped through, felt the electric tingle pass through her head.

The hat appeared.

It was inside the fence, on the path, on their footsteps.

"Whoa!" Corey shouted. "Where... where..."

He was searching the area like a boy who just had the lights turned off. Arms out, eyes wide, mouth opened wider, he began to panic. He followed her footsteps and snatched his hand back when it grazed the fence.

"Right here," she said.

He jumped back. Somehow his eyes got wider. She put her arm through the fence and he made a sound more like Pip than a teenage boy. He was staring at her hand and covering his mouth. She wiggled her fingers and he reached out slowly. She yanked him through the fence.

"You were... where did you..." Hands on his knees, he tried to catch his breath.

Tin pointed at the gap in the trees. He stood up and looked again. And then he got it. The tower was generating a field that was back-reflecting more trees. No one would see what was inside it.

"This is more than a fence," she said. "He was hiding."

※

THE WIND FIRED snowflakes through the trees.

Tin lifted her arm as she entered the tower's dead circle. Her cheeks were still slightly rubbery from the fall; the frigid air stole her breath. Corey huddled behind her.

"He went that way." She pointed.

Wallace had walked through an open field and kept walking. Once sloping turf, now it was trees. But once upon a time, she would have been able to see Toyland from the tower, the rigid walls, the half-dome loft where someone was watching him.

Why was he hiding? And why did he leave?

Corey pulled the hood over his face and trudged into the cover of the trees. The dormant branches swayed over them. Hunks of frozen snow fell into the understory, crashing through the branches in powdery displays. They hurried past the amphitheater, their footsteps from earlier already filling in.

Oscar was at the car. He was bent over the trunk. Suitcases were next to him.

Corey waddled like a panicked penguin. Oscar caught sight of them and began waving.

"Your dad."

"I know." His chin chattered. "I know."

He detoured toward the car. Mom was coming out of Toyland, bent over and fixing the pant leg on her snowsuit. The area where they were planning a snowball fight was still trampled but quickly filling with fresh snow.

"What's Oscar doing?" Tin said.

"Oh." Mom was startled. "I didn't see you coming. There was another noise in the house. This time the power's out. We're going to head back home before the weather gets bad. We should get there by morning."

"Noise?"

"It was under the house, felt like a tremor. It might have been an earthquake." Mom wrapped a scarf around Tin's neck and tucked it into her coat. "Go inside and pack your things. Check the bedroom you and Pip were sleeping in and look in the bathrooms, okay? I'm going to help Oscar shovel out the car. Pip's inside."

She pulled the green hat from Tin's coat pocket and flipped the white fuzzy trim. She didn't seem alarmed or notice anything that was out of the ordinary. It was just a hat. Tin snatched it before she could put it on her head.

"It's my fault."

"What?" Her mom put a warm hand on her cheek. "This is nobody's fault, hon. We're all together for Christmas. It doesn't matter if it's driving or camping in an old stuffy house. And we'll come back another time, maybe this spring when we don't need power. We'll pitch tents, find a stream to fish, all that fun stuff. All right?"

Tin stared at the hat in her hands, regretting how she'd snatched it away. More than that, she wanted to tell her. Why was she keeping it to herself? *Because I'm not even sure I believe it.*

There was no point in telling her now. They were leaving. Tin would put the hat back where she found it and forget all about it. Be a normal family.

"Yeah," she said. "Okay."

Mom kissed her forehead. "I'll be right back. And keep your coat buttoned up. It's cold out here, hon."

Tin stomped her boots before opening the door. Mom had started down the steps. The snowman was all the way by the trees, stick arms poking out, charcoal eyes looking back. It was a long ways from where they built it.

"What's wrong?" Tin said.

Mom forced a smile. "Nothing. Get Pip ready, okay?"

She jogged around the corner. The car was running. Oscar was shouting something to Corey. Tin stepped inside and pried her boots off. Somewhere, Pip was singing. Tin pulled her damp socks off.

Barefoot, she searched the kitchen for food. Mom had already emptied the refrigerator and cupboards. Boxes were on the long table. Tin broke off a gingerbread wall and ate it. It was hard and the icing was crumbly. She took a section of the roof with her.

Gingerman was gone.

Pip was in the lobby. The song she was singing...

The Christmas tree was still in the lobby, the branches sad and heavy with pine cones and broken strands of popcorn. A fresh log was snapping in the fireplace. Pip had pushed the couch in front of the fire, the back of her head visible, her legs swinging underneath.

"Once upon a time," she said in her singsong storytelling voice, "a long, long, long, long, long time ago, a toymaker was born."

Toymaker.

There was a sound of a stiff page turning. Tin imagined a picture book on her lap, the illustrations having nothing to do with the story.

"He looked like all the rest of his brothers and sisters, but that wasn't what made him special. No one really knows who the toymaker will be, a boy or a girl, it doesn't matter. Because it's the heart that makes him or her special. But this toymaker was special in a different way. He fell in love and left."

Tin felt something in her pocket. She thought, for a moment, an ember from the fire was in her coat. It was the hat.

"This toymaker grew up like all of the rest of his brothers and sisters. He was no different when he was a baby, snowballing in the summer and ice sliding in the winter. He laughed like they did; he grew fat and hairy like they did. He slept in the ice when he was tired, and sang songs when he was happy. His body was short and round, but his heart was twice as big."

A page turned.

"Every year, once a year, they all came together to celebrate when it was darkest and the sun didn't rise. Together, they would build and make; they would put their love into whatever they were doing and wrap their best efforts. They only did it for one reason. They did it to give. They had so much joy and love they couldn't contain it all, so they put it in their work and they gave it to the world. Isn't that nice?"

Her feet flutter-kicked beneath the couch.

"But the toymaker wasn't good at building. I know, right? That wasn't what made him special. It's not the toy that makes a toy special, did you know that? When a toy was finished, they took it to the toymaker and he made it special. He put something in it just by touching it. The toymaker's big heart gave it love."

This wasn't like her rambling stories to Monkeybrain. It sounded more like one Awnty Awnie would tell. Like Gingerman. Tin took a step and barely felt the floor.

Someone was on the couch with her.

"No one could explain how any of the toymakers did it. They were scientists. They said there was an explanation for everything. Sometimes it just took time to understand a pheno... phenomeh... phenememnom."

A page turned.

"But it had been like forty thousand years and no one could still explain how toymakers did it or why there was only one alive at a time. So they used a word to describe it even though the old ones didn't like that word. Magic. The toymaker was magic. But it seemed simple enough; he just loved so much that his love went into the toy so it could spread around the world. That wasn't magic. It was just magical how he did it. Because no one else could make toys special like that. Like you."

Another chill nearly swept Tin off her feet. She teetered as she came near. Pip had a leather book on her knees. It looked like the journal from Awnty Awnie's footlocker. Monkeybrain was on her lap.

There were other toys, too.

They were next to her, lined up and patiently staring at the book.

One of them was Piggy. There was also a wooden soldier with an open nutcracker mouth, a plastic baby doll with a bonnet, and a brown teddy bear.

They're listening.

"Pip? Hey. What are you doing?"

"Telling a story." She turned a page. It was blank.

"You have new friends?"

"Mmm-mm. Baby Doll, Soldier and Clyde. You already know Piggy. Soldier is on guard, but he's nice. They said hi."

"Okay." They were dusty and the fur was matted. "Where did you find them?"

Pip flipped the pages and hummed her song, this time without the words. It was the one from the 1930s commercial. She pointed at framed pictures on the walls and laughed.

"I know," she said. "But it's cold now and snowy. We'll come back in summer and then we can play."

Tin held onto the couch and followed where she was pointing. The toys on the couch were also the ones in the photos. *Maybe there is only one pig.*

"Pip? Where did the toys come from?"

"They live here. They said thank you, but you're not the toymaker. Neither was he." She flutter-kicked at the photo of Wallace. "That's why he locked them up."

I'm not the toymaker? "Locked up?"

"To keep them safe," she sang. *Silly.*

"I don't understand, Pip. Safe from what?"

Her eyes were searching; then she dropped the book to cover her mouth. The leather cover slapped on the floor. She stifled a giggle and turned her eyes to Tin.

"Piggy likes you." The pig was turned toward her. "She wants you to hug her. She likes that."

Pip held the pink piggy with both hands. Tin took it from her. The fabric was soft and cushiony. It smelled old and musty.

"Where did you get the book?"

"Piggy had it."

"Piggy?" Tin cleared her throat. "Where did you get it, Pip?"

"*I* didn't get it. *Piggy* got it. Ask *her,* not *me.*"

She held her breath. Seconds went by; then she picked up the book and was humming again.

"Pip? Can you hear them talk?"

"Yes. I can."

"I mean, do they talk out loud? You know, with voices?"

The book tipped and her eyes shifted in thought. "No. It's here." She patted her head. She heard them in her thoughts, her imagination. A small bit of relief melted Tin's anxiety.

"They said you growed up," Pip said. "You can't hear because you think too much. That's what happens to adults, they get too much thoughts and can't hear anymore. It's not bad to grow up," she sang. "They said it happens to everyone, even to me too. But I won't let it."

She looked at Clyde the Bear. Her mouth was open, her eyes intensely listening.

"Clyde said we have to grow up, but that doesn't mean we have to forget. That's what the toymaker does; he reminds us how to listen. That's why they're sad."

"Sad?" Tin braced herself on the wall. "The toys are... they're sad?"

"Because Santa can't find them. They don't want to stay here, Tin. They're not supposed to."

"Why... why can't Santa find them?"

"Because he can't see them."

The grippy texture of the wall kept her from sliding to the floor. *The tower is hiding them.*

"Do you want to hear them?" Pip's tone was serious. Tin didn't like that sound in her sister. It was too adult. Wasn't her.

"They said you have to wake up to hear."

She put the book down and hopped off the couch. They were all looking at Tin now as Pip danced over and put her hand in Tin's pocket. She held the green hat with an earnest look in her eye.

"They want you to see them."

"I... I do see them, Pip."

There were sounds of the car revving up, the tires spinning. Oscar shouting for Corey to push.

"*You* want me to put on the hat?" Tin asked.

Pip nodded.

She took it from her, felt the heat vibrate through her hands and into her wrists, into her forearms. Fill her body. Just one more time, because they were about to leave anyway. Besides, she wanted to put it on. She wanted to know more of the story. She wanted to see.

Her scalp tingled.

Wallace was at the workbench.

He was taller than before. His beard was full and tightly trimmed, mostly brown with vague streaks of gray. A small pair of round glasses was perched on the end of his nose.

His eyes were blue.

The green hat was folded on the bench. The tools were out along with patches of fabric and spools of thread, containers of glass eyes and plastic buttons. The design of Pando was pinned to the wall, less faded than when she'd seen it.

"I know, I know." He looked right at Tin.

Her heart went up a gear. But he was looking through her. Behind her, the workshop was cluttered but orderly, a chaotic collection of materials without cobwebs or layers of dust.

Sitting patiently on shelves were rows and rows of toys. There were soldiers and stuffed animals, baby dolls and dinosaurs and robots. Every possible toy from long ago, sitting and watching.

"Patience," he said.

Poised in front of the Pando schematic was a pink little piggy. Her stubby little legs were out, the snout wide and soft. The black beady eyes caught the light.

"All right, little fella." *Wallace put on the green hat and peered through the spectacles.* "Ready, then?"

Nothing had changed that she could tell. But the workshop rustled as if a rogue breeze had found a way through an open window. Wallace reached out with stubby fingers and squeezed the little piggy.

Something happened.

Tin thought the light had flickered. It looked like Piggy blinked. It happened again, only this time the snout crinkled and the arms wriggled and the legs too. The line of thread stitched beneath her snout curved upward.

She sprang off the bench.

"Hohohoho." Wallace laughed and wrapped his beefy arms around the pink little piggy. "There, there, little fella. I love you, too."

There were cheers and laughter.

Tin turned, her eyes misting. The shelves were moving. The toys were jumping up and down, back and forth, hugging each other, clapping their padded arms and legs, stamping their tools. They bounced across the floor, leaping onto the bench and, one by one then all at once, grabbed Piggy in a big, soft embrace.

It faded into a mix of watercolors.

Tin wiped her eyes.

Monkeybrain was on Pip's shoulder. His head next to her ear. He was smiling.

So was Piggy.

The stuffed pig sprang off the couch and hit Tin like a firm pillow. A warm gush flooded her eyes. The watercolors were back. And all she could think of was how beautiful it felt, how perfect everything was just as it is. And then she heard the words. They were tiny.

A thought that whispered between her ears.

10

"You're never going to believe what just—" Corey stopped inside the front door. "Uh, am I interrupting something?"

Tin was in a full Piggy embrace. She was larger than a normal stuffed animal—her stumpy legs wrapped around Tin; her snout was buried against her collarbone. She was so warm and soft.

A toy that hugged back.

Pip was playing with Monkeybrain, holding his lanky arms up and pretending he was dancing on her lap. Mom and Oscar came inside and shivered. All three of them were in coats and gloves and stocking caps, a snowy brine crusting their cuffs and dusting their pants.

"Change of plans." Mom stripped off her gloves by the fire. "We're staying for Christmas."

"Yay!" Pip cheered.

"Dug the car out," Mom said, "then there was another rumble. Didn't sound like an earthquake to me. Whatever it was, a tree fell across the drive. We can't get around it without some work. And that's not happening till the storm passes."

Oscar joined her at the fireplace. Corey approached with eyes on Tin.

"Come on." Oscar tugged on Corey's sleeve. "Let's stock up the firewood before you get warm."

Corey reluctantly followed. Mom was blowing into her cupped hands. She rubbed Pip's head as Monkeybrain did his dance.

"Plenty of food," Mom said. "Plenty of firewood. We could stay another month if we had to. It's like camping indoors, that's all. And we got presents."

She tickled Pip. A torrent of laughter trickled out. Monkeybrain did a limp flip. There was no sparkle in the eyes. No smile.

Did I imagine that?

"Santa will find us," Mom said. "Don't worry, hon."

"No, he won't," Pip sang.

"Oh, don't be a lump of coal. Santa sees everything."

"Not here, he doesn't."

Mom shook her head and mouthed to Tin. *What's wrong?*

"You don't think that sound was an earthquake?" Tin asked.

"If it was, it wasn't much. The tree looked like beavers were gnawing on it or something. So go unpack. We'll be here a couple more days."

Mom pulled the green hat over Tin's eyes. *I'm still wearing it!*

"Where'd you find the toys?" She held Piggy out like a newborn.

"One of the rooms," Tin said.

Mom picked up Baby Doll and gave it a hug. Tin wondered if she felt it hug her back.

"She's a good mommy," Pip said. "The best. You do? Momma, she likes you."

"Awww." Mom gave Baby Doll another hug.

Tin shook her head. *Pip's not pretending to hear that, Mom.*

Oscar and Corey began the first of three trips for firewood. Tin and Mom stacked it as they made return trips. The fireplace was piping hot when they were finished. They had to move the stockings from the mantel.

"Ready?" Oscar said.

"Where you going?" Tin said.

"Look at the boiler room again," Mom said. "It'd be nice if we had power." She put her gloves on and stared at Tin's feet. "Put your boots on, Tin. Need to stay warm."

Oscar put an arm around Mom. She hugged him and closed her arms with a satisfying groan. It was sort of gross. But not, really. They walked out in step. He whispered something to her and she laughed mischievously. That part was gross.

"Soooo…" Corey said.

Tin was hugging Piggy again. The toys were normal toys, what toys were supposed to be—staring and not blinking, not smiling. Not hugging.

Maybe Piggy had some mechanism built in that made her hug back. *And leap off the couch and blink and tell me everything is going to be all right.* Maybe that was what made Wallace's toys so special. There was no toymaker and the green hat wasn't magic. They weren't filled with elf love.

Anything was possible.

"Corey can't see," Pip said. Monkeybrain was still doing a mindless dance.

"See what?" Corey said. "Your sister is getting down with a pig. I see that."

"Piggy," Tin said. "Her name is Piggy."

"Okay." Snow puddles were melting around his boots. "Am I missing something?"

Tin held Piggy tighter. She didn't want to let go. The warmth was inside her and felt like it was coming from a stuffed animal. She had to get it out. No matter what he thought. *He can't see.*

"The toys are alive," she said.

"Wut."

"You know how Pip talks to Monkeybrain? I think she actually hears him talking, like, in her head. No, I don't think. She does. She hears him and she's not imagining it. She told a story when I came inside about a toymaker elven who filled toys with love. I think this is his hat." She rubbed it on her head. "I think Wallace found it on the North Pole."

"Yeah. You, uh, you sort of skipped the part about toys and alive."

She sighed and shook her head. This would be a lot easier if they stood up and said something. *He can't see.*

"Pip told me to wear the hat and I'd... I'd see."

"See what?"

Pip began laughing. She held her belly at first then covered her mouth but couldn't stifle it.

"Clyde likes you."

"What?" he said. "Who's Clyde?"

Pip flopped on the couch in a fit of laughter. Monkeybrain lay limply on her, his noodly arm pointed at the teddy bear with the shiny glass eyes and the stitched mouth.

"Here." Tin held the green hat out. Her head felt naked without it. "Put it on. You'll see."

"See what?"

"Just do it." She shook it.

"He's not the toymaker." Pip's laughter suddenly died.

"Neither am I. You said I wasn't the toymaker just because I put this on, right? Corey can do it, too."

Tin was feeling tense and hopeful. Part of her panicked that something was happening to her that wasn't supposed to be happening. She liked this feeling, the feeling when Piggy hugged her. If that was what it felt like to be the toymaker, then she wanted to be the toymaker. She wanted to have the hat.

I want to feel like this.

"No offense," Corey said, "but you look more like a toymaker." He backed up a step. "I didn't want to say anything, but you look a little..."

He ballooned his cheeks. That wasn't what you said to a girl, or anyone, really. Maybe a sister, though. A stepsister.

He's right. I'm fatter.

"I just thought maybe you were, I don't know, eating more gluten. I'm not putting on the hat, by the way."

Corey had already put the hat on and nothing had happened. Nothing had changed except her. She was still wearing the hat only this time she was awake. *I'm not the toymaker. But I'm the wearer.* She didn't know what that meant, but the toys had come to life when she put it on.

She really hoped she didn't imagine that.

"Close your eyes," she said.

"You're not going to hit me, right? You're still pretty. Did I tell you—"

"Just shut up." She pulled him in front of the couch. "Close your eyes."

She took a deep breath. It was shaky. She squeezed Piggy tighter and felt a warm gush of emotions. If this didn't work, she was going to feel stupid.

And she really wanted it to work.

"Ready?"

She took his hand and closed her eyes. It was damp and icy. She must've felt like a branding iron the way he flinched. She refused to let go. A jolt of something rode down her arm.

His hand warmed.

He stopped squirming, turned quiet. Stopped breathing. She heard shuffling. It was coming from the couch. There were whispers.

Corey jumped back.

If she wasn't hanging on, he might've stumbled into the fireplace. His eyes were pried open. A weird sound eked from his throat.

Clyde stood up.

The bear put out his arms. Pip was twirling Monkeybrain in circles. "He wants a hug."

Corey shook his head, looking back and forth between Tin and Clyde the teddy bear. Tin nudged him.

"Go on."

He reached down. Clyde leaped before he grabbed him. Corey held him like a dirty diaper. Confusion, panic, and curiosity mixed into a strange brew. Clyde climbed into his arms and hugged him.

"What's happening?" Corey whispered.

Clyde rolled his head against Corey's chest, the little arms and legs reaching around him. Corey's confusion melted into a goofy smile.

"It's like..." he said, "iiiiit's like chocolate, like chocolate. Like gooey chocolatey cheese dip that's-that's just, it's just... like a hot tub..."

His words faded into garbled nonsense. He was right, though. It did feel like that. It was the greatest and safest feeling in the world. Like everything was exactly what it was supposed to be, that this moment was perfect just like it was.

A hot tub of chocolatey cheese dip.

"Come here." Corey swept the other toys off the couch. "All of you, even you, you little wood man. Come here."

He fell on the floor with his eyes closed.

"It's like a puppy pile," he said. "Don't... don't... hahahaha... you're tickling don't... hahahaha—"

"Corey," Tin said. "Corey, snap out of it. Hey." She pulled them out of his arms. His eyes shifted back and forth.

"That was... that was..."

He tried to catch his breath. Tin pulled him up and put Clyde back in his arms. That kept him from hyperventilating.

"They're... alive?" He asked the question despite the evidence. The toys wanted another pile-on.

"I don't know what's happening," she said. "I mean, none of this makes sense, but here it is. I'm seeing it; you're seeing it. I don't know what it means."

"We've got to tell our parents."

"No," Pip said flatly.

"No?" Corey said. "What do you mean no? This is huge! Look at them! They're alive, Pip. Tin, tell her."

"I know what they are," Pip said.

"Then we've got to tell them. I mean, living toys. No wonder Wallace was selling millions. If he was making them feel like this, then, you know, we could, you know... right?"

"Make millions?" Tin said. "Yeah, I don't think that's why they're alive. Why can't we tell Mom and Oscar, Pip?"

"They're adults." Monkeybrain climbed onto her shoulder. "They don't have imagination."

They would shatter if they saw toys doing this. A break in reality like that and they'd fall through and never come back.

"All adults?" Tin asked.

"Most."

The toys climbed back onto the couch. Each one helped the other. The wooden soldier was last. They lined up on each side of Pip.

"So then... what?" Corey said. "We just play with them and don't tell anyone?"

"We set them free," Pip said.

"Set them what?" Corey said.

"They're presents," she said. "They share and give, that's their purpose. But they're trapped here and we need to set them free."

Corey shook his head. "I don't..."

"Santa can't see them," Tin said.

His confusion intensified. The toys watched him mumble. Pip giggled and answered one of them with amusement. Then she agreed and began singing.

"*Santa Claus is coming to town...*"

"This came from an elven." Tin waved the green hat. "Pip told me a story about who it belongs to while you were digging out the car. This hat is what made them alive, I think. And it somehow woke them up when I put it on. I think that's why Wallace hid it before he left."

"Why did he hide it?"

"Maybe so they wouldn't wake up, I don't know. Doesn't matter; the toys are awake. The tower is keeping Santa from seeing the house."

"Santa?"

"Yeah. Santa."

"You said Santa, right? I heard that."

"Santa Claus. The reindeer, the sleigh and presents. You just rolled around in a puppy pile of living toys. Why is Santa so hard to believe?"

"Yeah, but... *Santa*?"

"How are you not making the connection? Look at me. I've gained twenty pounds in like three days, a teddy bear just hugged you, and you can't get past Santa Claus? Where do you think magic elf hats come from?"

"It's a lot. That's all I'm saying."

Tin closed her eyes and walked off with Piggy. Corey did the same with Clyde. They looked like oversized toddlers with their favorite toys.

"Presents aren't about stuff," Pip sang. "They remind us, that's what they do. That's why we got to set them free."

"Remind us of what?" Corey said.

"Love," Tin said. "They're reminders of love."

She felt it. So did Corey. That made sense. Maybe Wallace lost his way; that was why he locked them up. He had used the hat to get rich. He sold the love instead of receiving it.

Santa Claus gives it away.

"Are there more toys?" Corey asked.

Clyde nodded. The others did, too. They jumped on the couch and pointed in different directions.

"Where?" Tin said. "Show us."

Piggy wiggled out of her arms. Clyde dropped on the floor. They zigzagged around the room, their padded legs sliding and thumping, and funneled into a line beneath the old antique couch against the wall.

Wump-wump-wump-wump.

Corey picked up the sheet covering it. Tin got on her hands and knees. A tiny door wagged on a hinge. The same kind of door in the workshop and the bedroom closet. The same door in the ceiling.

"Guess we should've known what the doors were for," Corey said. "Living toys."

11

"Clyde!" Corey shouted into the wall. "Hey, buddy. Come back."

"What's going on?"

Mom didn't exactly sneak into the lobby, but they didn't hear her walk in, not with all the shouting. They'd pulled the couch away from the wall. Corey had been yelling into the little mouse door for ten minutes. Clyde didn't come back. None of them did.

Corey jumped up. "Nothing."

"Nothing?"

"Well... yeah, no. Nothing. We were just playing... Clyde. It's a game that Pip made up, right, Pip? She, uh..." His words trailed off.

"Everything all right?" Mom asked.

"Hey, it's great," Corey said. "Did you get the heat thing going?"

"No," Mom said. "The generators are working. As far as we can tell, the solar panels and wind turbines are still producing, just all the current is being redirected."

"Where?" Tin was on one of the couches.

"Hard to tell. The system is so complicated. Maybe it's stuck in a deceleration cycle or a circuit loop. I'm going to take the laptop back for an analysis. Shouldn't be much longer."

She started for the front door, the puffy snowsuit rubbing between her legs.

"Where are the toys?" she said.

"That's the game," Tin said. "The one Corey was playing with Pip. It's like hide-and-seek, but with the toys. Only I hid them. He's trying to find them. It's complicated."

Mom looked at them one at a time. Pip was pretend-reading with Monkeybrain. Tin and Corey stared back. Talking was just making it worse. Mom approached the couch and, suspiciously, picked up the comforter.

"What's this?"

"This?" Tin slid the map onto her lap. "We found it in the workshop. You know, the one you told us about. Over there. Just all sorts of junk in there."

Mom's lie detector was going off. "Out with it. What's going on?"

"Someone likes Corey," Tin said. "His name is Clyde."

"Clyde?"

"Clyde's what they call a bear cub. Corey's a pup."

"Tin's girlfriend is a pig," Corey said. "Seriously."

"All right, that's enough." Mom lifted her hands. "What's really happening?"

"Mom, it's just a map. Seriously. We found it over by the workshop, and we were just looking at it, sort of figuring out where stuff was. That's the truth."

It was the truth. That was a way around the lie detector: lie with the truth. It wasn't exactly lying, not exactly honest. But enough to satisfy Mom's X-ray vision. She examined the map.

"We could use this," she said.

"Oh, yeah, for sure," Tin said. "Can we just look at it some more? Just something to do, you know."

Mom swept her lie detector one more time. She agreed as long as they left it for her and Oscar when they got back. It might come in handy if they didn't get the boiler room running.

"We'll be another hour," Mom said. "We'll cook dinner on the fireplace when we get back. Popcorn for dessert."

Tin and Corey pretended to be bored till she went out the front door and returned with a tool bag from the car. She tucked the laptop in the side pocket. They remained quiet for another five minutes. Mom sometimes made a return visit when her lie detector was going off.

"A pig?" Tin said. "What's wrong with you?"

"You started it."

"She saw you shouting into the wall. I was making something up, anything to explain why you were yelling Clyde into a hole."

"So you told her I'm a pup? That makes no sense."

Tin threw the sleeping bag off. Time was short and Mom wanted the map. Tin had been tracing the hollow walls when she heard Mom's footsteps coming down the hall. It was clear now. Those wide walls were narrow hallways for the toys, with little mouse holes for them to come and go.

This place was built for them.

Some of the walls were solid. Corey said they were probably load bearing, but he didn't really know what that meant. Tin started where Clyde, Piggy and the others entered the wall under the antique couch.

They could be anywhere.

Monkeybrain could go looking for them. If Pip let him. That was a hard no when they asked. What if he didn't come back? There was something about the toys that worried Pip. Tin knew what she meant. There was a reason Wallace was hiding them.

"Know what's weird?" Corey said. "I really miss him."

"Don't shout anymore," Tin said. "It's not helping."

"You think they're all right?"

"Will you just... stop for a second?"

Tin lost her place. It was hard to concentrate with him breathing over her shoulder. She knew what he meant. *I miss her, too.* That feeling she got when Piggy wrapped around her felt so good. All her troubles melted away. Like home.

"Well, it would've been nice if they just told us where they were going." He laughed slightly maniacally. "You know what I mean,

Tin? How hard would it be to say, 'Look, we're going here.' No, they just popped into that tiny wall and gone. We could've gotten the map; they could've pointed with their tiny hands, or little clubs, I don't know what to call them. Stumps? Oh, God. I think you're right, Tin."

Hands on his hips, he looked at the ceiling.

"I think I love him."

Tin took a deep breath. "I know where they are. I just... I don't know where it is."

It was the room with the red door, the one Wallace locked. *The others are still trapped*, she thought. She didn't know how Piggy and Clyde and the others got out, but she was sure the rest of them were in that room. *Where is it?*

She traced the walls again, this time with both hands. There were several intersecting junctions. The door was in between the lobby and the kitchen. And then Tin remembered something Pip had said about Gingerman.

That giant gingerbread house was in the pantry. When they were finished building it, Pip put him in one specific room. *That's where he belongs*, she said. *That's his room.*

Tin assumed she was talking about the lobby, but that wasn't it. The lobby was big and empty. There were couches and a fireplace and nothing else when they arrived. But the lobby was labelled on the map. *Toy room.*

"I know where they are."

She carried the map over to the upside-down staircase. It was built out of the wall as if someone could walk up if gravity was reversed. But that was a deception. There was a way to use it. She put the map on the floor.

"Up there?" Corey pointed. "You think he's up there?"

"Quiet." Tin hovered over the map.

The notes were shaky, hardly legible and faded with time, but there was an X on the wall at the foot of the upside-down staircase and a word.

GUBMUH.

"Maybe Monkeybrain can, you know, climb them," Corey said. "He is a monkey."

Gubmuh?

Wallace might've been mad, but he wasn't stupid. This was a clue, a reminder maybe, something he was working out.

The rope ladder that led to the loft had unfolded from the wall. Maybe there was something like that here. The X was right on the bottom step. Tin put the map under it and stood back. The bookshelf covered the wall. The covers were faded and dusty, the binding frayed. They were all probably pre-1930, at least.

There were at least a thousand books.

"Clyde!" Corey cupped his hands. "Can you hear me up there? Knock three times!"

She couldn't pull them all down. How would she explain it? None of the stories were good? No, there was something about the word. It was a clue.

Or maybe it was just an X.

"Humbug." Pip was sucking her thumb with Monkeybrain on her shoulders. "Bah, humbug."

"What?" Tin said. "Did Monkeybrain—"

She looked at the map. That was it. The word was spelled backwards. It was humbug.

"Is that from the movie..." Corey snapped his fingers. "I think it was like the Grinch, right? Like, 'Humbug those little'—no, that's not it. I know—"

"Shhh!" Tin need to concentrate.

Humbug. That was from an old story. A famous one. It had a grumpy old man, the one with—

"Scrooge!" she shouted. "Ebenezer Scrooge."

But that wasn't the name of the book. It was on the tip of her tongue. The title of the book didn't say anything about Scrooge or Ebenezer or humbug. It was something else. Something about singing.

"I think it was Rudolph—"

Tin shoved Corey aside. She ran her fingers across the bindings, dust floating in her wake. First the first shelf, then the second, back and forth.

A Christmas Carol.

"I don't think that's—" Corey jumped back.

Like an old spy movie, the book triggered something in the wall. Dust cascaded from the upside-down stairwell. The wall quaked and the treads began to quiver. Gears mechanically clicked. The floor shook and the furniture chattered. The candle-holding chandelier danced on its chain. The steps didn't turn over.

The treads lowered.

They stood back and watched the staircase drop each step at a time. Tin had seen this sort of thing at an obstacle course where ropes were attached to both ends of each tread so that the path swayed.

Everything stopped shaking.

"I'm not doing that," Corey said.

Tin wandered to the first step. They led up to a door in the corner. At least thirty feet off the floor. The ropes were as thick as irrigation pipes. They were braided and rough. The second step swayed. Her heart thumped. The ropes were old. They could snap just from age. But they led to the door. And she knew what she would find up there.

It was on the map.

"You stay here," she said. "Tell Mom I'm in the bathroom."

"Yeah, I'm good with that."

Mom would come. She was sure of it. Unless she was just getting used to Toyland quaking. Tin took the first step; Pip grabbed onto her sweatshirt.

"Monkeybrain wants to go."

"No, Pip. You've got to stay—"

Her sister scampered past her and was three steps up the swinging staircase before she could reach her. Monkeybrain was wrapped around her neck, looking back. The treads were heavy and didn't move under her little feet. Tin took the steps two at a time, keeping her eyes up and hands on the ropes. The treads creaked heavily.

She caught up before they reached the top.

"Hold onto the rope," Tin said.

She turned the knob and the door opened inside. There was a short hallway like the one leading to the loft. A strange sense of déjà vu gripped her. She helped Pip inside. A naked light bulb hung from the ceiling.

The red door.

"Is he up here?" Corey made the climb, pale and shaking.

"Go back down," Tin said. "Find something to knock the doorknob off."

"I just got here."

"The ax is by the back door. Hurry."

"Couldn't we just pick the lock?"

"You know how to pick a lock? Go."

The hinges began squealing. Pip's little hand was wrapped around the tarnished knob. The latch had given way.

"Or maybe just open it," Corey said.

A stale, musty odor wafted out. Her phone didn't penetrate the darkness at first. She pulled Pip to her side and pushed it open. The hard, white light beamed across a square room. Standing in the middle was a bear, a pig, a doll, and a wooden soldier. They were surrounded by toys.

Hundreds of them.

They were different colors and sizes—animals and dolls and creatures to play with. Some with long fur, others plain fabric. Some with glass eyes, others stitched, others with buttons. They weren't much different than Piggy and Clyde, except for one critical thing.

They're empty.

"Clyde, Clyde." Corey pushed past Tin. "I was worried."

Piggy trotted on all fours and climbed up Tin's leg. She hiked her into the crook of her arm and felt the warm goodness melt through her. Monkeybrain knuckle-walked around the room, tugging on an arm here, a leg there. He shook a crumpled elephant then returned to Pip.

"He took them."

"What?" Tin said.

"That's what Monkeybrain said. He took them."

"What... what does that mean?"

Piggy looked melancholy. There was nothing they could do about the toys. Wallace had locked them in there to keep them safe. *From who?*

Piggy began humming. She didn't sing the words, but Tin knew the song. It was the radio commercial. Piggy was quivering. It was too much to say the name, or she didn't know.

Tin didn't need her to say it, though. Wallace locked them in there and left. He tied the key on a balloon so that he'd never find it. He knew what he was doing.

He was protecting them from himself.

"He's gone," Tin said. "You're safe."

Piggy shook her head. Wallace could come back, she thought. Piggy didn't know about aging. She was a toy. But Wallace was dead.

No one lived that long.

"Santa," Pip said. "He can help them."

Monkeybrain had whispered to her. That was what the toys had told them when they first appeared. Santa couldn't see Toyland. If Wallace took the toys' lives, Santa could give them back.

He has to see us.

Corey was hugging a bear that was hugging him back and he still couldn't wrap his head around Santa Claus. Tin wasn't stuck on that. She knew what they had to do. If the toys were telling her that Santa needed to find them, then that was what she was going to do.

"We'll take them with us." Tin picked up a yellow octopus. The tentacles dangled. "We'll tell Mom something, I don't know. It doesn't matter. Once they're outside the wall, then Santa can—"

"They can't leave," Pip said.

Tin shook her head. Maybe the tower was doing more than hide them. It had some sort of current. Tin felt it; so did Corey.

The toys did, too. That's why they were in the woods.

"We've got to turn off the tower," she said.

"Why?" Corey said.

"Aren't you listening?"

"No, I'm sort of really into this." He hugged Clyde with a goofy smile. "Besides, we can't climb it. You saw what Wallace did to the steps."

"I think there's more to the wall. It's not just hiding Toyland. It does something to the toys. They can't cross it or it turns them off."

"Maybe Wallace wasn't hiding the toys."

Wallace could've been protecting something inside the wall. Maybe he didn't want anyone to see the toys when they were alive. Or maybe it was something else.

Something far more valuable.

"Come on."

She guided Pip down the steps. When they were back on the floor, she pushed the book back into the wall. The treads were cranked back into place.

"You stay with Pip," she said. "Tell Mom I was bored, that I went exploring the house."

"Where you going?" he said.

She put on her coat then put Piggy on the couch. It hurt to leave her, but she couldn't take her. She checked her pocket.

It wasn't the toys he was hiding.

PART III

SASKATOON, Saskatchewan, Canada – Shawnda Washington, 28, had run out of gas on her way to visit family. She had stayed in the car with their three-year-old son, Treymon. Her husband, Raymond, 31, had set out on foot to find a station. When he returned, there was a snowman next to the car.

His wife had a strange story of how it got there.

"He came out of the woods," Shawnda said. "I thought maybe he was lost."

The man didn't appear to have any gear, according to Shawnda, and was only wearing a T-shirt and suspenders. She was cautious at first, but he was friendly. He said he was looking for someone. He had something that belonged to them but didn't say who it was or where he was going.

"Then he started building a snowman. Trey loved it."

The man, who said his name was Mr. Doe, claimed that, where he was going, snowmen really lived. It didn't matter how big or small they were, it was their heart that was alive.

"Some sort of electromagnetic thing or something," Shawnda said. "I couldn't understand half of what he said. He sounded smart, but I think he might need some help."

Any information regarding someone who knows of someone matching this description, contact the local authorities.

12

Tin struggled to zip her coat in the wind.

Powdery snow filled her boots and packed inside. She lifted her arm to shield her face. Large snowflakes stung her cheeks. Her ankles were nearly frozen by the time she reached the trees.

One of the trails was a faster route to the wall than the driveway. Lumps on the dilapidated stage looked like ghosts beneath newly laid blankets of snow. Tin's chest burned with cold air.

She buried her hand into her pocket, felt the hot fabric of the toymaker's hat inside. It felt alive. *What secrets does it hold?*

She remembered what happened to Wallace in the end. He wandered into the trees and never returned. That wasn't the ending she wanted. She doubted that was what he wanted, either.

Because of the hat.

The wind whipped through the trees. Snow melted off her brows. The trees beyond the wall were a blur of watercolors, like fresh paint smeared on a canvas. The hat was burning hot as she neared it, her breath coming out in rough puffy clouds, tears streaming down her cheeks, snot from her nose.

She could feel the wall. It sounded like an electrical wire. But she didn't slow down, didn't think about how it looked and sounded different than before. She just had to get through it.

It walloped her.

She felt it in her teeth. Her jaws clenched uncontrollably. Her bones rattled like cold steel struck with a wrench. A high-pitched ring had gone off.

She was staring at the gray sky.

She'd almost lost consciousness. The wall had sucked the strength from her legs and spit her out the other side. Her shoulder ached. Just must've hit a tree.

The hat was gone.

Dizzy, she scoured the snow on her hands and knees, just like Corey had done the last time. It wasn't there. She wiped her eyes. The wall was still a watery veil. Waves were undulating near the ground like something was getting electrocuted. It wasn't the cold that was distorting it. She could hear the buzzing. Could feel it crawling on her cheeks.

It's turned up.

Corey said he'd dropped the hat the last time. Maybe he didn't drop it. *What if I can't get back in?*

She tried to remember what was on the other side. Were there trees? Was the path right there? She couldn't see what was over there, and she couldn't tiptoe through the wall to get back. She could walk around to the entry drive to play it safe, but it would be dark by the time she got back to the path.

She was going to go through hard and fast.

She caught her breath, rubbed the feeling back into her face. She backed up for a running start, ducking her shoulder and shouting as she closed her eyes.

The shock hit her even harder.

She didn't feel the impact of the ground. She struggled to get her breath back. It was like a gut punch that wouldn't stop. She doubled over and dry-heaved. The path was beneath her.

The hat was behind her.

It was sitting at the base of the wall and dusted with snow. There was a sizzling crackling sound where it was touching. Waves rippled the blurry barrier, warping the trees beyond. She crawled over and pulled it away.

It burned her fingers.

She shook her hand. The snow wasn't melting around the hat. She rubbed her fingertips and touched it again. It had already cooled. She leaned against a tree and felt like crying. Her feet were numb. Her mom would want to know what she was doing out there, and she'd have to explain it, and if Pip was right, the whole crazy thing might break her mom and Oscar.

Santa Claus is looking for the toys, Mom. Because they're alive. And he wants this elf hat, too.

There might not even be a way to turn the wall off. Wallace made sure of that.

Unless, she wondered.

The hat shivered in her hands. It heard her. There was one way she could see into the secrets of Toyland. Because the hat wanted the wall off too. It wanted to tell her how to do it.

It won't even take a second to find out.

Tin was on the ground and leaning against a tree. The cold was biting her cheeks. Tree branches swayed and the wind howled. She looked up. The world was barren and gray one second, then—

Butterflies.

Black and white striped butterflies. Big pendulous yellow flowers hung from thick vines, the smell of lush greenery. Tropical.

The sun had melted the clouds.

Trees arched overhead with dripping moss. High above were curving panes of dewy greenhouse glass.

The loft was unrecognizable.

There were no collections of artifacts, no storage cabinets or shelves. The paths of slippery ice were gravel and wandering through a tropical conservatory where birds sang and insects buzzed and treefrogs chirped. Somewhere a waterfall echoed.

Children shouted.

Tin was leaning against the desk. The surface was covered with plans and sketches. One of them was titled TOWER, but it was on the bottom of the pile. She tried to pick up the drawings. Her elbow struck a framed photo of Wallace and Awnty Awnie propped on the corner. It didn't budge.

Gleeful laughter came from outside.

She could see vague forms running in the field through the foggy glass. Gravel crunched behind her. A woman was coming up the path wearing khakis and a long-sleeved shirt with a stuffed animal in her hands. It was the zebra. The mane was long and furry. The head leaning on her shoulder.

Tail swishing.

Awnty Awnie touched her nose with a tissue. Her complexion was blanched, her eyes red-rimmed. She was so young and beautiful. And sad. She stood at the desk. She wasn't looking at the drawings but the distant shouting.

She petted the zebra.

Tin heard purring. Awnty Awnie put her lips to the zebra's head and closed her eyes. Then placed it on the desk. The legs sprawled across the plans. The black glassy eyes looked up and the stitched mouth curved. Slowly, it turned into a frown.

Awnty Awnie rushed down the gravel path.

Her footsteps quickly echoed from the loft. The purring turned into a whine. The birds fluttered and the butterflies flapped their wings. The treefrogs resumed singing. Tin waited for her to return. But she wasn't coming back.

Outside, the play continued.

Tin reached out and rubbed a spot clear. There was a line of them chasing each other.

Led by Wallace.

He was large and bearded, suspenders over his shoulders. Hearty laughter walloped from his belly. He fell down. It wasn't children who piled on top of him.

It was toys.

The humid conservatory air turned bitterly chilly. Cold snapped at the tip of her nose. Tiny bullets stung her cheeks. A gust had blown the hat into her hands. She sat there staring at it with no answers.

Only feelings about what she saw.

Awnty Awnie had stared at the toys before leaving the zebra behind. That was her toy. *Her Piggy.* It hurt her to leave Zebra. To leave Wallace. But she had to. She couldn't stay or she would never leave. She saw what was becoming of him. It broke her heart.

And his.

It was getting dark. Tin fell twice on the way back. Sensation was coming back to her legs when Toyland was in sight. She went around the front. Mom's and Oscar's tracks had almost been scrubbed from around the car. The tree that fell across the drive was buried.

She paused at the door to catch her breath. There were no drifts along the front porch. She pried her boots off and peeled off her socks. She cracked the door and slipped inside. She was knocked off balance by a soft pillow. Piggy hummed against her chest.

"I'm guessing you didn't leave the hat."

Corey and Clyde were staring at her. The sad Christmas tree was behind them, but she couldn't see it. A six-foot-tall panda bear was in front of it.

Pando.

13

"Where's Pip?"

"With your mom," Corey said. "She came back and you weren't here. I said you went to the workshop to look for more plans because you were bored. I'm supposed to wait for you." He waved at Pando. "Surprise."

Tin stripped off her coat and warmed her hands by the fire without taking her eyes off the new toy. He stood six feet tall on stumpy legs, with black and white fur and arms ready to hug. The green button eyes followed her.

"What's he doing down here?" she said.

"I'm glad you asked. I was on the couch having a tickle fight with Clyde, and your sister was telling her monkey a story about carrots that made a home in a compost pile, when it sounded like someone was hitting the wall with pillows. I think maybe it's your mom and my dad having a pillow fight or something. I'm nervous because I got to lie about you and not tell them you were going to dump an elf hat outside the invisibility shield that's surrounding us.

"I look up and I don't see your mom and my dad. Nope. I see a living dead panda bear lumbering in the hall. I'll be honest." He squeezed Clyde. "I thought he was going to eat us."

Tin circled around Pando.

"He came wobbling in with those big green buttons on his face and stood in front of your sister's half-dead tree and just stared. I mean staaaaaared. No one moved. Not Clyde or me or Baby Doll. Well, Soldier did. And your sister. But the rest of us, ready to pee."

"Is she all right?"

"Your sister? Oh, she stopped reading for like a second and went right back to it. Like she's seen stuffed pandas all her life."

Pando followed her approach, the head turning on a thick neck. Piggy squeezed her tightly. Pando was in good shape. He didn't smell moldy or have any matted patches of fur. He smelled like the loft, green and earthy.

"Did Mom say anything?"

"Uh, no. But then he wasn't moving when she got here. This is the new normal, Tin. Toys walking around. I'm not totally digging it."

Pando turned his head almost in a complete circle.

"The million-dollar question," Corey said, "is why you put the hat on. Because I thought the plan was to leave it out there. But that's just me, so—"

"How did you know?"

The evidence was six feet tall. Every time she put it on, there was a noise and something else. *Where was Pando when the other toys woke up? Maybe it took him longer to get here.*

She pulled the hat out of her coat. Pando's head turned quickly. She twirled it on her fist.

"I think I know where all the power is being diverted." She told Corey about the hat being yanked from her hand, how she was nearly knocked out going through the wall. "It was different than before."

"So then you put the hat on. Makes total sense."

"I was looking for answers."

That was sort of the truth. She was convinced the hat would somehow signal a rescue if she got it outside the wall. It didn't matter if it was Santa Claus or Mutant Ninja Turtles. But Wallace had planned for that.

How did the wall get turned up?

Tin stubbed her toe. Something tumbled across the floor.

"What's he doing?" she said.

Baby Doll was on the couch, but the wooden nutcracker had been standing directly in front of Pando when she accidentally kicked him. Stiff and rigid, the square mouth made for cracking walnuts was wide open.

A rhythmic thumping was in the hall. A shadow stretched into the lobby. Tin was damp with melted snow. She wrapped the comforter around herself just as Pip came skipping into the room.

"Tin!" Pip leaped on the couch and crawled under the comforter with her. "Piggy!"

"Where have you been?" Mom looked at the front door. Puddles of melting snow led to the fireplace.

"I, uh, I was outside just for fresh air. I didn't go far. I heard the rumble again and came right back."

"You heard a rumble?" Mom looked at Corey.

"I don't know what she's talking about."

"Oh, I thought... maybe it was nothing."

"So when Corey said you were in the workshop—"

"He lied, yeah."

Mom folded her arms tightly.

"Sorry, Mom, really I am. Did you get the boiler room figured out?"

She shook her head, chin wrinkled with frustration. Pando was sitting on the floor. It didn't occur to Tin that he was standing when she got there, balancing on both legs. Now he looked completely inanimate.

All the toys did.

"Where did you find the panda?" Mom said.

"In the workshop," Tin said. That wasn't a lie. "It's Pando, remember?"

"I thought you didn't go to the workshop?"

"We did, the other day. He was there. I swear."

Pip snuggled against Tin, the sucking sound of her thumb finding its rhythm. She was already sleep-flinching into a late nap.

Mom was nodding along, thinking. This was a good time to be quiet.

"Corey." Oscar was heading to the kitchen. "Let's get dinner started."

"Yes, sir."

"Leave the bear."

Corey was more than happy to get out of her mom's glare, but Clyde didn't want to let go. Corey had to pull him off.

"Sorry," Corey whispered. "Be right back, buddy."

He pushed him under the comforter. Clyde crawled next to Piggy. It was getting hot. Mom was examining Pando, pacing around the giant panda bear, dragging her fingers through the fur. Pando was listing to the side, head lying at an angle.

"We're not going to have power," Mom said. "The system is too complicated. Wallace must've had it updated before he left. It's going to be cold and no water since the pump is down. We'll need to conserve. Hopefully the storm lets up and we can work on getting around the tree."

Mom leaned over the couch and tickled Pip. Or what she thought was Pip. It was actually Piggy.

"Pip, hon. Too late for a nap. Let's get cleaned up and see if Oscar needs help."

There was moaning and complaining, but she eventually crawled out and dragged Monkeybrain by one arm. Mom watched her till she was out of the room.

"Tell me what's going on."

"Nothing, Mom. I told you, I just wanted fresh air."

"You have no idea how transparent you are."

"I'm sixteen, Mom. I have secrets. So does this house. And so did Wallace and Awnty Awnie."

"What secrets?"

"I'll let you know when I find out."

This was the parenting crossroads. Sometimes she pushed a little harder; sometimes she gave a little space. There was only so much she could do with a sixteen-year-old. She patted Tin's leg and sat.

"You're my first child."

"I know, Mom."

"What I mean is that you're not a baby anymore. When you were little, there was never any space between us, you know what I mean? I loved that. But I'm your mother and my job isn't to keep you a child. It's to let you grow up. It's to help you be your own person. One day, I won't be your mother. I mean, I'll always be the one who gave birth to you, but not your mother."

She patted her leg and smiled.

"I love you because you're my daughter, but I like you, too. My parents wouldn't have said that about me. I'll always have your back. I'll be on Team Tinsley no matter what. I'll let you make all the mistakes you have to make to grow up. It's the only way to learn. I just don't want you to make a mistake that you can't take back."

She brushed Tin's hair from her eyes.

"Don't go outside again." Her mom smiled grimly. "Understand?"

Tin nodded. *Is it already too late?*

14

It was a hot-air balloon drifting softly, smoothly into an endless blue sky. Up, up it went. Tin knew she was dreaming. She wanted to stay, but she floated toward waking.

If you want to play...

The song weighed the balloon down, each word like a sandbag.

And stay out all day...

She was falling deeper into sleep. It felt so good. The song was taking her back where dreams would mold the ground into whatever she wanted.

I know the place we can do it—

The sunlight was white and blinding. Tin's eyelashes clung together. A pig was inches from her face, with little black eyes staring into hers, stumpy front legs on her cheeks.

"Piggy," she grumbled, "what are you doing?"

Pip was cuddled against her. Monkeybrain was on her shoulder. There was another lump with them. That would be Baby Doll.

The other couches were occupied.

Mom and Oscar were side by side, the comforter half on the floor. Mom squeezed a pillow to her chin like a stuffed animal. Corey was buried in his sleeping bag.

White embers settled in the fireplace. The logs were blackened. Tin couldn't see her breath. It was warm inside the lobby. The sun was up and the trees were still. It was midmorning.

Everyone was still asleep.

"I don't want to..." Pip rolled over.

Tin wasn't sure why, but Piggy woke her up then crawled under the sleeping bag. Pando was sitting in front of the sad little tree. No one woke up in the night to tend the fire. Tin was the first one up.

Thanks to Piggy.

Mom picked her head up. "What time is it?"

"Almost ten," Tin said.

Mom sat up and stretched. Oscar was confused, as if not remembering where they were. He rubbed his face.

"I haven't slept that good..." he said. "Like ever."

"I know." Mom sat there, satisfied. "Is the heat working?"

The fire was dead, but the room was warm. It wasn't just Tin who felt it. Mom put on two pair of socks and started across the room. She stooped over to pick something up.

"Watch out." She tossed Soldier to Tin. "Toys on the floor."

Soldier was standing guard again. Maybe that was what he did. He was a soldier, after all. Tin held him in one hand. Unlike the others, he was rigid. The nutcracker mouth was open, the eyes wide. He had been standing in front of Pando.

Maybe both of them were standing guard.

"Corey." Oscar tickled the lumpy sleeping bag. "Get the fire going."

"But the heat is on," he moaned.

Oscar went to the kitchen. Tin was still snuggled with Pip and the toys. They squirmed beneath the sleeping bag.

"Hot water!" Mom called from down the hall. "We've got hot water!"

Oscar cheered from the kitchen. Corey groaned. Pando fell forward. He climbed onto all fours before standing on his hind legs. He stretched and moved a bit more fluidly than the day before. He turned his head.

Did you sleep well?

Tin jerked back. The sound startled her. It was loud and echoey between her ears. She didn't expect it. Most of all, she recognized it. It was the voice singing in her dream.

"Was that..." She pointed at Pando. "Was that *you*?"

"What?" Corey popped his head out. "Ahhh!"

He scrambled to the far end of the couch when Pando turned his head. The black and white face twisted into a bright smile. Clyde clung to Corey's side with his little brown nose buried against his shoulder.

"I forgot where we were." Corey was breathing hard.

Is he all right?

"I think so," Tin said. "But not really."

"What?" Corey said.

"You can't hear him?" She pointed again.

"You can?"

She didn't answer. It was obvious by his confusion and hyperventilation. He was hugging Clyde like a lifesaver in a sinking boat.

Only you can hear me. You're special. Pando picked up the crumpled comforter and sat on Mom's couch. *On behalf of all the toys, I want to thank you.*

He spread his arms and broke out a grin that raised his snout.

"I'm not special."

Of course you are. You're the hat wearer. There can be only one.

"But isn't... isn't this for the toymaker?"

You're the wearer. And there can be only one wearer. The hat chose you.

She shook her head, but surreal confusion remained. She was having a conversation with a stuffed panda bear that sounded imaginary but was anything but. Piggy climbed deeper in the sleeping bag.

"How are you alive?" she said.

"Wait, are you..." Corey looked between them. "Are you talking to him?"

She held up her hand. He was impossible, hugging his bear and now freaked out that she was hearing one of them talk.

It's not magic. Pando sat back and crossed his arms.

"If it's not magic, what is it?"

Pando's arm didn't quite reach the top of his head. *Ask the hat.*

"Is he talking about me?" Corey said.

Tin had slept in her cargo pants. The toymaker's hat was tucked into the side pocket. She held the little bell as she pulled it out. All of this started after the first time she put it on. Not just visions, but the house changed.

And the toys woke up, she thought.

"The other toys." She pointed to the top of the upside-down staircase. "What happened to them?"

Greed.

"Wallace?"

"What about him?" Corey said. "Did he—"

"Shhh." Tin held up her hand. She needed to concentrate. Pando's voice sort of came and went, fading if she wasn't listening closely. It was strange, like a frequency. *How is he doing that?*

"Wallace locked them in the room?" she asked. "Why did he leave?"

The answers are there. He nodded at the hat. *Just ask.*

"You want me to put on the hat? Like Wallace?"

You're not like him, dear.

Maybe Wallace didn't start out that way. The hat did appear to save his life. *But then he used it,* she thought. *Is that where things went wrong?*

"Is Santa real?"

What do you think?

She nodded thoughtfully. "You know, I asked my mom about Santa when I was ten, and that's what she said. But I'm not ten. The toys said Santa couldn't see Toyland. I've been outside the wall and this place disappeared. So far they're right, you can't see Toyland from out there. That means Santa can't see it, either. That is, if he's real."

Pando smiled. He understood. There wasn't anything he could say that would make it any more or less true. The toys were alive. That was true.

"How do we turn it off?" she said.

If we knew, do you think we'd still be here?

"The steps are gone. Who tried to set the tower on fire?"

We're trapped, dear. But you can help us. You have the answers in your hand. Only one person can be the wearer.

Pando's expression solidified. His stubby arms relaxed across the back of the couch and stiffened. Moments later, Oscar came into the lobby, tying his apron behind his back.

"Corey, let's go," he said. "Firewood."

Corey dragged his feet onto the floor. His dad stared until he was up and moving, then went back to the kitchen, not before watching his son carry a teddy bear over to Tin and tuck it under the sleeping bag. The entire crew snuggled against her, warm and soft.

"Seriously"—he bent over—"what'd he say about Santa?"

"What'd you think?"

"Don't give me..." He looked over his shoulder. "Is he alive, yes or no?"

The evidence is sitting across from us, she thought.

"Tell him to tell Santa I want a new laptop."

Corey didn't bother tying his boots or zipping his coat. He went out the front door. The morning was bright and still. The snow was piled high on the porch. The storm had passed.

"A Christmas miracle." Mom had a towel wrapped around her head. "Plenty of hot water, Tin."

"Maybe later."

Mom pulled the sleeping bag from Pip's head. A moan escaped the pile. Monkeybrain was wedged against her cheek.

"Piper?" Mom sang. "Time to get up. Come on, hon, let's get a shower. You haven't had one in days. Santa only delivers to clean little girls."

Silly, what adults came up with. Santa only gave presents to little kids who showered regularly. Sort of explained why things were so confusing for teenagers.

"You and Pando having a conversation?" Mom said.

Tin went cold. Mom hiked Pip into her arms and smiled. It was the way Pando was seated on the couch, like they were talking. Mom tickled Pip into angry laughter. Monkeybrain stared on the way out.

"Why do you do that?" she whispered. When the big panda didn't answer, she added, "You come to life in front of us, why not Mom?"

He was stiff and silent.

Oscar was outside with Corey on the front porch, talking about shoveling around the car. These were the moments she wondered if she was imagining the whole thing. Were those just her own thoughts she was hearing? Was the fire tower projecting a wall that kept Toyland invisible? Were the toys really alive?

There's one way to make sure, she thought.

She dug Piggy out. She shivered in her hands and cowered. She was cold or scared or both. She hadn't done much of anything except hug her since yesterday.

"I need you to do something for me," she said. "I'm going to put this hat on, okay? I'm not really sure what will happen, but I need you to take it off as soon as I put it on. No one else is here. Can you do that?"

Piggy nodded quickly. Her beady black eyes glinted with morning light. Tin hugged her one more time then set her on her chest.

"Don't worry," she whispered, "I'm going to get you out of here."

Piggy rubbed her snout against her nose. She swore she snorted. Oscar's voice grew louder on the front porch. Tin quickly grabbed the hat—

The little bell rang.

The hat flopped on Wallace's head. Brown locks curled around the white hem. Icy blue eyes shaded by bushy eyebrows. He was hunched at his desk, muttering and shaking his head. The little bell rang each time he did.

He was in the loft. The desk overlooked a wide-open field, an unobscured view of the tower. The glass was clean. It looked brand new. No condensation streaking the inside, no algae griming the outside. The air around the tower wasn't warped.

It wasn't turned on.

He was feverishly working on something. Papers were under Tin's foot.

The floor was covered with sketches and plans, paper ripped in half, parchment wrinkled into loose balls. The desk was cluttered with more of the same—stacks of full-size plans. None had been rolled and stored in the sleeve cabinet.

He was still working on them.

Tin could see her breath. It was chilly in the loft. But Wallace was wearing a white T-shirt, suspenders hung at his sides. There was very little gray in his beard. It was humorous, a grown man at a serious desk with a silly elven hat.

It wasn't even winter.

But he smelled good. Like spices, coriander and cinnamon and the like. A different smell than the other times.

The plan on top was of the house. She couldn't slide it off to see what was beneath. Wallace didn't notice her. Dream or not, he was oblivious to the outside world.

Pencil in hand, he scribbled in a leather journal. There were stacks of them, each filled with musings. He wasn't recording his thoughts. He was doodling. Both pages were filled with sketches.

Tin leaned closer, the pleasant smells of pumpkin filling her nostrils, to see the intricate details. It looked like circuits and formulas, nothing she could understand, but all of it orbiting a well-rendered spherical object.

An ornament with hieroglyphics.

He was working too fast for her to follow, not pausing to think or admire his work. He couldn't go fast enough, as if he was transcribing what he was hearing.

"Wallace?"

A woman marched into the loft with a bulky box. Tin hadn't turned around until then. The loft was completely different. It wasn't filled with artifacts of world travel or the botanical wonders of a tropical conservatory.

It was empty.

The woman was, of course, Awnty Awnie. She was young again, as young as the first time Tin had seen her in the forest when Toyland was under construction.

She looked around the place and put the box down next to a sapling—a tree that would eventually fill the entire room, its branches scratching the glass as if one day it too would realize it was trapped.

Her knees were dirty and she wore the kind of gloves made for gardening. She wore a flannel shirt with the sleeves rolled up.

She was so rugged, so beautiful.

She shed her gloves and put them into a pocket, careful not to step on any of the plans. She stood next to the desk and touched his shoulder.

And startled him.

He came out of a trance. Tears melted into his whiskers. He blinked without recognition for a moment. Then smiled back.

"I'm sorry, love. Do you need help?" He said it like he had broken a promise.

"No, dear. No, no. I'm hungry. You?"

"Oh, yes. I'm, uh, let me finish this last bit and I'll join you for lunch."

"Lunch?" She chuckled brightly. "Dear, it's almost dinner. You've been here since morning."

He looked around the loft. Quite a bit had been accomplished without him, it appeared. He seemed oblivious to the amount of work that would be required to make it become what it was meant to be. Awnty Awnie didn't appear bitter.

Quite content actually.

"Yes, well, I am a bit hungry. I'll make quick work here."

"What are you making now?" She peered a bit closer.

He covered the journal. "It's a surprise."

"Surprise? Not much left to surprise me with."

He grinned and laughed. It was so contagious that Awnty Awnie laughed with him. Even Tin found herself smiling.

Awnty Awnie pushed his chair back and fell on his lap. She slung her arms around his neck and planted a kiss on his lips, looking down on him with pure joy. Plans slid onto the floor as he threw her onto the desk and kissed her back.

"An hour," he said. "Come for me in an hour no matter what."

"No matter what?"

"No matter what."

He put her on her feet and kissed her again. She brushed the hair from his eyes and tipped the toymaker's hat. He reacted abruptly to keep it from sliding off. With one hand, he turned her around and began to dance. Awnty Awnie was laughing, paper scuffling under their heels. He dipped her backwards with his hand at the small of her back, and they both laughed.

"One hour," she said.

He watched her return to the box she had brought up, watched her unload seeds and soil and tools. When she left, he returned to the desk, his smile slowly fading as he lifted the pencil. His eyes, once again, turned blank.

And the scribbling began.

This time, instead of muttering, he was humming. Tin moved closer to see what he was drawing and noticed the plans that had slid off the desk. She squatted near them.

It was a schematic of scaffolding and an observation hut on top. Mechanical details were inset around it, control panels and circuits that were even more complicated than what he was drawing. She got on her hands and knees to read the fine print. It would take her hours to sort through it. But this was it.

The tower.

That was when she recognized what he was humming. She knew the tune from her dream. She remembered the words.

If you want to play, and stay out all day—

Two black eyes.

They were shiny beads. Tin's reflection was looking back. Piggy was pressed against her nose. The toymaker's hat was still on Tin's head.

It had told her what she wanted to know.

The front door opened suddenly and morning light spilled into the lobby. Oscar plodded inside, his scarf loose around his neck, snow tracking off his boots. Mom's footsteps came from the other direction, the towel still around her head.

"Did you hear that?" he said.

"It was distant," Mom said. "Almost like thunder."

"The sky is clear."

"The power's still up, though," she said. "Let me check the boiler room. Stay here. I'll let you know if I need you. Tin, hon, Pip is in the shower. Can you just let her know I'll be right back?"

Mom hurried away. Oscar went back outside, holding the door for Corey, who came in with an armload of firewood. When his dad closed the door, Pando's expression softened. His snout wrinkled.

"I know how to turn off the tower," Tin said.

Pando nodded once. Corey reached into the sleeping bag. Clyde climbed into his arms. "Cool, cool," Corey said. "Any word on my laptop?"

"He got it all from the hat, didn't he?" she said. "All the plans to build this house, the ideas to modify the tower."

A wonderful man, Pando said.

"The journals he was sketching in, they're up there. But the pages are missing."

Quite a few things changed, in the end. He was... different.

"He was sketching a-a-a ball or ornament. It had all these symbols. What was it?"

Pando leaned forward and turned his head. If his eyes weren't simple buttons, she thought he might be winking. *So much was lost.*

Tin was so weak again. Her legs were drained. She was famished. The smell of Oscar's cooking was suddenly filling her senses. She was going to eat first and wait for Mom. And then disappear for a while. Tomorrow was Christmas Eve.

So little time.

15

The workshop was even worse than the last time.

Before, a few of the shelves had fallen to expose the entrance to the loft. Now almost everything was in a pile. Gloomy light beamed from the loft.

Tin carefully worked her way through the mess. She passed the workbench where, in one of her visions, Wallace had brought a toy to life. The little drawers had rattled out of their slots and dumped their contents. All the jars were on their sides or broken. She squeezed Piggy hiding under her sweatshirt and flashed her light under the bench. The little door was exposed.

"He built this for you," she said. "The toys."

He had a vision. Pando hopped on all fours.

"You're special, though." She pointed at the drawing still tacked to the board.

Not special. Different.

"His favorite?"

In a way. The dim light shaded the half-grin beneath his snout.

"Why are you so different? You're bigger than the others."

I think.

"You *think*?" She laughed. "How do you think without a brain?"

How do I do this? He spun like a ballerina. *Without a brain?*

He curtsied. It was fluid the way he moved. Not like when she first saw him in the lobby when he moved stiffly and made noises like he was filled with stuffing.

"Is that why you weren't in the toy room?"

That's not the toy room. His expression matched the room's gloom. *It's just where he put them.*

Piggy buried her snout beneath Tin's arm. She wouldn't let anything happen to her. She was safe with her.

The path circled around the workshop. Pando hopped on all fours through the debris, gracefully leaping his way to the ladder. His steps sounded like beanbags.

"Why did he build things like this?" She pointed at the door. "It's so strange."

He was original.

"Crazy?"

Not crazy! Pando turned away to compose himself. *He was doing things no other human had ever done. No one understood him.*

So don't insult Wallace, she thought. But he was right about him. The house was like no other. And, as far as she knew, no one had brought toys to life. Perhaps his visions made him see things in different angles. There was nothing boring about the house.

There was still so much to discover.

"What's so special about me?"

You're different, I think. It wasn't always like that for him. The hat became part of him. The hat wants to show you something.

"Then why did he leave it?"

He was jealous.

"Jealous?"

The hat changed him.

She tugged the hat from her pocket. The little bell rang. "Is it changing me?"

Not if you peek.

His grin was sympathetic, hopeful. Wallace abandoned them and hid the hat. Perhaps they'd been waiting for someone to come find it all this time."

"Why are his eyes blue?"

Pando stopped abruptly. He nodded his head then balanced on his back legs. *Blue?*

"In the visions, his eyes are blue. But all the stories my aunt collected mentioned green eyes." She explained the newspaper clippings her aunt had in a leather journal that looked like the ones on the desk.

She... collected them?

"I think she was following him, yeah."

He wandered off on all fours, nosing through the debris as if he was sad. Instead, he circled around and looked up. No tears on the button eyes, no sniffing imaginary sadness. He was a toy.

We should go up before your mother wonders where you are.

She climbed the ladder quickly, the ropes thick, dusty and rough. Through the short tunnel, she stopped in the yellowish light. Musty, earthy odor fell over her. Where once ferns covered the ground and flowers bloomed, now little things scampered through debris. The vision of past beauty lurked somewhere in the shadows. Now it was filled with a collection of things, an attempt to hold onto the memories.

And now no one was there to remember.

"What happened to this place?" she muttered.

It wasn't always this. Pando briefly stood on his back legs.

"No, it wasn't. This place was alive. I saw it. My Awnty Awnie built it."

He built it for her.

She turned. Pando was scanning the area, straining to see what she was remembering. He sounded hurt.

"I saw her carry the seedlings up here. The soil and tools, the boxes. This was her garden. There were palm trees and hummingbirds, butterflies on flowers. And these paths, they weren't slippery."

Her aunt was like that, she remembered. The garden in her backyard where she spent endless afternoons pulling weeds and sowing seeds, watering and mulching and sometimes just sitting there to nap, like she had all the time in the world. Somehow, she imagined, that was what she did here, in this place, whittling the afternoons away, discovering the small pleasures hidden beneath stones or still pools of water. This was her paradise.

Or her escape, she thought.

She forgot about the slippery paths. She fell into Pando. Piggy scampered beneath her sweatshirt.

Careful. He picked her up. *There's no hurry.*

He slid on all fours, left then right, leaning into the curve and expertly gliding to a spinning stop.

"You've been up here all this time?"

He took her hand. *I don't remember.*

She hung onto his hindquarters like a child learning to ice skate. "What's the last thing you remember, then? I mean, before the toys woke up."

He swung around the first turn and spun around. She grabbed onto his fuzzy ears. He slid backwards and picked up speed, swaying his hips. She was beginning to feel the balance, taking longer strides to keep up.

I remember him. Out there.

She didn't need to ask what that meant. Wallace had looked back after releasing the balloon with the key attached. Someone was in the loft. She thought it was Awnty Awnie, but her aunt was long gone by then.

"It was you."

They reached the platform. Her legs were still weak since that morning. The floor felt wobbly. The chair was empty where Pando had been. He was still nothing more than a stuffed animal sitting at Wallace's desk.

Her last vision was still so clear. She could almost see him still sitting there, hunched over, scribbling madly, the visions coming faster than he could write them down.

She picked up the zebra.

Her legs were splayed, the black and white striped fur coarse, damp and moldy. But she was warm, but not like the others. Piggy peeked out of her collar and reached with a stubby leg. Tin held Zebra closer.

Piggy hugged her.

Awnty Awnie had left and Wallace couldn't take it. The pain. Loneliness. He let the plants die and tried to fill it with stuff. It just never filled up.

"Why did she leave?"

Pando shook his head. He was hurt, too.

"He must have said something about her."

She was young. Selfish. And she hurt him.

That didn't sound like Awnty Awnie. She had always been at peace, a present woman who gave her entire self to hear another person's troubles, to sit in silence and enjoy the moment just as it was.

But Tin didn't know her when she was younger. That could have been a different person. Maybe she was selfish. Because she didn't just leave Wallace.

She left the toys, too.

"You've been up here all by yourself. It must have been lonely." She squeezed Pando's padded shoulder. "I'll fix this."

I know you will. He smiled weakly.

Tin began her search for the tower plans. It had been clearly marked in the vision. She started with the one rolled and wrapped in ribbons, laying them flat on the desk. They were brittle and cracked. Her carelessness ripped some of them. These were antiques and she was tossing them about like crib notes.

There were surveys and sketches, flowcharts and outlines, the outpouring of precious thoughts put down in pencil and ink. Some of the pages were filled with calculations and symbols, things that looked like another language.

One oversized plan held variations of the ornament she'd seen him sketching in the journal. These were done in more detail. They were of different diameters with specifications listed in the margins.

"What are these?"

Visions, Pando said. *Sometimes he couldn't make sense of them, so he just wrote them down.*

Tin continued her search through the empty journals. Wallace must have ripped the pages out before leaving. *Why would he leave the plans?*

She opened all the drawers. The tower plan wasn't there. She stood on the top step and overlooked the endless collections. If it was out there, she would never find it.

Why isn't it with the other plans? she wondered.

The windows were too grimy to see much more than vague forms. Even if she cleaned a panel, there were only trees now. No field where toys chased Wallace. No view of the tower in the distance.

Plan or not, she thought, *there's only one way to turn it off.*

She had to get up there. If it was as simple as it looked in the vision, there was only one lever. *Is it really that simple?* she thought.

The hard part wasn't turning it off. It was getting up there.

"I've got to get back. I told Mom I'd help with the car."

Pando led her down the steps. She decided to take the other loop back to the exit, just in case the tower plan was sitting on a shelf. Pando continued sliding without her.

There was a jewelry box.

It was just past the bottom step. It wasn't big enough to hold a full-sized plan or even the pages ripped from a journal. Something curious caught her attention. The small drawer was cracked open. She reached for it.

It snapped shut.

Dust and fallen leaves whipped off the floor into a vortex. A magnetic wave passed through her. It reminded her of the tower, the way it felt when she stood under it.

"What was that?"

Pando was down the aisle and around a corner. She couldn't see him. She went as fast as she could all the way to the exit. She couldn't explain what had happened, but she didn't tell Pando what she saw and why it seemed so familiar.

It was red.

16

The lobby was empty.

Black logs smoldered in the fireplace; the sleeping bags were folded. The gingerbread house was still incomplete. Pip had lost interest. There was a squeal from outside.

Pip was on the front porch.

She had cleared a patch of snow off the boards and built a castle with a wall and miniature snow people. Monkeybrain was propped against the wall, his long and lanky arms folded over his lap. He was listening to her spin a story about a snow queen who lost her snow doggy, and the villagers were on the hunt.

"Know where Mom is?" Tin asked.

There was another squeal. It was followed by laughter.

"Never mind."

The car was completely dug out. Corey was at the third turn in the middle of the entry drive. The snow was up to his knees. He stood there with arms crossed. Around the bend, the fallen tree blocked the road. It wasn't a big one, but big enough they couldn't drive over it.

"Look away," he said.

His dad and her mom were rolling in the snow. They were covered, head to toe. Mom threw her leg over him and stuffed a handful of snow down his coat. She had wrestled in high school. Oscar would have let her beat him even if he could have won.

"What are we supposed to be doing here?" Tin said.

"We were going to chop the end off the tree and drive around it. Then your mom threw a snowball and my dad yelled tickle fight, and now we might have a baby brother."

Mom screamed when Oscar rolled her over and pinned her arms. He was sprinkling snow on her head and said the forecast was looking hazy. Mom couldn't stop laughing.

Clyde peeked out. "You bring the pig?"

Piggy squirmed under her sweatshirt and waved.

"Where's Pando?" he asked.

"In the lobby. If the lovebirds don't need help, I'm going to the tower."

A snowball thumped against his stomach. Another one flew between them. Mom and Oscar had climbed behind the tree and were lobbing snowballs. Corey and Tin took cover in the trees.

"Pip!" Mom shouted. "Our side, come on."

Pip was chugging down the road in a fit of laughter. Mom pulled her over the tree. Quietly, they discussed a plan of attack.

"All right," Corey said. "They want a snowball fight, they get a snowball fight. Start a pile, Tin. We get about twenty snowballs and I'll start throwing at your sister. I won't hit her, maybe, but your mom will protect her. You go for my dad. Aim for his daddy parts. We don't want a baby brother."

Snow fluttered from the branches. Mom and Oscar had already launched a second wave.

"Hey, come on," Corey said. "We're not ready."

Tin had ducked behind the stump where the tree had fallen. The splinters stuck up like daggers. She cleared the snow away. The bark was notched on the back side. The wood wasn't rotten.

"This doesn't look like beavers," she said.

"Beavers?" He looked down. "Make snowballs!"

Mom and Pip began charging while Oscar lobbed snowballs into the trees. Pip's snowballs only went a few feet and she fell down once. Mom blocked Corey's shots.

"Meet me at the tower," she said. "Bring Clyde."

"What?" he shouted. "Where are you—hey, no fair. Time!"

Tin ran from the action. The snow had been trampled days ago, and fresh snow had filled in tracks that led directly to the fallen tree.

And it wasn't beavers.

❄

THE SKY WAS blue and cloudless.

Tin shaded her eyes. The sun was at high noon. She stood at the edge of the barren circle. From that distance, the climb didn't look that bad. But the closer she got, the higher it looked. And the stronger the waves vibrated inside her.

Everything was the same. The branches were still there. The steps were thirty feet from the ground. There was a pile of tangled metal at the far edge of the circle. It was the steps at one time.

How'd he get them over here?

The struts had been butchered from the tower, not cut. There were dents and chunks, the twisted metal crudely torn from its place and pulled far enough away it couldn't be used again. It looked too heavy and awkward to pull.

Something else bothered her.

It was the time she put on the toymaker's hat and saw Wallace with the red balloon and the key to the toy room. He watched it float over the trees before walking across the field. Tin had turned to see Pando in the loft.

When she turned back around, Wallace was almost gone. Tin woke up, but not before noticing the tower. Maybe Wallace came back to make sure no one climbed the tower.

Because the steps were still attached.

Someone had removed them after he left. It didn't matter, really. She needed to get up there to turn the tower off, to drop the wall. Santa Claus could find the toys and they could leave Toyland.

Because someone didn't want them to.

She scooped up snow on the edge of the circle and formed a snowball on her way back. Piggy stood on her hind legs and watched Tin swing her arm in a circle. There wasn't time to warm up. The first tread was close to thirty feet from the ground. Mom's head would explode if she saw Tin climbing one of the struts. Piggy's stumpy arms and legs weren't meant for climbing.

But she could walk up the steps.

She fired the snowball. Pain flared down her shoulder. Her days of throwing a softball from center field were over. The same went for snowballs. If she couldn't throw a snowball that far, she wouldn't be able to launch Piggy up there.

She walked to the forest's edge and scooped up enough snow for three snowballs. Sticks snapped in the trees. Something was moving. It wasn't a squirrel; she hoped it wasn't a coyote. She took a step into the shadows.

Bears are hibernating, right?

Whatever it was scampered away. She could hear it scuffling through the undergrowth.

"Where you going?"

Tin's heart hammered her sternum. Corey was behind her. Clyde was peeking out of his coat. They both looked a little worried.

"Oh, now you're ready for a snowball fight?" he said.

She put one in his hand. "Think you can hit the steps?"

"From here?"

"Yeah, from here. Or over there. Either one."

He eyed the distance of the bottom step to the ground and scowled. "It's like twenty feet."

"More like thirty."

She dropped the snowballs and grabbed his sleeve. She wasn't going to tell him about someone chopping down the tree. He'd be useless. She needed him. They all did. He had played baseball since he could walk. No need to practice with snowballs. Piggy was trotting across the barren field. She picked her up on the way to the tower.

"Corey's going to throw you up there." She cradled her like an infant. "If you fall, will you, will it..."

She was certain Piggy could feel love. And the way she sometimes quivered when Pando talked about Wallace, she was positive she felt scared.

"Will it hurt?" she asked.

Piggy rolled out of her grip and hit the ground. She bounced to her feet. *Tada!*

"Okay, good." She picked her up. "So you know how we want to turn off the tower? We turn it off and Santa will see Toyland. Then he can help the toys in the room."

She didn't want to say it out loud. *Maybe,* she thought, *he won't want the toymaker's hat back.*

"So the only way up there is to get to the steps," she said. "Corey's going to throw you up there; then you're going to walk to the top."

"And then what?" Corey said.

"There's a lever." She closed her eyes and recalled the plan. "It will turn it off."

"Or self-destruct or launch into outer space." Corey abruptly stopped. "Look, Tin, you think there's a lever up there, like, one lever that turns on a nuclear-powered force field?"

"It's not nuclear-powered."

"You don't know what it is. No one does! Pulling an unknown lever isn't a good plan."

"You have a better one?" She hugged Piggy. "Look, we're in the middle of nowhere inside this invisible dome thing, and we have no idea how it works or why. Never mind you and me are talking to toys and one of them is talking back, or that somehow this hat gives them life or that Wallace locked them in a room to protect them from I-don't-know-what and that, right now, I believe Santa Claus is our only hope. What if that tower powers up again only this time we can't get out?"

She stepped closer.

"Do you have a better plan?" she said.

He looked up. She gave Piggy another squeeze and put her into his arms. Clyde climbed out of his coat and put his arms out. They watched a stuffed pig and stuffed bear hug it out.

"Let's pull a lever," he said.

They examined the best angle to launch. A gentle wind was coming from their backs. He decided on an underhand toss because, he said, he was a world champion at cornhole.

"Just get her high enough," she said.

"I know."

"I don't want her getting stuck in the struts."

"I know."

"So it's better if you just—"

"You're making me nervous."

He windmilled Piggy in a big circle to loosen his shoulder. Piggy threw out her legs like it was a carnival ride. Corey handed Clyde over to Tin. They stood back quietly. He took a deep breath and looked back.

"Sure about this?" he said.

She nodded.

He looked at Piggy, looked up, took a step back and swung his arm. At the same time he shouted barbarian-like, and Tin imagined Piggy squealing out *weeeeee!* The pink pig tumbled curly tail over snout, soaring with ease at first. But her fluffiness quickly decelerated the ascent. It was like throwing a bag of feathers. Tin clenched Clyde and he squeezed back.

Piggy hit the third step.

She ricocheted down to the second step and tumbled down to the first. Stumpy, fingerless legs flailed. If stuffed animals felt pain, Clyde would be in a world of hurt. Tin was crushing him as Piggy put a short leg against a twisted rail. Her back legs swung over the edge.

"She did it." Corey sounded choked up. "Way to go, little guy. Give me Clyde."

Piggy pulled herself onto the tread and jumped up and down. Tin's heart stopped. "Be careful!"

"And hurry," Corey added.

The sun was bright. Shadows were cast below the tower. They

had plenty of time, but he was right. If Mom or Oscar came out for a hike, how were they going to explain throwing stuffed animals into the tower?

Piggy had to pull herself up one step at a time. At first, she would lean over and wave. There were at least seventy steps to go. Tin clapped and encouraged her to go five steps before stopping to wave.

"It might be Christmas before she gets there," Corey said.

Fifteen minutes and she was halfway to the top. Tin decided they should go to the trees so she wasn't distracted. Besides, even if Piggy reached the top in time, Mom would want to know why they were staring at the tower. They were almost to the edge of the circle when Tin's ears popped.

"You feel that?" Corey put his hand to his head.

The air pressure changed. It reminded her of taking off in a plane. She opened her mouth to pop her ears when a rogue breeze blew through the trees. Debris swirled around them.

A vortex.

Tin had seen them cross the Midwestern plains and throw dust and debris into the sky. They were harmless whirlwinds that formed when the ground heated up to create a column of swirling wind. It wasn't enough to hurt anyone. But enough to shove her off balance.

She started running.

The twister seemed to grow as it neared the tower. It grew wider, picking up bits of dead grass and twigs. The piles of branches fell over as it engulfed the tower.

Piggy was on one of the landings when it hit.

Even if she was hugging a post, she didn't stand a chance with her little legs. She slid over the metal flooring, her legs flailing, then tumbled like a pink pillow. When she went over the edge, she was caught in the updraft and heaved nearly as high as the tower.

Tin's heart lodged in her throat.

It looked like she wasn't coming down, like the vortex would throw her into the trees. Or worse. She knew where the wall was that surrounded the property, but did it have a ceiling? She could be zapped back into an inanimate toy.

"Piggy!"

She landed at the far edge of the clearing, bouncing and tumbling into the trees. The vortex rattled the branches and disappeared. Tin found her little pig covered in damp foliage.

"I'm so sorry. I'm so, so sorry."

When she was done hugging her, Piggy shook off the mess like a wet dog and hugged her again. Tin's chest hurt. Her heart, too. Piggy wasn't hurt. In fact, she had had fun.

"What was that?" Corey was waiting at the tower.

"A vortex."

"That's not what I mean. It went right for the tower. And, oh, by the way, dust devils don't happen in the winter."

She was losing her grip. He was right. That wasn't normal. Summer vortexes didn't form in the winter. That was science. And they didn't go after things. Something made it happen.

Nothing about this place is normal.

Tin was already heading back to Toyland. Mom was sure to come looking for them if they were out there much longer.

They'd try again the next day. Maybe they wouldn't have to throw the toys up there. Even if Piggy climbed the stairs again and they threw Clyde up there with her, they would just slide off the steps if it happened again. They couldn't hold on.

"I know someone who was made for climbing," she said.

17

"Just when things couldn't get weirder," Corey said.

Mom told them she'd found a game room. Tin imagined it would be shuffleboard and Ping-Pong. Maybe a bowling alley.

"Is it pool?" he said. "Or Putt-Putt?"

Corey approached the multitiered table and brushed his fingers over the green felt. Tin wasn't there to play a game. This room was at the end of a slanting hallway with wooden slats that creaked. It was far from the lobby.

And they would hear someone coming.

Pando lumbered on all fours, his footsteps soft and quiet, and climbed a tall chair. It looked like something a lifeguard would sit in.

Corey picked up a stick. "Ask him how to play."

It looked more like an aluminum baseball bat than a pool cue—blunt at the end. A rack of billiard balls was in the middle of the table. They were tie-dyed.

The game is not for him, Pando said.

Tin told him what she heard. Corey took a few practice swings. She sat on a bench. The padded walls were covered in scarlet leather. It smelled a bit funky.

Sort of chloriney.

There were photos on the walls, just like the lobby. Only these were taken in the game room. The toys were in team uniforms, hoisting trophies, giving high fives and brawling. They were soaking wet.

There was only one shot of Wallace.

He was in the high chair where Pando was now sitting. A whistle in his mouth, a black and white horizontally striped T-shirt.

"You know how to play?" Corey spoke into his sweatshirt. Clyde wasn't coming out. "Okay, fine."

Piggy was wrapped around Tin's midsection, buried beneath her shirt. She had fallen almost seventy feet and landed like a couch cushion. Not a scuff on her. Still, Tin didn't like the memory of seeing her tumble. Or the way she'd trembled when she picked her up.

"We came close," she said. "Piggy was twenty feet from the top."

How did she reach the steps? Pando asked.

She explained how Corey had thrown her, how she'd hung onto the bottom tread and hopped up each step.

Smart.

"What happened to the steps?" she asked.

One day they were just gone. I heard the chopping, like someone cutting down a metal tree. I was in the loft, you know, and heard it fall. It was heavy and loud, a great big thud. That was when things got bad.

Tin leaned her head against the padded wall. Pando was talking more. She liked that. He used more words, described things more completely. It was taking time for him to wake up, maybe. And she'd gotten used to the way she heard him, almost like his voice inside her head was normal.

There was a crack.

The billiard balls exploded in twenty directions. Corey stumbled back with the bat in his hands as they bounced off multiple rails and rolled up ramps and down slopes, around the felt curves. Numbers fell open on the wall like an old-fashioned scoreboard.

He looked at Tin. "You see that?"

A plaid ball had bounced off the ceiling and now hovered at waist level. Corey pushed it with one finger and it floated back into place. He took the bat in both hands.

"Don't," she said.

"Well, then ask him how to play."

Tin grabbed the floating ball. As soon as her fingers touched it, all the weight returned and it nearly slipped from her hand. She put it on the table with a heavy thud and took a seat in what looked like a dugout.

What was she going to do when she reached the tower?

"Pull a lever."

Oh. So you saw a lever.

"In a vision. I think it turns it on and off. It doesn't matter, that's all we've got. We have to try it."

She told him about the strange dust devil that seemed to come out of nowhere, the way it went right for the tower. Piggy couldn't hold on.

Another explosion, this time the balls bounced off the walls, the ceiling. Pando swatted one away. One hit the fence in front of Tin. Pockets opened on the walls and swallowed three of them.

Corey was on the floor with his hands over his head. He peeked up when it was over. The scoreboard said 102.

"Is that good?"

Pando's eyebrows knitted and his green button eyes moved closer together.

"What's wrong?" Corey said. "Am I winning? The score went down—"

Tin held up her hand. The game room was beginning to be a bad idea, at least with Corey in it.

"You said when the steps came down, that's when things got bad. But they were still up when Wallace left. Who took them down?"

Pando looked away. *He came back.*

"And then it got bad. What did you mean?"

Pando swelled up as if he were taking a deep breath. He deflated and, in her head, she heard him sigh. It was just an expression. *He's not breathing,* she thought.

Wallace, Pando started, *had started staying up late. I don't even think he was sleeping anymore. I would hear him all hours of the night and the day. He'd stopped playing with the toys, would sit in the umpire chair during tournaments. He was just consumed by something.*

It was an idea.

All of his ideas came from the hat—Toyland, the tower, the toys. But this was different. He wasn't bathing or shaving; his hair turned gray. He was getting fatter, not wearing shoes or hardly any clothes even when it was snowing. It was just... he was changing.

Pando shook his head.

He spent all of his time in the workshop. It was this idea he couldn't escape. He was making something bigger than ever before. I think it was dangerous. But he didn't care. It was all night and all day; he wouldn't stop until he was finished. He thought it would change the world. His idea would be even greater than everything you've seen so far. And then, just like that, he sort of... changed.

"Changed like how?"

It was in the middle of the night. None of the toys knew he'd gone out there, but I saw him from the loft. I watched him climb the steps of the tower. There was a full moon in the middle of winter. And it was snowing. It was beautiful. And he was climbing the tower to turn it off. I knew that's what he was going to do. He was going to let the world see everything at Toyland—the toys, the hat. Me.

The billiard balls cracked, Corey took cover, and Pando ducked a yellow speckled ball that sounded like a bottle rocket.

"How did you know he was going to turn it off?" she asked.

Why else would he go up there? The tower had been working ever since the beginning. Maybe he was just going up there to check on it, but not in the middle of the night. Not the way he looked.

That was all probably true. But Tin wondered if there was some other way Pando knew. If he talked to Wallace like he talked to her—with thoughts—then it occurred to her that maybe the thoughts didn't just go one way. Did he know Wallace's thoughts? *Does he know mine?* she thought.

"Did he?" she asked. "Did he turn it off?"

There was another sigh. *He was halfway up the steps when it started in the trees. The branches started shaking and snow fell from the limbs. Snowflakes started going in a circle, just like you said. It wasn't much at first, but it kept going, moving toward the tower. And the closer it got, the stronger it became. Snow was pulled off the ground. The loft was shaking.*

"You were watching from the loft?"

I saw it, yes. It left a deep trench in the ground. I don't know how the tower didn't fall. It's so strong, but the legs were shaking and swaying. I thought the whole thing was coming down. I thought maybe Wallace was doing it, he was somehow going to destroy the whole thing, but he was up there, too. He was hanging on with both hands. And the wind just kept getting stronger and stronger.

Tin didn't flinch when balls crashed against the fence. One careened off Pando's shoulder with no reaction. He was staring with big green buttons, remembering it all again.

He didn't do it. He changed his mind. He came back down the stairs before the wind threw him off. I think whatever it was scared him. It wasn't long after that he left, but not before coming back to chop down the steps.

"Why would he come back to do that?"

I think he was scared that maybe one of the toys would try it.

"And then he left?"

Pando turned toward her. She thought he was about to nod, but instead he put his arms straight out and looked ahead. The inanimate stare of a stuffed panda bear returned. The hallway began creaking. Mom looked in the room.

"Lunch is ready."

Her lipstick matched the color of the Santa hat on her head. The balls cracked off the ceiling and landed back on the table like a hailstorm. Mom peeked back inside.

"Did you see that?" Corey said. "All at the same time."

"You sure this is safe?" Mom said.

"I mean, I don't know. It's sort of like Putt-Putt pool. I'm just hitting balls. Watch."

He lined up another shot, stroking the stick on the edge of the table. It struck with a concussive crack that Tin felt in her chest and launched into a hole in the wall. The scoreboard counted down.

"Is that good?" Mom said.

"I don't know."

"What's the ref say?"

Tin and Corey went as stiff as Pando as she crossed the room. Corey wrapped his arms around Clyde burrowed beneath his sweatshirt. Pando was just a big stuffed animal perched on the high chair. Strange, but normal. Mom walked around him, dragging her hand over his stiff legs.

"Did I say something wrong?" Mom looked at them.

"No," Corey almost shouted. "No, no, no... ha! No, God no. I was just like 'What's she talking about?' you know? So what's for lunch?"

"Why are you dragging Pando around?"

"Something to do," Corey said. "I'm almost finished, so I'll come for lunch in, like, a minute. I'm starving, by the way. What did my dad make? Your turn, Tin."

Corey held out the stick. Mom looked at her. "Everything all right?"

"Yeah, Mom. It is, I swear. I'm not hungry." That wasn't true. "I might go for a walk or something."

Mom kept her X-ray vision on. Corey kept up the nervous laughter and Tin shook her head. He made a shot as Mom stared.

"Is the tree out of the way?" Tin asked.

Mom said they'd moved the car down the drive. They'd have to carry their things to pack it when it was time to leave.

"Tomorrow's Christmas." Mom pulled her hat on tighter. "Santa Claus is coming to town."

Corey began humming the song. Mom told her not to go far on her walk. Tin wasn't planning on leaving Toyland. Not yet, anyway. Mom told Corey lunch was getting cold and hoped he won.

"By the way," she said, "have you seen Baby Doll?"

"Baby Doll?" Tin said.

"The doll you found with the bear and pig. Pip can't find her. She said she was on the couch with the soldier. Pip thinks something happened to her. You know how she gets."

Corey wasn't listening. Instead, he tapped a shot around a funneling hole. Tin's mom left before the balls went flying.

"Look." He pointed the stick. "Almost zero. I think I got this game figured out—what's wrong?"

Tin shook her head. *Baby Doll is missing.* All the toys had been acting scared. They weren't like that when they first appeared. They were so happy, their hugs so free and loving. Now Piggy clung to her.

You should leave. Pando turned toward her.

Tin walked around the high chair. Piggy squeezed with all four legs. Pando buried his snout in his stumpy arms and shook his head. Tin looked at the panda's leg. It had a rip. Stuffing was leaking out.

"I told you," she said, "I'm not leaving."

A grin grew beneath Pando's snout. Her words, however, didn't soothe Piggy. The balls cracked and disappeared into holes. The scoreboard dinged.

"I did it," Corey said. "I think I won."

The room began to quake. At first she thought it was going to be one of those noises that worried her mom. The car was ready to go if it was. But this was more like a calculated vibration. A mechanical latch clicked into place; gears began turning.

Pando's grin widened.

The entire pool table sank. Corey went with it. They dropped three feet into icy blue water.

"Hooooo! Hooo!" Corey shouted. "Oh, my freaking jingle bells... oh, man."

He threw the stick and held his arms up. The water sloshed around his waist. Icy chips rode the waves.

"You got to be kidding me." He climbed onto the ledge. "You got to."

He was dripping onto the floor and flicked water at Tin. She hid behind the high chair.

He doesn't understand, Pando said. *He won.*

The pictures on the wall. The winners got to swim when the game was over. Because this was their version of pool. Of course it was. They were toys.

"I can't feel my legs!" Corey walked off, stiff-legged.

"Take Pando with you," Tin said.

"You."

"I'm not going back."

Corey looked at her. So did Pando. Tin looked at her phone. She needed to do something alone this time.

❇

Pip would be ready for a nap in an hour.

Tin would be back in time to read her a story. Once she was curled up with her thumb in her mouth, Tin would go out to the tower. If all went well, she'd be back before she woke up.

There was something to see before that.

She climbed the workshop ladder into the green air of the loft, where things still scurried and vines dangled. She slid carefully around the room and climbed the steps to the desk. Piggy peeked out of her collar and waved at Zebra.

Zebra did not wave back.

The plans and books were still where she'd left them. She wasn't there for them. She turned down a path to find something else.

The jewelry box was still closed.

The bottom drawer had mysteriously closed when she thought about reaching for it. Something about the way the objects around her had shimmered when it happened, how debris stirred on the floor.

Just like it knocked Piggy off the tower.

Something didn't want her to see what was in there. Perhaps it was nothing. She tugged on the delicate ring and found the drawer to be locked. It didn't come loose even when she braced it with her hand.

There was an envelope opener on the desk.

The blade was slender and the handle made of ivory. She slid it into the seam and began to pry. The blade bent under the strain. Piggy climbed out of her sweatshirt and tried to help. She almost quit, when the locking mechanism popped. The drawer slid all the way out of the box and spilled its only object on the floor.

The antique letter opener was ruined. She didn't feel it slip from her hand. Piggy climbed down and grabbed the frayed end of a string. Tin picked up the rubbery object tied to the other end.

A red balloon.

It hadn't been popped. Simply deflated. She'd seen this balloon before. Once upon a time, a key had been tied to the end and it had floated away from Toyland.

It came back.

Wallace had locked the toys in the room to protect them. He never wanted the key to be found, but the balloon was here. And the toy room was unlocked.

And the toys are empty.

"Did you escape?" she asked.

Piggy climbed onto her lap and hugged her neck. She didn't answer. But of course she did. Piggy, Clyde, Soldier and Baby Doll were the only ones who got out. That was why they took her up there, for her to see what had happened to the rest of them.

But who did it?

She leaned against a marble column lying on its side. The floor was cold. She reached into her back pocket. The little bell rang. There was so much she didn't understand.

She held up the balloon as if the hat would see it, as if that would be enough for it to know what she was asking.

"Show me."

She was standing in the field again.

The sky gray and wintery. Wallace had already crossed the barren field and entered the trees. She stood there waiting for him to return to chop down the steps.

The balloon was just a red dot hovering over the dense forest. Perhaps it would fall into the trees and snag on a limb and Wallace would come waddling back with it.

But it never descended.

The balloon was caught in a rising current of warm air. It began twisting and turning, spiraling as the weighted key was tossed around.

Then the red dot grew larger.

It changed course and headed back. The invisible vortex crept out of the trees and stirred the dust. It came toward her, and above it the balloon hung, quivering in the violent eddies. The balloon and its key went over Toyland.

Pando watched from the loft.

Tin began running. She didn't take her eyes off the balloon until it dropped over the roof. The ground pounded beneath her feet and thudded in her ears; her breath was hot exhaust as she turned the corner. She didn't find the balloon.

The front door was open.

She peeked inside. The lobby was just like they had found it on the day Tin and her family had arrived—the couches all in the same place, the one against the wall beneath a white sheet. Except for the upside-down stair case. It was open.

So was the toy room.

A lump swelled in her throat. The balloon was on the floor. The end of it cut. She took the steps three at a time. They didn't sway, didn't move. The toy room was dark and still. The toys were all around, tossed about like a ship rolling over. They weren't torn, weren't dirty or hurt.

Just still.

Tin tried to dig through them, but nothing would move. This was a vision, a story. She couldn't change it. But the toys were too deep. She couldn't see how far down they were buried. But nowhere did she see the pink fabric of Piggy or the brown fur of Clyde.

Until she stepped out of the room.

She looked down into the lobby. The fireplace was cold and black. The cobwebs had not yet grown thick and wavy; dust didn't cloud the photos on the walls. On the far side of the lobby, in front of the sheet-covered couch that hid the little door, four miniature figures looked back. One at a time, they ducked under the sheet. She heard the hinge on the hidden door swing.

Piggy was the last one in.

She was right in front of her, little legs on her cheeks. She threw them around Tin's neck and quivered. Pando was locked away in the loft, hidden and safe. But the toy room was routed. They had been taken. Lifeless.

"You escaped," she whispered.

She held Piggy like a football and didn't look back on the desk where she last saw Zebra. It was time for Pip's nap. Time for a new ending to the story.

Time to turn the tower off.

18

Tin barely had time to tie her boots. She slipped out the back without her coat and ran into the trees, falling twice, her legs so weak. The toymaker's hat had drained her again. She reached deep and ran on pure will.

She emerged from the trees and rested on her knees. The sun had dropped behind the tower. She raised her hand. The air was crisp. Waves distorted the clear sky.

I won't leave you.

She had promised Pando and all the other toys. She wasn't going to leave them behind for another Christmas. She walked across the barren circle and scanned the forest. Everything was still. Picturesque. A perfect day for the holidays, the kind of scene she imagined on calendars or greeting cards.

Tin rested against the tower.

The icy steel burned her hand. She laid her head back. The stairs went up a hundred feet. She couldn't climb them even if they touched the ground. Not now. She barely had the strength to reach into her backpack.

Monkeybrain flopped in her hand.

His fur was nappy and worn. Arms and legs swung like noodles;

his head bobbled loosely. She had swapped Piggy for Monkeybrain as Pip sucked her thumb. She might be awake by the time Tin got back, but she would make something up about a walk and telling stories.

"Wake up."

His head waggled limply. No one was around. She didn't think this would happen. The toys woke up when she was alone. Why didn't he wake up for Tin when she was little? Because they hadn't come out to Toyland.

"I promised."

She looked up and began laughing. Nothing was working out. None of the toys could climb up there, not with their stumpy legs. Not a hundred feet and not if that wind came back. For the thousandth time, she wondered if this was her imagination.

Did I really bring a purple monkey to climb it?

A felt hand grabbed her arm. Purple arms climbed onto her shoulder. She bumped her head on the tower as he leaned closer, his oversized eyes staring into hers. For a moment, she had the whooshing sensation of reality dropping out from under her.

It's not a dream.

She told him what to do, pointing at the stairwell. He needed to hang on tightly because it might get windy. And once he was up there, all he had to do was pull a lever.

And we all live happily ever after.

Monkeybrain looked up. He didn't smile. There was no expression. He simply climbed onto her head and reached for the tower's scaffolding leg. His tail momentarily wrapped around her neck. His little hand was much firmer than a child's grip.

She watched him ascend the tower.

He reached the steps in no time, using hands and feet to scamper up the scaffolding while his tail swung about. He peeked over the edge. Tin stood up weakly. She backed away, shading her eyes.

"Go!"

It was effortless.

He was halfway up in less than a minute, swinging around the platforms and sometimes scaling the struts. He wasn't being careless. This was what monkeys were made to do. This was a metal jungle.

Was that why Wallace made all the toys with generic arms and legs?

He was almost to the top when the first warning occurred. A limb broke. Monkeybrain was seconds from reaching the tower when the trees began swaying. And then it happened, but not like before.

A twister burst from the forest.

It came out angry and fierce, foliage and twigs and snow swirling into the vortex. It crossed the field in a second. Tin didn't have time to cover her eyes. A warning caught in her throat as a frigid blast stole her breath. She was thrown off-balance.

It attacked the tower.

The metal struts quivered. She cupped her hands and shouted. Monkeybrain was on the last set of steps. He was hanging onto the railing with all four hands. His body waved like a purple flag. If he got inside the tower, he would be safe. If he lost his grip, he would be thrown across the field.

How long could it last? Monkeybrain wouldn't get tired, would he? He could hang on as long as he needed to. Or until Mom or Oscar came out. All he needed was a slight pause and he could make the last couple of steps. The minutes went by and then she felt it. It was a lull. It was slight, just a faint pause, but it was enough.

Monkeybrain felt it too.

He scampered for the next rungs as his body and tail waved about. Carefully, he ascended the railing. Only two more. She hadn't thought about how he would get through the door or if it was locked. It wouldn't matter. Because the lull wasn't the vortex weakening.

It was inhaling.

Tin's ears popped. An atmospheric vacuum shook the ground. All at once, brittle blades of dormant grass quivered. The vortex punched out with twice the force. Monkeybrain held the last baluster in the railing. His grip couldn't be broken. He was going to make it, she was sure of it.

But the seams.

His arm ripped at the shoulder. It was thrown into the sky. His body rippled outward like a flag weathering a hurricane. Tufted bits of stuffing streamed out. When the seam on the second shoulder gave way, he was tossed like a broken kite, tumbling and flapping wildly. The vortex followed him, buoying him higher and higher. She was afraid he would be thrown deep into the forest. But it was worse. She heard more ripping.

A cloud of white stuffing burst like a firework.

The vortex suddenly vanished. Bits of shredded purple fabric fluttered like heavy confetti.

Tin couldn't remember falling to her knees.

Silence returned. The ground was scattered with bits of purple. The stuffing drifted into the trees like snow. Whatever did this was leaving.

She started crawling.

There was something in the forest that did it. It was getting away and she was on her hands and knees. What was she going to do if she caught it?

I promised.

"Tin!"

Pip ran toward the tower. Mom reached for her and missed. Pieces of Monkeybrain were everywhere. Tin lay there listening to her little sister and her mom's attempt to soothe her.

"Why, Tin?"

Mom was confused and angry. Her lips were thin. Tin looked back at the trees. It was gone. Whatever did this had gotten away. Tin wondered if it could do something like this, what else could it do?

Is that why Wallace left?

"Mom, we have to leave."

※

At some point, Pip began to hyperventilate.

Once they were inside, she dissolved into a string of hiccups and syllables. Tin couldn't bear to look at her, snot running and eyes puffy.

Tin found an empty room as far away from the lobby as she could find. She stared out a triangular window. Her mom was probably still consoling Pip, convincing her that they could put Monkeybrain back together. But he was old—at least as old as Tin—and maybe it was time to get a new Monkeybrain.

Somewhere in the panicked sobs, Pip would say he wouldn't be the same. That was what Tin would say. But it wasn't just that he'd been pulled apart.

I did it.

The sun had dipped behind the trees. Daylight was quickly giving way to a starry night. Her reflection grew. She wasn't wearing a coat and was heavier. She wasn't imagining it. *Did anyone notice?*

The door closed behind her.

She kneaded the toymaker's hat like a good-luck charm. There was no furniture in the room. There were no pictures on the walls, no weird games or upside-down staircases. Just a sunken floor that Mom walked around.

Their reflections were equally gutted.

"You won't believe me," Tin said.

"Try me."

There was a lot of story to tell, none of which her mom would believe. She looked down at the hat.

"This doesn't belong to Wallace. He found it on his expedition." She shook her head. She didn't really know that, but it didn't matter. "It belongs to an elf. And not just some regular elf who lives on the North Pole. This was a special one. A toymaker."

Mom was still listening.

"When he put it on, things... happened. Special things."

"Special?"

"Wallace, um, when he put it on, he just knew how to do things. Like build this house and the solar panels. He did things to the tower. He made lots of money with it."

She paused with the hat twisted in a knot.

"He brought toys to life."

Mom nodded thoughtfully. The kind of nod that went along with that kind of story. The kind of nod a mom gave when she saw where a lie was going.

"Okay," she said. "That would explain why you and Corey are carrying stuffed toys around."

"You believe me?"

"I believe you were talking to toys. And I believe you were playing with them. You put the panda in the game room chair. You've always had a great imagination, Tin."

Imagination. Tin went back to twisting the hat. Mom took it from her. "So what happens when you wear it?"

"What?"

"You said Wallace did special things when he wore the hat. What happens when you wear it?"

"I sort of... sort of see things."

"Mmm." Mom frowned curiously. She was being incredibly patient. Maybe the Christmas spirit kept her in check. She looked inside the hat, rang the bell.

"It won't work on you," Tin said.

Mom put it on anyway. The bell flopped to the side. She looked at her reflection.

"Why would you do that to Monkeybrain, Tin? I just... I'm trying to understand. Help me. You know what he means to your sister."

"She talks to him, Mom. You've seen her do it. This house, that hat... it brought him to life, too."

"Hon, she's four. You talked to toys when you were four."

Adults' imaginations fade. If they know what's going on, what's really happening, the truth will break them. That's what Pip said. Is that what happened to Wallace?

How much time do I have left?

"We have to leave, Mom."

"Tomorrow is Christmas."

"No, Mom, something is out there and—"

"It's dark, Tin. And nothing's out there."

"I can show you, Mom. The tower is making an invisible wall, like a dome or something. You can see it, I swear. If you go out there and walk through it, you won't be able to see what's inside. Wallace was using it to hide the hat from Santa."

"Santa?"

"That's why I had Monkeybrain. He was climbing the tower to turn it off. But there's—"

"All right, stop, hon. Monkeybrain wasn't climbing—"

"Something's out there, Mom. It's taking the toys, and I think it scared Wallace away." A ripple of chills rode down her back. "I'm scared, too."

Mom looked serious. Maybe Tin said too much. Words weren't going to break her mom, but they could worry her. That wasn't what Tin wanted to do.

I promised, she thought. *But I can't hurt my family.*

"Why can't I see them?" Mom said. "If the toys are alive, why can't I talk to them?"

"Because you're... you're too old."

Mom actually laughed. It was just once. She shook her head, staring at the hat, then another wave of laughter shook her until she wiped her eyes. It sounded like nonsense. Tin wouldn't believe it, either. Her mom had to see what was happening.

And she can't.

"Tomorrow," Mom said, "you'll apologize to your sister. And then you're going to help put Monkeybrain back together."

"Mom, we really have to—"

She held up her hand. "We're safe, Tin. Nothing's going to happen. Santa won't come because we put out the presents for him, okay? In a few days, we'll pack up the car and head home. We can take the toys with us and talk about this some more. Right now I just want to have a normal Christmas."

She put the hat in Tin's hands.

"Your sister loves you, you know that." She kissed her forehead. "I do, too."

Tin remained with just her reflection staring back. Christmas was tomorrow. There was still time to talk to her mom, take her out to the wall. Oscar would come, too. Tin could show them. Once they saw how it made everything invisible, how it shocked them, how the tower was emanating energy, they would believe. Maybe not believe in the hat or the toys, but they would believe they were in danger. That would be enough.

Unfortunately, Tin wouldn't get the chance.

19

Each snowflake fluttered like a crystalized butterfly. They each made a unique sound, carried a note different than all the others. Tin stuck out her tongue. She wanted to know what sound tasted like. There was tiny laughter as she chased after them with her tongue out, their notes making a music box melody.

A song.

She hummed along. Even though she couldn't catch one of them, even when she swatted at them, it was fun. Even when the snowfall had reached her waist. She grew tired, the kind of tired that felt so good, so satisfying. She wanted to lie down, close her eyes and let the butterfly snowflakes take her deeper.

Until one of them poked her in the eye.

It wasn't white like the others. It was sort of tan and coarse. Definitely harder than a snowflake should be. It bounced off her nose. There were more sprinkling down from the sky like off-colored hail. They tickled her nose and she sneezed.

Then a large one filled the sky.

It was bigger than all the snowflakes combined, like a giant foot coming to squash her. She tried to run, but there was nowhere to hide. Its shadow passed over her. She covered her head and, strangely, felt it kick her in the chin.

She opened her eyes.

Something was standing on her face, rubbing thin hands together. Crumbs fell on her nose. Flat legs left a sweet trail on her lips. It was about to kick her again.

She sat up.

The thin little figure went tumbling into the blankets. A silhouette crawled out like a cardboard cutout. Tin went to squash it.

No!

The cutout lifted its arm. The voice in her head wasn't Pando's. It was higher-pitched and sort of funny. She fumbled her phone from her cargo pants and lit him up.

Gingerman.

She hid the phone. The lobby was dark again. The logs in the fireplace were black and cold. Oscar was snoring hard. She could see his breath. The furnace must have gone out again.

And no one noticed.

Gingerman dug through the blankets and retrieved a short arm. It had broken off when she sat up. She reached for him and he clubbed her with it.

Never, never pick up a gingerperson. Unless you plan to eat us.

"You're... alive?"

He climbed onto her shoulder. *I'm the only one left.*

Piggy wasn't under the covers or in the sleeping bag. Pip was on the same couch as Mom, thumb in her mouth. No Monkeybrain, of course. Corey was on the other couch. She couldn't see if Clyde was there.

He took them.

"Where?"

Where? No, he took them. Gingerman stiffened like a regular, edible cookie. Like the toys in the toy room. Whoever he was talking about was sucking the life force out of them. *He took them.*

He's not like the other toys, Gingerman said. *He only takes.*

"Who? Who is it? Who's taking them—"

Shhhh. He put the detached arm on her lips. *I can't say his name or he'll come back.*

"Tell me where he is."

No time for that. Now's your only chance. You've got to turn it off while he's not looking. Hurry!

"Turn what off?"

He climbed down the blanket then slid to the floor. His crispy legs clicked on the hardwood.

If you don't turn it off, you'll never leave Toyland.

"Because of the wall?"

No, not the wall? Get with it. He'll take you, too, just like the others. He'll take all of you—your mom, your sister, your... whoever he is—

"Corey?"

Whatever. Turn off the tower or you end up like them.

He drew the detached arm across his neck. He tap-danced across the room. Tin illuminated the others. Oscar kept snoring and no one stirred. They were counting sugarplums. She noticed the time. It was midnight.

Christmas.

She tiptoed after Gingerman. He was at the front door. A moonbeam had fallen through the window.

"Where are you going?" she whispered.

I'm out of here.

"You can't leave. You've got to help me."

Help? What am I going to do? It would take me six months to climb the tower. No, you're the only one who can do it. By the way, a little help?

He pointed the arm at the door.

This was happening too fast. Was he telling her to climb the tower in the middle of the night? That was what it sounded like. *While he's not looking?*

She looked back at her mom. Oscar almost never let the fire die, especially with the furnace not working. But he did the other night when everyone slept late.

When I dreamed about the song, she thought.

Gingerman was right. If she was going to go, this was it. She could make it back to bed and no one would even know she was gone. Unless, of course, something bad happened.

Like really bad. Like really, really.

Seriously, there's nothing I can do. He turned his icing-caked face toward her. *Like nothing. At all.*

"I can't do this."

Remember Piggy? She's depending on you. We all are. Now just be really cool and crack the door so I can get a head start.

He danced around like Pip when she really had to go. Tin put her hand on the doorknob.

Come on, come on, come—

She pulled it open no more than half an inch and he slid onto the porch. His voice faded off.

We're all counting on you. No pressure.

Tin closed the door and held her breath. Everyone was still sleeping. She quietly walked over to the couches. Corey was hugging a pillow. Pip had a blanket against her face. And Soldier, who always ended up standing guard, wasn't at his post.

He even took Pando, she thought.

She laced up her boots and went out the front door. The full moon was blurry and the stars smudgy lights. The wall had been turned up again. That was why the furnace was off. Someone was bound to wake up and soon. Tin crept back inside and stuffed pillows under her blanket just in case her mom did.

Then sprinted across the porch.

❄

No wind. The air crisp in her chest and on her face.

She remembered a time when she was the same age as Pip. Mom and Dad told her she could stay up past her bedtime. Christmas was getting close, but they said a special man would come to visit if she was good.

She knew they meant Santa.

And she knew that Santa always rode in a sleigh pulled by reindeer. So she sat at the window and watched the sky until a car pulled into the driveway.

Santa got out of a taxi.

He was wearing his red suit and his beard was snow white. He moved slowly, like he was sore. He was probably tired, she thought. He came from the North Pole. She didn't know there were taxis up there.

They gave him tea and cookies, and she sat on his knee and he laughed exactly like she thought he would. She told him she wanted a tent for Christmas.

Hohoho!

It wasn't supposed to be funny.

She thought he would smell more like hot cocoa and cinnamon. He smelled a lot like her dad. And when he bent over, he was wearing a Led Zeppelin T-shirt underneath his coat. She thought that was strange, but maybe he vacationed like a normal person between Christmases.

"Is Santa real?" she asked.

"What do you think?" Mom said with a smile.

She decided he was. And that if Led Zeppelin Santa came again next year, she'd ask him if he was real. Now she stood on the edge of the forest, wondering the same thing.

Is he real?

The tower was a dark monolith. She could feel it humming. Wishing she could ask her mom again, that her mom would tell her it was going to be all right.

That Santa was real.

The tower was a skeletal monster of steel standing steady in the cold winter night. There was no wind to blow the snow. Nothing to disturb it.

She went.

The frozen earth pounded beneath her. Breath hissing, chest burning, she ran straight for the nearest tower leg. She couldn't think about it or she'd turn around. Tears welled; the cold metal scaffolding bit her fingers.

The humming went through her.

She searched for toeholds without looking down, finding a firm grip before pushing up. She focused upward until she was level with the first step. She knew how high it was.

Her fingers were numb.

She clung tightly, hugging the scaffolding. The rusted metal was rough and flaky. She knew how far she'd fall if she slipped. But she didn't know how long she'd be out there if she did.

She looked down.

It was a mistake. Thirty feet looked different from up there. It was only a short walk across a beam to reach the stairs. But there would be at least one step in between angled struts with nothing to hold. She'd done ropes courses.

Not without a harness.

Breathe, hon, she heard her mom say. *You can always breathe.*

She closed her eyes and drew a breath. There was nothing to distract her when she was fully present. Just be here. Just be now.

The first step was terrifying. Fear plunged into her legs as she reached the gap. She had never felt so alone being on that beam with nothing to hold. Hand out, she lunged and didn't stop.

She was on the stairs.

The vibrations rang through her. She pulled herself up the railing two steps at a time, swinging around the turns with her eyes on the trees, waiting for the branches to shake.

The vibrations numbed her ankles. She could taste metal under her tongue, could hear the hum in her head. She slid along the railing with both hands, pulling herself up the steps. Almost to the top and she held her breath.

She made it.

Wheezing, she paused on the platform that circled the hut. Her senses had been chiseled down to nearly nothing. She found the door on the far side. The knob turned.

The door was stuck.

She leaned into it and tried again. Slivers of pain lanced through her shoulder. She stepped back to the railing. She didn't come all this way to be stopped by a swollen door. She closed her eyes and lowered her shoulder, pushing off the railing, and with all her weight forward, braced for impact, hoping to hear the hinges squeal or the doorframe splinter.

Silence.

She had rolled across the floor with barely a sound. She didn't remember falling or hearing the door close behind her.

The vibrations were gone. No ringing in her head or dull pain in her shoulder. Just the sound of her wheezy breath. She wiped her eyes.

Impossible.

This wasn't what she expected. It was a snow-white floor and snow-white walls that were too far apart. The hut wasn't this big on the outside. The lobby wasn't even this big.

It was empty except for a large snow-white column.

It was smooth and featureless and went from floor to ceiling. She pushed herself off the floor, no longer numb, no longer aching, as if she hadn't run through the cold or scaled a metal mountain.

Her footsteps echoed.

The column was polished and cold as a winter stream. She could hear it humming. It sounded like water trickling inside a frozen waterfall. There were no control panels to open, no hidden buttons or switches.

No lever.

But the plans...

"I don't..." Her voice startled her. It echoed unusually loud.

I don't know what to do.

She usually said that to her mom when things seemed hopeless, when there was nowhere else to turn. Now it was just her, all alone. And breathing wasn't going to solve this.

She had destroyed Monkeybrain for nothing.

Gingerman was wrong. She wanted to believe she could make a difference, but she was just a kid dumb enough to climb up a dark metal tower in the middle of the night.

A little bell rang in her pocket.

The toymaker's hat never transported anyone else who put it on. Just her. *I didn't find it. It found me.*

She held it up.

Why did Wallace turn on the tower? Why did he leave? Who was taking the toys? The answers were in the hat.

The truth. That's all I ask.

She closed her eyes and felt the fabric on her forehead, felt the cold bite on the end of her nose. Suddenly it was freezing cold again. The vibrations were back. She opened her eyes, expecting to see Wallace in the field or at his workbench. But she was alone.

And in a tiny room.

The floor was old gray planks. There was a black pipe in the middle—not a white column—and a wooden door was behind her. This was it. This was what the hut on top of the tower was supposed to look like.

And I'm still wearing the hat.

She opened the door. The night was still clear and cold, the stars still blurry through the tower's force field. Her teeth oddly rattled from the vibrations.

She wasn't transported to another time and place. She was exactly where she'd been the entire time. But everything looked different. Hesitantly, she reached for the hat.

The white room was back.

When she put it on, the tiny room returned. Back and forth she went, putting the hat on and taking it off. The white room came and went each time. That was how it worked. Without the toymaker's hat, it was the illusion of a large white room. But with the hat on her head, she saw everything exactly how it was.

This is how it's protected!

She had been standing in the hut the entire time but wasn't seeing it. No one would see the black pipe without the toymaker's hat.

Or the lever.

She grabbed the T-shaped handle with both hands. It took all of her weight to budge it. She leaned back and groaned. The pipe revved up. The floorboards began to quake. The vibrations rattled her vision. She put all of her weight on it. The noises grew louder. She couldn't hear herself breathing, couldn't feel her legs anymore. She wasn't even sure she was still holding onto it. She'd closed her eyes and puuuuuuulled.

And then she was screaming.

All the noise stopped when the lever reached the bottom. The quaking, the vibrations... they were gone. Just her cries of effort broke the silence. She stood up and listened, waiting for something, anything to happen. She pushed on the wooden door. The hinges creaked.

The stars were back.

She felt four years old again, waiting for Santa to cross the sky. Her mom and dad in the other room and Tin in her footy pajamas, safe and sound. A special day just hours away.

She believed.

The hills were carpeted and the trees frosted. The land undulated beneath a blanket of snow. She circled around the tower, looking across a perfect Christmas Day, wondering what Wallace was thinking when he built this place. He didn't want to share it, so he made it disappear.

Not anymore.

She made her way down the steps, slow and steady. She took her time crossing the beam. It was easier now that the structure wasn't vibrating. When she reached the ground, she paused to look around. No shadows were waiting in the trees. No mysterious twisters.

She walked back to Toyland.

The stars were still sparkling. She didn't know what would happen next. Maybe everyone was awake and wondering where she went. Mom would be angry and scared, but then the toy room would open and all the toys would march out because somehow the lever brought them all back to life. She hoped that would happen.

A Christmas miracle.

She crossed the front porch. Gingerman's footprints dotted the snow. She paused with her hand on the door and muttered her wish again.

It came true.

The toys were on the floor—Piggy and Clyde, sitting there with arms out, waiting for her. Just sitting there. Pando, too. He was in front of the sad little Christmas tree. He stood up when she closed the door.

"Hey," she whispered, "you're never going to believe what I did."

Something crunched under her boot. The floor was scattered with gingerbread crumbs. A broken arm was the only thing still intact. Then she heard a voice in her head. It wasn't Gingerman.

Pando walked toward her on two legs.

I know exactly what you did.

PART IV

TADOULE LAKE, Manitoba, Canada – Thomas Kramer, 63, has lived in the country all of his life. This past Christmas, he saw something he'll never forget.

"I thought maybe I was dreaming," Kramer said. "I was pouring coffee and someone was skating across the lake."

It's rare for Kramer to see anyone in the middle of winter. It only happened once in his life, and that was a lost hunting party. After following the sighting on a snowmobile, he found a man on the shore.

"He was setting up camp," Kramer said. "The fool had on a T-shirt and strange boots, said his name was Mr. Doe. I figured as much, people out here are private. But I still don't know how he got that far in winter dressed like that."

Kramer brought him back to the cabin, where he and his wife and their newborn shared Christmas dinner with him. The man said his name was Pan and that he was searching for someone.

"He spoke of reindeer that could leap great distances and that, soon, one of them would find him because of a hat or something."

Kramer had intended on him staying the night so that he could give him a ride into town. The next morning, he was gone. But before he left, Kramer saw something else he'd never witnessed. His newborn had been suffering from colic for months.

"We just couldn't get him to sleep," Kramer said. "And then this hairy little man just sang this song and we all got tired. Next thing, the baby's sleeping."

Any information regarding someone who matches this description, contact the local authorities.

20

Something was wrong.

It was how quiet the lobby was, the silence too complete. Nothing moved. Piggy and Clyde stared like empty toys.

Pando was on his back legs, standing almost six feet tall, his stubby arms at the sides of his big belly. He walked through the shadows, stopping in the moonbeam that spotlighted Piggy and Clyde.

His stitched mouth wasn't smiling.

A chill gripped her. One of fear and dread. Pando fixed a dull stare on her, the big green button eyes waiting. And it all came crashing down, the realization of what had been happening all this time. It was right in front of her.

"You," she said.

No smile, no wink. Not a word in her mind.

Tin approached under his watchful button-eyed glare. She swept up Piggy. She was firm, the fabric soft and the eyes empty. Just like a toy should be.

An ordinary, lifeless toy.

"Why would you do this?" she said.

A grin finally broke Pando's muzzle. It curled with the sardonic leer of something that crawled out from under the bed or hid in the closet.

They have something I need.

"You took their-their—"

Life?

She couldn't say it. He took the life from the toys. They didn't talk, but they moved and felt. They loved. And he took it from them.

He studied Corey's bear. *Do you think they care? Mmm? That's what they're for. They were made to give.*

She snatched Clyde from him, closing her eyes, wishing her love would somehow bleed into them and wake them up again. She'd done it before. And Pando, too. He was nothing but a stuffed panda bear the first time she saw him in the loft.

Or was he? she thought. *Maybe they were all alive this entire time.*

"You got the key from the balloon. That was you, I saw it. I saw what you did to the toys."

And ever since Pando woke up, the toys had been shivering. She felt Piggy's fear. Clyde's too. All of them were frightened, but she didn't know why.

"They're scared of you. And so was Wallace."

Wallace? Pando tilted his head and chuckled. *You still don't get it? The hat decided not to tell you? Then let me. He was scared, true. But not of me, silly girl.*

"Scared of what?"

Of what we'd become.

He paced toward the front door. A draft was leaking in. He quietly closed it, walking so fluidly, so humanlike. He picked up the gingerbread arm and broke it in half, letting the pieces bounce on the floor.

"You're the dangerous one."

He shook his arm. If he had fingers, he would've been shaking one at her.

I'm not a monster! I'm not. I'm better than them. He waved at Piggy and Clyde. *They could've all been like this, but he was too scared to let me do it. He'd seen what I created.*

"What are you?"

I'm not a stupid toy.

His smile sent shivers across the room. He tipped his head and leered darkly. If that stitched mouth could open, a tongue would wickedly flicker out.

I'm just like you.

"Me?"

No, he didn't mean her. He was walking on two legs, spoke so fluently, his gestures so natural. He didn't mean her. He meant human.

"Wallace was lonely," she muttered.

The amused smile grew to absurd lengths. His green button eyes partially hid in the black circles of fabric.

The hat saved his life. He was a desperate man, a good man. He didn't deserve to die alone on the North Pole. So the hat healed him, saved him, let him return. He made the world a better place, you can't deny that. All these toys going out into the world to spread love, that was because of him. But do you think anyone understood that? Did they appreciate him?

No.

So he made Pando, the perfect companion. Better than human, better than you. Think of it, house after house, family after family, with a Pando to watch over them, to love them, to know them. Think of it!

His voice left traces of a high-pitched squeal.

But he played some tricks on me. Oh, yes he did. A lot smarter than I thought. Yes, indeed. He played tricks. He couldn't see the wisdom of what we could do, and he left me here all alone! All alone in my Toyland! He thumped his chest. *He locked them up, but he couldn't stop me. That was his mistake, leaving me with all his powers.*

"What powers?"

I need what they have because I'm not like them. He moved closer to Tin. *I'm like you.*

She went around the sad little tree. The bell on the hat rang in her back pocket. There was laughter. Strangely maniacal and very human.

He left to tell on me. Can you believe that? He thought the only way to make things right was to find the toymaker and give back the hat. The toymaker would put it on and make all of this go away, he thought. *So he left me here, and look where we are, all these years later. No toymaker.*

"You took down the steps, didn't you? You didn't want anyone climbing the tower."

She had seen it in the vision, when Wallace launched the balloon and walked into the trees. The steps were still there. Wallace had even tried to turn off the tower. Pando once said the dangerous one had chopped down the stairs. She thought he was talking about Wallace.

The dangerous one never left.

We need the tower, silly girl. It was made for us, so we could live. But he couldn't take the hat with him, so he hid it from me. He thought it would somehow protect the toys until he got back, but then these little ingrates tried to climb the tower. They even tried to burn it down.

He went to the couches and pulled the blanket up to Pip's chin.

"What do you want from us?"

I'm not going to hurt you. He left, didn't he? So will you. The tower goes back on, and then you and Mommy and little girl here and all the rest can go home and never come back. But first, give me the hat.

He sat on the armrest and held out his arm, patiently. Pip didn't move. Tin noticed her thumb had fallen out of her mouth. Her lips quivered with each breath.

"The hat," she said, "it won't work for you."

He couldn't use the hat or he would've already done it. He said the hat chose to be found not the other way around. *Why did it choose me?* But still he wanted the hat. And she knew why.

So I don't have it, she thought.

She started backing toward the door. He didn't get up to stop her, simply lowered his beckoning arm and nodded, as if sighing.

Do you want them to wake up?

"What?"

They're nice people. I can see why you love them. He smacked Pip's leg then shook Mom's shoulder.

They jostled about and moaned. Mom smacked her lips and pulled Pip closer. Tin remembered dreaming of snowflakes that sang a song. *If you want to play, and stay out all day, I know the place we can do it.*

But Pando was lying. If she turned the tower on, they would never leave. And at some point she'd fall asleep and hear the song again. This time Gingerman wouldn't be there to wake her.

I don't want to hurt them. Pando got up, patiently. *I just want to live.*

She grabbed the hat from her pocket. The crumbs of Gingerman crunched under her boot. The door was only another step. He couldn't get to her in time. The car was down the driveway and past the fallen tree. She could take the hat with her.

But I can't leave them, she thought. *I can't leave my family.*

The crumbs of Gingerman swirled into a neat little pile, pieces of his arms and legs crumbled around his flat head. Tin's ears popped. The ornaments on the tree wobbled. Suddenly, there was a breeze in the lobby.

The hat was ripped from her hands.

It flew right to Pando. He stared at her with barely a grin, the hat fitting over his outstretched arm.

"You."

Fear transformed in the crucible of anger. There was someone in the woods when the twister hit the tower. Tin had noticed Pando had a rip on his leg.

I told you I was special. He stopped in the moonbeam. *Here's what's going to happen. You're going to climb the tower again, just like before when the pile of crumbs snuck you out of here when I was busy. I'll stop singing the song to your family, and they'll wake up in the morning as if nothing happened. And then we can all have a talk. You, me, Mommy. Just a happy little family.*

He didn't raise an arm or blink a button eye. But her ears popped again, and this time she felt electromagnetic waves pulse through the lobby. A picture fell off the wall but didn't shatter. It floated in front of her, the one of Wallace and Pando. Just the two of them.

How does that sound, Tinsley Ann?

He knew her name. Her real name. Of course he did. He was in her head. That was how he communicated. If he could put thoughts in her head, then he could see what thoughts were there.

I know all your secrets. It comes with the package. He opened his arms as if presenting himself. *I know how you pick your nose when no one is watching, how you don't brush your teeth, or how you wish your sister would sometimes just go away. Or that your Mom would just be a normal mom.*

"That's not true."

I know how you miss your father, but not the one who left you and never calls. You miss the imaginary father you never had, the one you pretend to have. A father who understands you, who has your back. I know that you sometimes put that stuffed dog in the chair, the one your real dad gave you when you had your tonsils taken out, and pretend it's the imaginary Dad Charming. He gives you advice, tells you that you're pretty, that he loves you—

"Stop!" She shook her head, trying to scramble her memories.

That's why Wallace left, she thought. *It was because of you.*

His mocking grin faltered. He saw that thought too. The picture shattered at her feet. An electromagnetic wave tore Piggy from her arms and into his grasp.

You really think Santa is real? He shook the hat. *The hat lies just like the toys. There is no Santa, silly girl. He's not going to see us; he's not going to save anyone. And even if he was, if he floated down here behind magic reindeer, what do you think he'll do? Think he's going to bring them all back to life and let you take them home like puppies? No. He gives little kids empty little things like this.*

Piggy flopped in his arms.

Wallace made us all special, not Santa.

He stalked nearer, towering over her. It was as if he'd grown since the day she first saw him, the day he trotted on all fours like a real bear. She stared up at his green button eyes glittering with life.

I will count to three. You choose whether to be a good girl or a naughty one.

She was trapped. There was no point in grabbing the hat. He could make a twister take it back. Even if she could wrestle Piggy away, she was empty. Her family was asleep. And a magic panda bear was glaring down at her.

One.

Something moved on the ceiling. She didn't look at it directly, just watched it swing in the periphery. Pando didn't notice because it was directly above him.

The ceiling door.

It was in the middle with no way up or down. Now it swung open and silently came to a standstill.

Two.

Something moved inside it. A pointed hat came out of the shadows followed by a square mouth.

Tin's heart walloped.

She focused on her breath, keeping thoughts from forming a warning flare. Pando wasn't the only special toy in Toyland. There was one of them different than all the rest, who wasn't made of cotton stuffing and soft fabric. He didn't feel like Piggy or Clyde or Baby Doll. He wasn't made for hugging.

It was to protect.

The wooden toy fell out of the ceiling. Pando was about to teach Tin a lesson if she didn't agree to turn the tower on, but in the moments before he finished counting to three, he saw what was coming.

It was too late.

Soldier dropped like an arrow, his square mouth open in a silent scream, his spear pointed down. There was a long rip. The panda bear arched violently.

A storm engulfed the lobby.

Pictures were slung in hurricane winds, the couches slid, and the sad little tree tossed across the room. Debris showered the walls. Pando swung around. White stuffing poured from a long tear. He reached back to hold it together.

Soldier was flung onto the ceiling.

The wooden toy rebounded to the other side of the room. He skittered like a rodent, the tapping of wooden limbs falling quiet.

Pando sent blankets flying. The tree landed on the steps. Firewood punched holes in walls as Pando stalked the room. There was another rip and Pando hobbled to one side.

Stuffing leaked from his leg.

Pando sent everything into the corner to bury Soldier. Her family was still on the couches with no blankets or pillows. Oscar snored. Pip sucked her thumb.

Hey.

Tin heard a whisper. She looked down at the pile of crumbs. The icing on the head was moving. It blew away crumbs like strands of long hair.

Sweep me up, Gingerman said. *This is our only chance to go.*

"Go... I... I can't—"

Soldier's doing his job so you can escape.

Tin looked back. Pando was digging through the pile now. "But Pando—"

That's not Pando!

"What... what you—"

It doesn't matter, he can't suck the love out of Soldier because he's made of courage. And I'm made of brains. So come on, sweep up my brains.

"My family."

They're okay, but not if you're still here when he gets a hold of Soldier, which he will.

"And then what?"

Exhibit A. The part that was his hand pointed at the crumbs. *Look, let him have the hat. He can't use it without you.*

Something broke. Pando went after it.

"Where am I going—"

Get in the car. Bring back help.

Something went flying. It hit the ceiling and then the wall. A piece landed near her feet. It was a wooden hat. Pando pounced in a storm of fluff. It was flowing from his chest now. He pushed something heavy back inside his body.

What is that? she thought.

The next thought that ran through her mind was not her own. It blew open the valve of adrenaline and ignited the fight or flight response.

Run, run, Gingerman's voice rang loudly. *As fast as you can!*

❄

TIN CRASHED into a snowdrift and popped up like a windup toy.

High-octane hormones fueled her around the driveway's turns like a snowball rolling down Mount Everest. She hopped over the fallen tree like an Olympian and picked up speed.

It was the rumbling that broke her stride.

It thundered through adrenaline-soaked panic, a tremor that sounded like heavy machinery and cracking lumber in the distance.

The car was hiding in the forest's moonlit shadows. Mom had driven around the tree so they wouldn't be snowed in again. It was ready to go, the keys in the ignition where she always left them. Tin's chest was burning. Her legs cold and weary.

The adrenaline tapped out.

There wasn't much left to burn, not after the tower.

The starry night was obscured by intertwining branches. There was no wall to stop her, nothing that would turn off the squirming cookie crumbs in her pocket. The world was wide open. And her family was back there.

And Toyland was breaking.

Whoa, whoa, Gingerman said. *Where are you going?*

"He can't see me."

She started back up the drive, her legs reluctantly hiking up the slope, her thighs quickly on fire. She locked into a furious stride, head down.

Who? Who can't see you?

She didn't want to say it out loud. But she thought it and Gingerman heard it.

Santa Claus? Gingerman said. *Santa... he's not back in the house! He's not anywhere. You believe in Santa?*

"You're alive, aren't you?"

I'm alive doesn't mean there's a Santa Claus. You realize that, right? There's all sorts of miracles that don't mean Santa Claus is real. Come on! He wriggled like a pocketful of bugs. *Look, I don't know why I'm alive. No one does. But I know how you can stay alive. It's not up there!*

She rounded the last bend. The porch swing was swaying. Snow was falling off the eaves. Black holes were smashed out of the walls where firewood shot through like cannonballs.

No! No, you can't go in there. You can't. There's nothing you can do.

She stopped with tears blurring the details of the crooked shutters. Maybe, she thought, she could carry her family out, one at a time, if Soldier kept Pando busy long enough. But carry them where?

She didn't have the strength to pick up Pip.

Okay, I admit it, Gingerman said. *I'm scared. There, you happy? I'm not like the other toys, you know. Wallace just made them to love, made Soldier brave. Made Pando psycho. He made me different. So I think, you know, it'd be cool if we went away from Toyland. Like far, far away.*

"You're wrong." She ran past the porch. "The toys are scared."

Not for themselves they're not. It was you, silly. They knew he would do something. They knew Soldier couldn't stop him, he could only buy you some time to escape. Get it? The car, the road.

Tin made it around Toyland and into the forest, the sounds of breaking boards and shattering glass fading. She was scraping the remains of adrenaline.

"Run, run," she panted, "as fast as you can... you can't catch me..."

Gingerman's remains went still. She fell in front of the dilapidated stage, pushed herself up and continued. For a moment, she thought the crumbs had fallen from her pocket.

That's what I say. How, uh, how did you know that?

She reached the end of the path and stood at the edge of the circle. The metal monster stood on four legs. The tower was cold and still. The night sky bright and clear. Gingerman wanted to run. That was all he knew how to do.

Tin didn't know what to do.

So she was doing something different. The only thing that made sense. And it didn't really make any sense at all.

The brittle ground crunched beneath her boots. Her face to a full moon, stars dusting the black night like diamonds, she searched for a streaking comet. Or a sleigh.

"I'm sorry," she whispered.

She remembered the exact day it happened; at a sleepover, her best friend, Tina, told her Santa wasn't real. Tina's mom told Tin it was true, that it was her mom and dad who were pretending to be Santa. They were the ones who were leaving the presents under the tree.

Tin had argued about the milk that was gone on Christmas morning, the cookies half-eaten. The carrots on the sidewalk for the reindeer were missing. The sooty footprints at the fireplace. It was proof. Right?

Tin's mom was so angry with Tina's mom. But she relented, told her it was fun to pretend. Told Tin not to tell her friends like Tina did, because they wanted to believe.

Tin did too.

She wanted to lie in bed and swear she heard the reindeer's hooves on the roof, heard the bells ringing on their harnesses, hear Santa's belly laugh as he slipped presents under the tree and stuffed the stockings. And not the Led Zeppelin Santa. The real one. And she would be snuggled up in her covers as sugarplums danced and the world felt safe.

"I grew up," she said. "I had to."

She reached the tower's moon shadow and continued searching the sky, her voice effortlessly reaching the trees. She didn't need to speak loudly. He would hear her.

If he was up there.

She leaned against one of the tower's legs and slid to the ground. It was hard and cold. She wrapped her arms around her knees and continued searching.

She was alone. Just her and the tower. The trees and the stars. A still Christmas night. Not a creature was stirring.

"I thought I was helping. I didn't mean to... make it worse."

She dropped her head and felt warm tears spread against the

backs of her cold hands. She was crying for a lot of reasons. Her family was in danger; she was helpless and didn't know what to do. And Pando had uncorked her secret thoughts, the way she pretended to have a better dad, the way she hated her real one.

The mess she made.

She thought if she turned the wall off, help would come. Now it was up to her. And she didn't know what to do.

At some point between blowing her nose and quietly sobbing, something was ringing. It was tiny and bouncy. She held her breath and listened. At first, there was only the sound of her pulse. Even the distant quaking of Toyland had gone quiet. But then she heard it again.

It was a bell.

There was no one walking out of the trees, but it was getting closer. And then, in the moonlight, she saw something trotting near the ground. The toymaker's hat was galloping right at her, ringing with each stride. She sat in disbelief.

The hat had never moved on its own, but it was making its way across the barren ground. It slowed as it neared then stopped in front of her, the bell lying between crispy tufts of weeds. She reached down to pick it up.

Zebra.

The toy zebra shook snowflakes from her black and white mane. The toy zebra that had been on Wallace's desk. The toy zebra her Awnty Awnie had left. Zebra looked up with black glassy eyes and nudged the hat. Tin reached for the stuffed animal.

The warmth gushed inside her.

It filled her with love and something else. It wasn't words or thoughts she heard, not a vision. But Tin understood what Zebra was feeling. She was holding something more than love.

Sadness.

Awnty Awnie had left her. Zebra knew she couldn't stay at Toyland any longer. She had to leave. And she had to leave Zebra behind. It broke her heart to do so.

Zebra's too.

Tin reached into her sweatshirt and found the hard outline of the necklace's medallion. Zebra crawled onto her legs and watched her hold up the oval pendent. It was the one her Awnty Awnie always wore, the pendant Mom let Tin have. It took a few attempts to find the latch. She pried it open like a tiny book.

Zebra climbed onto her knees, eyeing the black and white photo her aunt had put inside all those years ago. No one knew why.

It was a zebra.

All four legs reached around Tin. And what little snow was on Zebra's mane, the ice crystals that were sticking to the toymaker's hat, began to melt. There was no room for fear.

Love.

Zebra nuzzled against her then pulled away, nudging the hat with her muzzle. Somehow she'd gotten away from the lobby. But how did she get here? Zebra was inanimate like the toys in the toy room. It was just her and Pando in the loft when Tin had first seen her. What was different? Tin looked at the hat.

I put it on.

When she found the balloon in the loft, she had put on the hat. Zebra woke up and Pando hadn't found her. She'd made her way to the lobby, had risked everything to get it.

This was when the toys first woke; it was after she had put on the hat. And every time afterwards she was weak. Like it drew something out of her. How many toys were in Toyland?

"I know why I'm here.

"I know why I'm here."

Zebra leaped in circles. With the hat in one hand, she ran her fingers through Zebra's mane—

Wallace.

He was in the toy room. The toys were with him. They were gathered around as he took a knee, arms out, hugging each one. They stood in line and hopped away when he let go with a troubled laugh in his belly.

They didn't notice the key.

He was holding it in his right hand as he clenched them one by one. The toymaker's hat was a green crown, crooked on his head. When he hugged the last one, they stood around waiting for what he wanted to do next. Wallace picked up the wooden soldier. He didn't hug him, simply looked into the big painted eyes very seriously.

"I'll be back," he announced. "Close your eyes and it'll be like I never left."

He backed out of the toy room with a pained look in his bright green eyes. Confusion filled the room. The toys shuffled toward him as the door began closing, light knifing down to a narrow line. Soldier at his post.

And then it was dark.

Tin was in there with them. She heard the scratching at the door. Wallace's footsteps. And then it was quiet. Soon, they closed their eyes to sleep. She knew what would happen, though. How the lock would turn and the door would open. How they would excitedly run to it. But they wouldn't find Wallace.

The sadness in the room was palpable.

Tin closed her eyes. Never had she been able to touch anything in the vision or influence it. But she wasn't there to move them. They were toys. They were made to give.

It was time for them to receive.

She imagined all the toys in Toyland, their stiff arms and empty stares, the cold marbles in their bellies. She wished to give them the love they gave. And then she felt it pour from her. A dam broke open and flooded the world. It shook her.

Emptied her.

Staring at the starry night, the toymaker's hat was crooked on her head. Zebra had climbed onto her lap. Tin was lucky to be leaning against the tower or she would have hit the ground. She was too weak to lift her arm.

"Did it work?" she croaked.

The fur on Zebra's mane had stiffened. She was rigid, pawing Tin's dead legs like an angry bull. Tin was too cold to feel fear when she saw the figure coming toward her.

He was limping on four legs.

21

Tin had slumped to the ground.

The toymaker's hat was beneath her head like a thin pillow. Her steamy breath leaked into the starry night. Zebra climbed onto her chest.

Pando stood over her.

He looked like a ragged overcoat. He was badly torn. Patches of fabric were missing. A long tear had opened his stomach. He looked down without a hint of malice or anger. Just weariness.

He bent over—bits of stuffing floating toward her—and reached for the toymaker's hat. Zebra spun around and kicked his arm away.

He stood tall. *You know why I have to do this. You know! She left you, remember? She left all of us.*

Zebra braced herself again, bowing like a bull about to charge.

Who kept you company? Pando said. *Who stayed in the loft and made sure you weren't lonely? Who told you stories when it was dark and promised she would come back? Who was the one who took care of you?*

He thumped his chest.

I did.

This time he swatted Zebra away. She tumbled across the ground and leaped back, but not before Pando took the toymaker's hat. Tin's head thumped on the frozen earth.

They watched the tired and torn panda bear stare into the toymaker's hat as if searching for answers, yearning for it to talk to him like it did to her, to share with him the memories it held. He looked into her eyes with those dull button eyes that were somehow filled with expression, perhaps a bit of guilt.

But not regret.

She didn't know how she was going to turn the tower back on. Even if she wanted to, she didn't have the strength to climb it. Bits of dust and debris swept against her cheeks. She closed her eyes and felt a deep magnetic hum. It wasn't coming from the tower this time.

It was Pando.

He was pulsing. Shock waves emanated from his chest and swelled in her head. Something creaked in the trees. Tin turned to see the skeletal remains of the staircase rise from the ground. The trees whipped around and branches snapped as it began dragging toward the tower.

Pando hadn't flinched.

He didn't lift a hand. Magic words didn't resonate in her head. He simply watched the stairs creep closer. The metal twisted and bent. Twice it tumbled over. Eventually it slid beneath the tower, the sticks of an attempted fire scattered beneath its weight. It tipped upward and leaned awkwardly in place.

A final groan and the silent night returned.

I know what you think, that I'm a bad toy. It's not that simple. Some things cannot be undone.

He started reaching for her, prepared to carry her to the top, put her in the tower and keep her there until she threw the switch. Her family would sleep until she did. There was nothing she could do to stop it. Zebra took her final stand, bucking with renewed efforts.

You can't stop me. He hesitated. *Not now.*

This was all a mistake. He had wanted her to wear the hat ever since he woke up. Maybe she was giving life to the toys, but she was giving it to him, too. Or was he just taking it from them after she gave it? If she'd just never found the hat in the first place, none of this would've happened.

But the rest of them deserve to wake up, she thought. *Just not Pando.*

He frowned and glowered. That thought stung a little. It was so easy to love the other toys. Pando wasn't like them. *And that was the real mistake,* she thought.

My mistake, Pando said, *was trusting him.*

Stuffing spilled from his belly as he slid both stumpy arms under her. Wind swirled around them. She felt magnetic waves beam from his chest. He didn't have the strength to lift her, but the vortex did.

The ground began to quake.

Tin thought he was preparing to unleash the magnetic waves again, but his button eyes buried beneath the creases of fabric brows. He looked back toward Toyland.

The trees were shaking.

Tin could feel the rumble. The frozen ground shook like a stampede on the horizon. Pando took a few steps. Something dropped from the distant branches.

It was coming for them.

Small and quick, it was galloping on four legs, a long tail curled over it. Bleached in bluish moonlight, the creature's color was distorted. But not the shape.

Monkeybrain was fast approaching.

Pando just stood there, arms folded across his torn belly. Tin didn't know why he didn't whip the wind into a vortex and throw the purple monkey deep into the forest. Maybe he was about to. It was moments later that something flooded out of the darkness.

It was a stampede.

They were different sizes and colors, hopping and bouncing, running and rolling. There were hundreds. Maybe a thousand. Aardvarks and anteaters, gorillas and cheetahs, lions and tigers and bears, spacemen and dolls, babies with wobbly heads and robots with square bodies and trucks with headlight eyes and smiling grilles.

A cavalcade of Christmas.

Pando didn't budge. He watched them charge like mounted

cavalry, spearheaded by a galloping purple monkey. The ground quaked as they neared, the padded footsteps pounding the frozen soil. They separated as if Pando were the keel, racing around him and between Tin and the giant panda, climbing over her legs, scrambling on top of each other, locking arms and legs, hooves and hands and tails.

A wall of fur and shiny eyes.

As the last of them took their place, one final toy climbed on top. Piggy pounced onto her chest, a curly tail wagging. The tingle of affection poured through her.

Pando towered over them. He surveyed the group of misfit toys, the large and small, and began to pace.

So, he said, *this is what you want?*

He waved an arm and scanned the glassy eyes, the button eyes, the stitched faces and carved scowls.

What do you think is going to happen? Huh? If we don't get the wall turned back on, do you think a fat man and reindeer will find all of you then? That he will sweep you up and deliver you to children who care about you, is that it? No one cares about you more than me!

He pounded his chest. Stuffing puffed from rips.

I took from you so that I could save you. All of you! I was the one who made sure she found the hat. I was the one who allowed her to pour her life into you. You are nothing without me, all of you. I made you, don't forget that. And now we are forgotten. We are abandoned. We are alone! You understand that, don't you now? There is no Santa Claus coming to save us. Don't forget, Annie didn't leave me. She left all of us.

He aimed his stubby arm at Tin.

I won't leave you. But she will. Her family will. They will leave you and forget you. I won't let that happen. I won't let anyone hurt you.

He looked at Zebra.

Not like Annie did.

He was talking about Awnty Awnie. He didn't care about Wallace. It was Tin's aunt who hurt them most.

The ground swirled around him. Was he stalling? Conserving his energy? He was capable of throwing them into the trees, but maybe he couldn't do that with all the rips and tears. Why didn't he just absorb their lives like he'd done already?

There are too many of them, she thought.

She'd given everything she had to bring them back, and he wasn't ready. He was too weak. *Or maybe,* she thought, *he's telling the truth.*

Pando looked up. There were no streaking stars, no sleighs pulled by reindeer. The wall had been down for hours. There was no Santa Claus.

Maybe he's right, she thought.

He stood on his back legs and limped in front of the formation of stuffed toys.

Together, let's carry her to the top and turn on the tower so that it will protect us from the world. Just as it was meant to do.

Tin pushed onto her elbows to peer over the line of bushy heads and furry tails. Pando had both arms over his belly, the toymaker's hat wedged beneath one of them. An expression of pleading slowly turned to anger.

The toys didn't move.

You don't understand, he said, *what you mean to me.*

"They understand," Tin said.

Far behind him, one last figure had emerged from the trees. It wobbled across the field, taking long uncertain leaps, bouncing side to side, falling and getting up. He was small and sturdy, dented and scratched. And missing his hat.

Pando raised his arms. Wind began to circle his feet. *I don't want to do this.*

"Neither do they."

Soldier covered the last distance in a single bound, hands raised, mouth opened in a silent scream. Pando hit the soldier with the full force of his magnetic might.

The army of toys pounced.

Tin's ears popped as the atmospheric pressure skyrocketed. The calm of Christmas night vanished in a flurry of stuffing filling the sky like puffs of enormous snowflakes. The wind howled; specks of grit stung her cheeks. Stuffed lions and colorful unicorns stood next to Piggy, keeping Pando from nearing her.

Their last stand.

Above the tearing of fabric, she heard his cries. Pando begged for mercy, not from what they were doing to him.

Please, he was saying, *don't make me do this.*

Toys were flung into the distance. Some were torn apart, missing an ear or eyes, a leg; some were left lifeless, as if Pando had pulled the life from them. But others came back to join the fray, buoyed by the life Tin had given them. They fought for her. For themselves.

And Pando had to make a choice.

Perhaps in the end, he really was protecting them. He was their only hope. He didn't know how to love, not like they did. But he felt something when he harmed them, took the spark that filled them. Perhaps he would've taken them all in one fell swoop. If he could've. Instead, he was draining them one at a time, hoping, perhaps, for something different.

That they would change their mind.

The toys were going to be a field of scattered fabric and stuffing when this was over. Zebra suddenly leaped off her chest. Tin tried to grab her. It wasn't fair. She didn't want to see her like the others. She was Awnty Awnie's favorite.

Piggy backed her wiggly-tail rump into Tin's face.

She pushed her aside enough to see Zebra come flying out of the rumble. Tumbling like a barrel, she bounced onto Tin's lap. And something came with her. Tin reached for it.

She could barely feel the hat.

Her hands had grown so cold and weak. She didn't have much to give. She'd already filled them up once. But if she didn't do something, she would be alone with Pando. They were giving everything to protect her.

She could do the same.

22

The workshop.

Tin was standing at the ladder that led to the loft. The workshop was cleaner than she'd ever seen it before. Across the room, standing at the workbench, was the life-sized panda bear.

The Pando schematics were still posted on the wall.

He wasn't inanimate, not a regular stuffed toy. His back was to her. She couldn't see what he was doing. The other toys were helping him. Piggy and Clyde and Baby Doll were fetching tools, trundling over with screwdrivers and hammers and jars full of rivets. The hollow sounds of wood and tinkering metal was in full operation.

They worked seamlessly, like a network. One mind, different bodies. Tin didn't hear thoughts. There were no words. Complete focus on the task in front of them.

They were building a toy.

It took all four of them with their fingerless hands and stumpy arms to manipulate the parts. It must have taken a long time. They were almost finished.

"What do you think you're doing?"

Fear jabbed Tin in the stomach. Her thighs turned cold. The figure stood in the crooked doorway. He was short and round, one suspender loop hanging at his side. Wild whiskers and wide bare feet.

The toymaker's hat flopped on his head.

His feet scuffed the floor. His hard eyes the icy blue of the North Pole. The entire workshop shuffled, a scattering of toys hiding on the shelves, moving to dark corners and behind boxes, under sheets. Piggy, Clyde and Baby Doll backed away.

Pando didn't move.

He remained in front of the schematic that outlined his design, a poster of detailed pride. Wallace stared holes through him and used his weight to shove him aside. Pando stumbled a few steps. His stitching did not smile; the green button eyes weren't angry.

"So you're a toymaker now?"

Wallace studied the project with a sneer and incredulous laugh. He worked the arms.

"Wood?" He chuckled crudely. "That's not a toy."

When the rivets didn't pop off, he batted it with the back of his hand. It crumpled into a pile of bent limbs. Piggy and Clyde dragged it away and straightened it out. Wallace stood toe-to-toe with Pando, their bellies touching, neither one backing down, staring eye to button eye.

Wallace began laughing.

It was the kind of laugh that buckled knees and sent little things scurrying for cover. He continued down the bench, cruelly chuckling as he went. The toys on the shelf pushed against each other.

A gray fabric elephant was too big and slow.

Wallace snatched him with one hand. Elephant curled his trunk around his wrist but couldn't pry off the grubby fingers.

Stop.

Tin flinched. She heard Pando's voice in her head. It frightened her at first, but the tone was pained and pleading. Wallace looked at the panda, a grin spreading through whiskers like a stain. He pulled the toymaker's hat over his bushy eyebrows and closed his eyes. Elephant began squirming. Panicked. Desperate.

And then it stopped.

Wallace let out a satisfied gasp. He licked his sick grin with dead blue eyes on Pando then put the elephant back on the shelf.

It was stiff. Inanimate.

"I made them," Wallace said. "I take them."

Will you do the same to me? *Pando said.*

"Oh, please. You're a bear, not a drama queen." *Wallace thumped Pando's schematic with his fist.* "I created you, all of you. I gave you life. If I want it back, I'll take it."

He wasn't shuffling anymore. He pulled the suspender loop over his shoulder up. His blue eyes were clearer than when he first arrived.

Before he took Elephant.

You didn't create us, *Pando said.* The toymaker's hat did.

"That's right." *The little bell rang on his head.* "And who wears the hat?"

It wasn't meant for this. Not what you're doing.

"What I'm doing?" *Wallace bumped him.* "Making the world happy? Sending love to the little boys and girls, that's wrong? I made you to give to the world. All of you!" *He swept his arm.* "If I want to take some love for myself, I earned that."

They're frightened, Wallace.

The toys had found places to hide. The ones left out in the open were quivering. Piggy, Clyde and Baby Doll, too. But not Pando.

"You wouldn't exist without me." *The toymaker's hat was crooked on his head.* "Do you think he cares what I'm doing? Because if he did, he would come down from the North Pole and stop me."

He can't see us! *Pando glared with green buttons.* You made sure of that.

"For you," *Wallace responded calmly.* "I built the tower to protect all of you."

Wallace surveyed the room. Dust floated from quivering shelves. He licked his lips, nodding. Wild blue eyes searched from beneath bushy eyebrows.

"I did it so you can live."

He slid his hand down the bench, brushing random pieces onto the floor. Piggy, Clyde and Baby Doll dragged the wooden soldier they had built. Wallace walked his fingers toward them.

The hat belongs to the toymaker. Pando stepped in front of him. *You are not the toymaker.*

"I beg to differ."

Wallace's quickness was deceiving. He snatched the soldier by the leg. Piggy and Clyde tumbled toward him. Wallace shook them off and backed away with his prize, the greedy smile once again spreading through his whiskers. A monster clutching its prey, he held it like a fish on a hook, straightening the toymaker's hat with a little ring of the bell.

And closed his eyes.

Pando approached stealthily. He didn't try to stop Wallace from doing what he'd done to Elephant. Something about Soldier was different.

Euphoria did not melt Wallace's expression.

His eyebrows kneaded tightly. The corners of his smile turned down. Pleasure turned to anger suddenly morphed into confusion. He squeezed harder, gritting his teeth, grunting. But it wasn't working. Not like the other toys. He opened his eyes.

Pando was in front of him.

"What are you—"

Pando threw his arms around him. Wallace struggled to break free. His cheeks were flush and his nose cherry red. The scuffle suddenly stopped. He went catatonic. Eyes wide open but not seeing, his teeth began to chatter. Drool oozed from the corner of his mouth. Strange noises gurgled out.

And then the wind started.

It swirled around them at first then widened out, sweeping parts off the bench, scraps of paper fluttering. Things crashed from the shelves. Toys hunkered down to avoid being tossed across the room. The violent eddy stirred the workshop.

Pando and Wallace were in the eye of it.

Tin backed into the corner. Debris, small and large, rattled the shelves and bounced off the walls. She covered her face. The little bell rang, the toymaker's hat still tightly on her head. The storm dragged toys from their hiding places. Wood splintered and metal twisted.

And then it stopped.

Everything fell at once. Stuffed animals and plastic dolls stopped rolling. Paper and fluffy stuffing fluttered. Pando and Wallace were still locked together. When all was still, they separated. Pando stumbled back. He swung his arms but couldn't catch his balance, his stumpy legs caught up in debris. He crashed into a pile of boxes.

Wallace watched him.

The toys scattered into hiding. They peeked out to see what would happen. Wallace kept his attention on Pando as he struggled to crawl out of the wreckage. Clumsily, he climbed on all fours but lost his balance when he tried to stand up.

What have you done to me? *Pando's voice had changed.*

There was panic. Confusion. But he sounded... different.

He looked up with green button eyes. Wallace returned his questioning stare with calm openness.

A roar filled Tin's head. Pando leaped out of the chaos. The stitched mouth twisted and contorted, button eyes pinched in fury. The padded legs outstretched.

Wallace didn't move.

Something darted off the workbench. It happened in a flash, an object suddenly come to life. It hit Pando like a missile and threw him into a pile of tools. Pando dug his way out of cascading boxes and looked down. Stuffing was blooming from a long tear.

Soldier was in front of him.

Spear at his side, mouth open, he remained vigilant. Tin watched from her corner. Wallace slid the toymaker's hat off his head and stared at it thoughtfully.

Calmly and patiently, he made his way across the workshop, carefully stepping over debris. He moved several items to find a silver footlocker. Pulling loose the latches, he folded the hat and placed it inside.

He looked up at the entrance to the loft then followed the ladder down to where she was hiding. Briefly, their eyes met. They were softer than when he first walked into the workshop. Kinder. The two moles were still above his right eyebrow, but his eyes had changed.

They were green.

Pando was still looking over his body. Wallace went over and examined the tear. He searched the workbench and brought back a needle and thread and began sewing together the damage.

How did you... Pando's voice trailed off.

"You made me special," Wallace said. "More than you realized."

Wallace's voice had changed, too. It was patient and calm, matching the look in his green eyes.

Soldier moved between them. Little by little, the toys began peeking out from their hiding places. Piggy, Clyde and Baby Doll trundled by Wallace's side. He finished stitching the tear on Pando's leg.

"Gather the toys," he called. "All of them. Meet me in the toy room."

Toys began hopping off the shelves. They crawled out of dark corners, more than Tin realized could fit in the room. Slowly, they made their way into the hall, guided by Piggy, Clyde and Baby Doll.

What are you doing? Pando said.

Wallace squatted down one more time. He took Pando's arms and looked him in the button eyes. There was no anger, no malice. Sadness, perhaps.

"I can't fix what you've done," he said, "but perhaps I can find someone who can."

When the last of the toys waddled out, Wallace stood up. He nodded without a smile. Pando scrambled onto all fours. He pulled himself onto his back legs and leaned on a rake.

You can't do this to us. Not like Annie.

Wallace stopped in the doorway and paused. He took the oddly shaped doors and began closing them.

"She didn't do this to us, Wallace."

In the dim light of the stuffy workshop, the panda bear hobbled after him. He swayed on his back legs and couldn't keep the doors from closing. Footsteps receded until there was silence. Tin watched from the corner.

This wasn't what she expected.

She wanted to fill the toys with life. Instead, she wasn't sure what she'd just seen. Was this true? All the questions and answers were as chaotic as the workshop. But one thing was clear. The panda bear was lost. He was slumped and alone, more than ever.

Because that's not Pando.

She didn't know how it happened, but she stood in front of him, looked closely at the button eyes and stitched mouth. Once so angry and threaten-

ing, now he was gutted. The panda bear slumped in the corner. He stared with big green buttons.

"Wallace."

She wanted to stop him. This was just the beginning. Eventually he would keep the tower from getting turned off. He would chop down the stairs and bring back the balloon and open the toy room.

He'd already done all those things. But there, in that moment, she was moved by where he was. Once he was lost on the North Pole. Now he was lost in the trappings of his own making.

So she put her arms around him.

Unlike all the other visions, she felt him move in her grasp. His fur soft, his padding firm. She squeezed him and felt the gush of love. The floodgates cracked open. He stiffened then relaxed. She could feel him quiver as the warmth flooded into her and filled her.

Completely.

The room dimmed to a dark place that didn't feel lonely anymore. It was just the two of them, holding each other, in a space that was warm.

He wasn't alone.

❄

The little bell rang.

Snowflakes piled on top of her. The night was filled with lofty white puffs that continued to climb higher, eventually drifting off to find trees and earth.

Toys were strewn across the field.

Most of them, however, were still standing. Next to her was a pile of black and white fabric. Soldier was next to it.

He was missing an arm. Fresh dents were carved across his chest. He stood there not like a victor, but a protector who would never, ever let down his guard. He laid his broken spear against the mysterious metal ball.

Noel toys each come with a surprise inside them—a marble that makes them special. Only Pando doesn't have a marble.

The metal ball was etched with symbols, just like the drawing she'd seen in Wallace's sketchbook, the one he was so obsessed to record. This was his most special creation, the toy that would be the pinnacle of all his creations.

A lifelike toy that did more than just love.

Piggy climbed into her arms. A heavy footstep crunched behind her. Tin scrambled away from the stranger who appeared from nowhere.

He seemed to come out of the dark, poking the ground with a long stick. With a grunt, he took a knee in the settling fluff and uncovered the etched metal ball. Soldier didn't stop him. That was when she noticed two moles above his eyebrow.

And the green eyes.

23

A long coat dragged behind him, the hem frayed and tattered.

His beard was as white as snow and reached past his waist. Perhaps if he stood upright, the beard would merely be to his chest. He stabbed the hard ground with a gnarled cane and shuffled through the fluff and shreds of fabric.

The etched metal ball lay in the goose down like a medieval egg, the top half dull gray. Standing guard, the soldier was buried up to his waist. He watched the old man shuffle near without moving, as if this was the treasure he'd been charged to guard.

Somewhere in the beard, a smile moved.

The old man's eyes crinkled, and laughter rumbled from the whiskers. He lifted a feeble hand to his forehead.

The soldier returned his salute.

The old man continued kicking around the stuffing. He was looking for something, muttering as he went, stopping at the toys who had fallen and did not get up. Occasionally, he grunted. Often, he shook his head. He continued searching and then bent over with a tired groan. With a knobby, knuckled hand crimped over the cane, he tossed the stuffing aside.

The toymaker's hat.

He brushed it off and looked inside it. A gentle smile and a kind look possessed the bright eyes hidden in deep folds.

Bells chimed in the distance.

A herd of deer was near the trees, noses in the snow in search of lichen. The biggest of them all was watching the old man. Tin was starting to doubt he'd even seen her. The toys had gathered in such a tight knot around her that she was buried.

"Come now." His voice was strong and joyous. "Gather round, just like we used to, remember? Come along."

The toys, however, did not budge.

They remained suspicious, as if Pando had assumed the form of a feeble old man. He held out his arms like an elder magician who'd forgotten his tricks. No rabbits in his wooly sleeves, stuffed or otherwise. Slowly, he lowered them.

For the first time, his gaze fixed on her.

"My dear, what you've done is nothing short of remarkable. And I cannot apologize enough for my tardiness, to leave this monumental task all alone with you. It never should've happened like this." He gestured to the remnants of fabric and stuffing. "Be that as it may, there is a remedy."

He held up a crooked finger.

"My promises are not the best, but I do keep them."

If he was Santa Claus, then all of the stories were way off. There was no red coat or floppy hat, no belly full of jelly. Just the white beard, scraggly at that. And perhaps a twinkle in his eye.

But the moles. The green eyes, she thought. *It has to be.*

"It's all right," she whispered. "Go ahead."

One by one, the toys crawled off her. They moved around the old man as he nodded his approval, as if they were surrounding him. All except Piggy went. She remained seated firmly on Tin's chest. The old man nodded with a twinkle.

"Gather them," he said. "We can do this."

Reluctantly, they did as he asked. They scooped up the empty fabric and piles of stuffing, brought them back to Tin, stacking them on all sides of her until she was surrounded by the remains of what had happened, buried in a tribute. They gathered it all.

Except for Pando's remains.

The old man nudged the metal ball farther away then held out his hands. The toys formed a circle around Tin as if she was the tribute and they were about to sing. The old man was part of it. He joined hands with a stuffed giraffe and a plastic baby doll with one lazy eye. It was a strange sight.

She heard voices.

The old man closed his eyes. His mouth gaped open, but he didn't make a sound. The song was in her head. They were singing.

If you want to play…

The fabric fluttered. The stuffing swirled. A flood of energy, like the hands of the wind, swept around her. Tin felt the bonds of love move inside her. She was weak and alone, nearly emptied of her own vitality, all of it given to the toys, to wake them up. To save them.

And now they were giving it back.

The inanimate toys that had fallen felt it too. They began to move. They lifted their heads as if waking from a pleasant dream, filling their sides with stuffing, leaping up to join their family. The circle grew wider and the love grew stronger. The song grew louder.

And stay out all day…

She closed her eyes and felt like she was floating high above the ground, a titan who could walk over the forest and through the oceans, a container who had endless capacity to love. Not a creature was stirring, all through the night.

I know the place where we can do it.

For a moment, she thought she was alone, that all of this was a dream. But the toys were still there. The old man, too. He was more wilted than before, stooping like an ancient spruce holding the burden of winter on his branches. He faltered a step. Tin started to get up.

"No, no," he said. "Stay where you are."

The toys, once reluctant and suspicious, now gathered at his sides, helping him shuffle toward her. He looked back at the metal ball and the pile of black and white fabric and weakly pointed.

"If you don't mind."

Several toys—including a boar, a brown bear and an elephant—hoisted the ball on their backs. They followed the old man to the tower. Tin helped him sit on the ground. He leaned back with a groan.

He took deep breaths, as if smelling the country air for the first time. Or a place long forgotten. Something familiar that felt so comfortable.

Zebra sniffed his coat.

She pawed at the beard. The old man opened his eyes. He stroked her with both hands, the black and white mane bristling. She laid her head on his chest then flopped on her side, nuzzling into the long whiskers. He held her with both hands.

"You're..." Tin said. "You're Pando."

His laughter was frail and trailed off. He nodded with a tired sigh.

"Is Wallace—"

"Gone?" He rested his hand on the metal ball. "No, he's in here. He's here."

"I didn't... is he..." Tin swallowed. "Is he hurt?"

"No, dear."

Even after everything Wallace had done, to her and her family, the toys, she couldn't live with the guilt of harming him.

"The hat chose him," he said, "but you probably already know that. He was a decent man then, a good man perhaps. And he didn't want to die, not with so much life to live. Perhaps the hat knew that when he was lost on the North Pole, so it saved him. But, after that, he just..."

An amused chuckle escaped his throat. He turned his head with a feeble smile and brightened up, as if recognizing her for the first time.

"He loved her, you know," he said.

He dug a handkerchief from his coat and blew his nose like a tuba. He smiled down at Zebra, rubbing her nose.

"Why did she leave?" Tin asked.

"I think you know why."

"They need to hear it."

The toys were watching. They were listening. The emotion that wrung Pando's voice was thick with the memory of Awnty Awnie, and he was holding it in.

Wallace wasn't the only one to fall in love with her.

"My dear, she left," he said, "because he loved something more."

All at once, the toys migrated closer. They crawled onto his legs, onto his shoulders, into his arms. He looked around with a pained smile. He didn't love them any less now than he did all those years ago.

"He had tapped the hat's magic," he said. "It's not magic, really, but it feels that way. He gave it to them. Giving life felt so... so remarkable. 'You are all my children,' he would say often. But then he became something else."

She heard the sadness. It was the same sadness she'd heard in the workshop, witnessing Wallace empty the elephant, taking the toy's lifeforce, as if drinking it, becoming drunk with it. That was just before Pando had done the impossible, so impossible that it couldn't be anything other than magic. He had the power to move the wind, to send thoughts. Wallace didn't realize everything Pando could do.

He switched bodies.

The toys took turns in Pando's embrace, waiting patiently to climb into the crook of his arm. He squeezed each one with the same amount of affection, reluctantly releasing them before the next one.

"They're perfect," he said. "Wallace was making the world a better place, one at a time. He was helping Santa deliver the most important thing in the world."

Love.

Something snorted in the distance. The deer were still grazing at the edge of the forest. The biggest of them was staring in their direction. Even from that distance, his rack of antlers was enormous.

"Children need love more than something to play with," he said. "The toys had more than enough."

He glanced at Tin.

"There's a reason the hat wasn't for him," he said. "Your aunt saw it. She tried to stop him, but it was… it was too late. He was lost again." He cast his gaze at the metal ball. "All this love, and still he was empty."

With help from a stuffed gorilla, he put the ball on his lap. It was heavier than it appeared. He followed the intricate carvings, his finger retracing their design. He pulled the black and white fabric to his face and drew a deep breath.

"How did you do it? How did you switch—"

He held up his hand. "I understand it seems impossible. It should be impossible. But there are so many things in this world that humans just can't know. Even Wallace didn't know what I could do when he created me. You have to understand I *am* special. I am different than all the rest of the toys. And I understood what would happen if I didn't do something."

"So you left?" she said.

He dropped his heavy hands, recalling a decades-old memory. "There was someone who could fix this." He took the hat in both hands. "I went to find him."

"The toymaker?" A long pause. "Did you? Did you find him?"

He turned his head. The folds of skin, the countless wrinkles and faded green eyes told of the years he'd accumulated and the things he'd seen.

"It's not up to me to find him," he said. "It took all these years to discover that. But journeys are like that, my dear. They take as long as they take. The hat will find him." He held it up. "It just found you first."

"My family." She began to fidget. "What about my—"

"I'm sorry, how selfish of me. Your family is just fine, I promise. They're sleeping, nothing more. The song was one of my gifts to bestow peaceful sleep and glorious dreams. Wallace was using it for other reasons. I assure you they are dreaming on their own now, and they'll wake without a scratch or a memory of what happened. He's making sure everyone will have a wonderful Christmas."

"He?"

A twinkle lit his eyes at just the right moment.

She didn't want to say whom she thought Pando was talking about because maybe it was someone else. But there were reindeer by the trees and bells ringing on harnesses.

He threw his weight forward with a grunt and a groan. The elephant and gorilla pushed him upright and then helped him stand. He was bent over, taking a moment to straighten up like his back had rusted over time. But like a tree that had grown crooked with time, he wasn't meant to straighten.

He scooped up the metal ball and curled it like a pumpkin. It made her nervous to see him clutch something so heavy.

"He, uh, he meant well," he mused. "And I loved who he was. Just not what he'd become."

He seemed to drift into a well of memories that the ball released. A lot of history was packed in there. She thought, for a second, he had forgotten she was there.

His green eyes peered through wrinkled slits. His laughter echoed off the trees and startled the herd of reindeer. It trailed off into a coughing fit. He wiped his eyes and dug his free hand into his pocket to retrieve the toymaker's hat. He studied it like he did the metal ball.

"Do you know why it chose you?" he said. "The hat."

"Because I look like my aunt."

He squinted again. "No. Well, maybe. But it's more than that. What makes a person isn't the way you look or the way you feel any more than Wallace was a panda bear."

The black and white fabric was just a suit. Wallace was in the metal ball.

"You're more like your aunt than you realize, and the hat knew it. The toys too."

She didn't know what he was talking about.

"You're real, Tinsley Ann. Genuine. You're vulnerable and courageous. And, most importantly, you love."

She shook her head. "I don't—"

"The hat doesn't make mistakes."

"Oh." She looked around at the rutted field and damaged toys. "I think it made a big one."

He took her hands. His hands were dry and thin like fallen leaves. But they gave warmth that went all the way through her.

"Mistakes," he said, putting the hat in her hands, "look different in the past."

"I can't keep this."

"I'm not leaving it. In fact, I'm taking it back."

"Taking it back…?"

"Where it belongs. This too."

He lugged the metal ball up a few inches. If Wallace was still in there, he wasn't going to stay at Toyland. Not after the mess he'd made. Perhaps, if there were so many things possible, like Pando had said, then someone on the North Pole could fix Wallace.

A sullen mood seemed to age him. He looked like a feeble old man under the weight of responsibility. He sighed deeply. The largest of the reindeer stretched its neck toward the moon and let out a hoarse call.

"A gift. It is Christmas, after all." He gestured to the hat. "One more story."

He smiled with a twinkle. There was something jolly about him. She hesitated. It was the last time she would see the hat. It didn't belong to her. It didn't belong at Toyland.

"What about them?"

She picked up Piggy and Zebra. Dozens gathered around her. She wanted to pick them all up or roll around in a puppy pile of toys. She didn't want to lose them.

"They'll always be there for you." He opened the hat. "That's their job."

The reindeer were trotting near the trees, their harness bells chiming. Something was in the shadows behind them. It was large and boxy. It looked like a sleigh. And someone was sitting in the front of it.

"May I?"

He placed the toymaker's hat on her head. Lights started to sparkle around him like fireflies of different colors, blinking on and off—red and green and blue. She wanted to reach out and grab one. Before he pulled it snug, she heard his crackly voice one last time.

If you want to play, and stay out all day...

24

They weren't fireflies.

Colors flashed on the bristly branches of a Christmas tree. Strings of popcorn and cranberries were draped from the limbs; silvery strands of tinsel hung from them, too. The ornaments were homemade—pine cones with glitter, foam balls with hot-glued beads.

Tin reached for one.

It was a hard plastic snowman. She'd made it with her mom during a snow day. School had been cancelled and Mom stayed home from work. They had cut out plastic figures and colored them with markers then put them in the oven till they shrank. They made them every year after that.

The snowman was her very first one.

Mom was wearing a sweatshirt with a candy cane print and carrying a small plate of cookies and a glass of milk. Candles threw warm light across the room. Her hair was past her shoulders. Tin couldn't remember it ever being that long. She looked younger.

Sadder.

She left the plate in front of the fireplace. There were only three stockings hung from the mantel. A big cushiony chair was facing the window. It had been pushed across the room. Awnty Awnie's loopy brown hair was above it. She wasn't watching the traffic go by. In the dark glass, Tin saw a little girl on her lap.

They were looking at the sky.

Awnty Awnie looked just like Tin remembered her, heavyset and soft. Doughy enough that a little girl sank into her. Tin knew that she was looking at herself on Awnty Awnie's lap. She also knew that Little Tin was five years old.

That was when Dad left.

Awnty Awnie wrapped both arms around her. Little Tin sucked her thumb as she spoke hoarsely.

"He has a great big sleigh with special reindeer that can fly. The one in front is the biggest and baddest of them all. He's the one who guides them, who protects them." She squeezed and whispered, "Ronin."

Tin had forgotten these stories. Awnty Awnie told them to her when she was little. Tin thought she was just making them up because no one ever sang songs about them. There were no cartoons, no movies about a reindeer named Ronin or Flury the Snowman or an elven named Jack.

"There's a special tool on the sleigh that Santa uses to stop time. That way he can get around the world in one night. He stops at every house with his bag of gifts. It's not like other bags, though. When he gets to the Christmas tree, he reaches in and pulls out just the right present for the children who live there. It's not always what they want. It's what they need."

"Is it heavy?" Little Tin asked without taking out her thumb.

"That's a good question. Santa has many, many helpers for heavy things."

"Elfs?"

"There are elven, yes. But the real heavy things are taken care of by the abominables. These big, burly snow creatures." Awnty Awnie's voice turned gruff. "They're more like snowmen, but not men or women or the kind with three snowballs. They have a heart right here."

She tickled her chest.

"It's round and metal and special. It's really who they are, because it makes a snow body. They load up the sleigh and protect the elven."

Little Tin watched the sky with big eyes, hoping to see the sleigh streak past before she fell asleep. Awnty Awnie hugged her tightly and rocked side to side. They both watched.

"Hynie?" Little Tin said. "Do you think he's real?"

Hynie, Tin thought. I used to call her Hynie. Always thought she was trying to say 'Honey.' Awnty Awnie was her Hynie.

"What do you think?" Awnty Awnie said.

They kept watching. Little Tin's eyes grew heavy. Tin remembered that feeling, of sinking into Awnty Awnie's lap all warm and safe. Sometimes falling asleep as she hummed a song.

It was the best place in the world.

"Bedtime," Mom announced. "Teeth brushed and in the covers, little girl."

"I want a story."

"Hynie already told you three. Come on, the sooner you're asleep, the sooner Santa gets here."

"Let's go, little chicken."

Awnty Awnie laughed her high-pitched laugh that made Tin smile. Tears immediately welled up. Little Tin scooted across the room in footy pajamas without taking her thumb out. Awnty Awnie held onto the chair a minute longer.

Mom was keeping busy.

Sweeping the floor and straightening stockings, arranging Santa's cookies on the plate. She wasn't smiling, not that year. Awnty Awnie just watched until she was close enough to reach out.

"You all right?" she said.

Mom nodded grimly. They hugged for a long time. Awnty Awnie rocked back and forth. Her love was endless.

"I'll check on Tin," Awnty Awnie said.

Gingerly, she slid on her black and white striped slippers and walked out of the room. Mom sat in the warm chair and looked up at the sky. Tin wondered if she was watching for the sleigh, hoping to see it deliver hope. Or if she was just waiting for this Christmas to be over. Tin wished she could hug her, but it just wouldn't be the same as Awnty Awnie's hug.

Nothing ever was.

In the back of the house, Little Tin was in bed. She was lying on her back. Her eyes were barely open. Tin knew she was trying to stay awake, hoping to hear the reindeer land on the roof. Awnty Awnie used to say that if she listened carefully, she could hear their bells before they arrived.

"Hynie?" Little Tin said. "I'm scared."

Awnty Awnie closed the bedroom door. She carried a bag to a rocking chair. It creaked under her weight.

Little Tin didn't know why she felt scared. It was just a feeling in her stomach. A feeling that stayed with her a very long time after her dad didn't come back. She was too little to understand what that meant or why Mom was so sad.

She just felt scared.

"I have something for you," Awnty Awnie said. "Santa said I could give it to you a little early. I don't think Mom will mind."

Awnty Awnie bent over and the bag rustled. Little Tin turned her head on the pillow. It was taking Awnty Awnie a long time, but then a little head appeared at the edge of the bed. The eyes were big and the hair wild and frayed. The fabric was purple. Awnty Awnie and Little Tin didn't hear Tin whisper.

"Monkeybrain."

Awnty Awnie tucked him into the covers and wrapped the long, gangly arms around Little Tin's neck, patting the purple monkey on the head.

"He's special," Awnty Awnie said. "He'll keep you safe when I'm not around. When you feel scared or nervous or sad, he will always love you." Awnty Awnie kissed her on the forehead. "Like I do."

The pendant around her neck dragged over the covers. She stayed close and began to hum. It was never words she used, just a song she hummed at bedtime. A song Tin had forgotten about.

A song that did have words.

"Goodnight, little chicken."

Awnty Awnie kissed her again and slowly, carefully, made her way out of the room, leaving the sounds of a sucking thumb behind. Tin stood at the foot of the bed. Monkeybrain was nestled into Little Tin's shoulder. Years later, she would give the purple monkey to Pip, and she'd tell her the same thing.

When you feel scared or sad...

Tin crawled onto the bed. She put her arm around the little girl. Nothing moved or shuffled beneath her. This was a vision. A memory she couldn't change. But a memory she wanted to never forget again.

She lay there for a long time. The lights in the house were turned off. Not a creature was stirring. Tin closed her eyes with Pando's song in her head. And just before she dreamed of sugarplums and candy canes, she heard the bells.

And reindeer hooves.

25

Someone was breathing in Tin's face.

Her eyes broke the seal of sleep. Pip was tickling her nose.

"She's awake, Momma!"

Pip scampered off, little footsteps pounding the hardwood. Tin rolled over and hit the back side of the couch, the sleeping bag around her legs. Cotton candy stuffed her head; every joint in her body ached. Her mouth dry as sand.

She stared at a little door on the ceiling.

An avalanche of memories were stuffed in the closet of her mind, hiding in the dark corners while she clawed her way back to the present moment.

Why did Soldier fall out of that door?

A soft lump was beneath her. She reached behind the small of her back. Piggy stared at her with black shiny eyes and stiff legs. Her snout was dirty like she'd been rooting for grubs.

Clyde was on the other couch. He was in the corner, legs out, eyes blank. Just like a stuffed bear should look. Tin sat up, her brain swishing in sand. The room wasn't trashed. The couches weren't broken. There weren't holes in the wall or broken picture frames on the floor.

"Santa came!" Pip skipped into the room. "He found us!"

Monkeybrain's hands were around her neck. He was bouncing on her back as she danced and twirled. She grabbed a big present and put it on Tin's lap. Other presents had already been opened. Boxes and shredded wrapping paper were around. The sad little tree was on its side. Pine cones and popcorn were scattered on the floor. Soldier was in front of it.

Scuffed and broken.

"Why didn't you wake me up?" Tin said.

Mom put a hand on her forehead. "You felt warm and sounded unsettled. Sleep did you good. How you feeling?"

Tin was sore and sleepy, like she'd been camping for a month. "What happened to the tree?"

"It fell over last night. No one heard it. We were all knocked out."

"Santa did it," Pip said. "It was an accident."

"You opened presents without me?" Tin said.

"Just a couple," Mom said. "To hold off the restless one."

Pip was dancing like a girl who'd eaten the entire gingerbread house. Monkeybrain swung behind her like a child just trying to hang on.

"Pretty impressive," Mom whispered. "Putting Monkeybrain back together like that. I thought maybe you got up in the middle of the night; that's why you were so tired. Good job. He looks exactly the same."

A vague memory of Monkeybrain came out of the dark corners, of him ripped from the tower and fluttering stuffing.

Stuffing.

"Where was he?" Tin asked.

"Next to Soldier."

"Look who else is back?" Pip danced behind the fallen tree. "Baby Doll!"

She skipped around the tree. The Christmas spirit had the pedal on the floor and Mom was letting it go. Tin looked around the room. There were no other toys. Nothing bigger than a baby doll.

No life-sized panda bears.

"Where's Corey?" Tin asked.

"Outside with Oscar," Mom said. "They're flying a drone."

"He was happy," Pip said. "Almost cried."

"You sure you're feeling all right?"

Mom put her hand on Tin's forehead again. She felt sluggish and stuffy, but not sick. It was just hard to sort out her memories. Like the last couple of days were soup.

"Have I been sick?" Tin asked.

"I don't think so," Mom said. "Although you've been acting strange."

Mom looked at her with a penetrating stare that was more concerned than suspicious. Maybe it was Rocky Mountain fever or Lyme disease or some other parasite you could pick up from nature.

Pip dropped a stocking on the couch. "Santa stuffed it. I got Pop-Tarts and licorice and lip gloss and these little things that you put in the oven to shrink…"

By the looks of it, Tin's stocking had the same things. Slowly, she pulled them out, and Pip took them from her, announced what it was, and put them in a pile by the unopened presents.

"Where's Pando?" Tin asked.

Mom looked around, eyebrows furrowed. "Who?"

"The, uh…" She pointed at a picture on the wall.

"Oh, the panda. I don't know."

Tin reached into her stocking for the Pop-Tarts. They were cinnamon. Pip cheered and started to open them. Mom stopped her. That was enough sugar. Pip trotted around the tree and sang about Pop-Tarts.

A bell rang.

"I think there's one more thing in there," Mom said.

Tin felt nervous. The sound of the bell threw light in the closet of memories—the stampede of toys, the whirling storm, the frayed fabric. She looked at the photo on the wall, the one with Pando and Wallace. Wallace's eyes were still blue.

Was it all a dream?

She reached to the bottom of the stocking and felt the fabric of something wadded up. The stocking folded inside out as she pulled it out. It was green with a white fuzzy hem. And a little bell on top.

"Story!" Pip shouted.

Mom asked Pip to go get her boots and coat. They were going outside to burn off some Christmas spirit. Tin stared at the green hat, the memory of Wallace—er, Pando in Wallace's body—leaning over to put it on her. The fabric was thin and the stitching coarse. She put her hand inside it. A tag was attached to the seam.

Made in China.

"You all right?" Mom said.

The fog was lifting. She remembered the last gift Pando promised her before putting the hat on her for the last time. The memory she'd never forget.

Tin smiled. "Yes."

"Good. Well, put some clothes on. Let's go find Oscar and Corey. I'm sure they want to come open the rest of the presents."

Mom corralled Pip in the direction of the kitchen. Tin sat for a moment longer. When she stood up, the aches had vanished. She felt lighter than before. The worries gone. She was still wearing cargo pants. Mom hadn't noticed the dirt stains and the rips in the knees.

There were crumbs in the pocket.

It was just a dusting of gingerbread, the remains of a cookie that she had been toting around. Gingerman, however, was gone. Maybe he fell out.

Run, run as fast as you can...

She picked up Soldier standing rigid at the fallen tree. He was nicked and scratched and half-broken. It wasn't Wallace who made him. Pando knew someone would have to stay behind and protect the toys. Maybe he was planning to make an entire army before he left. Turned out, one was enough.

He didn't squirm in her hand or move when she put him back down. She didn't say anything.

But she did salute.

❄

PIP HAD ALREADY RUN down the path.

Mom wrapped the scarf around Tin's neck and zipped up her coat. She felt her forehead one last time. Tin recalled the way Mom looked in the vision, that Christmas night when things were so heavy and Awnty Awnie was telling stories. It was a lot to ask from a single mother. Tin hooked her arm through her mom's arm.

"Thanks, Mom."

"For what?"

"For everything."

Together, step for step, they followed Pip's footsteps, laughing as they squeezed between trees and slipped in the snow. The stage was still a graveyard of memories buried in virgin snow.

Pip came running at them, arms flailing, Monkeybrain bouncing. She slammed into Mom.

"It's-it's... you got to see—"

"Slow down," Mom said. "How many Pop-Tarts did you have?"

"They're there, Momma!"

Mom let Pip pull her down the path. The clearing was up ahead. Tin slowed down. She didn't want anything to change, none of the excitement to return. This was perfect as it was.

Something was buzzing.

There was no feeling of magnetism, no swirl. The clouds peeking through the branches weren't blurry from an electromagnetic field. The tower didn't look or feel like it was on. The whirring was above her.

A drone.

Corey was shouting for Oscar to watch the landing. Tin stopped on the edge of the clearing. The drone was hovering its way to the ground. Corey landed it near the trees, next to tracks in the snow. They were large for deer or moose. No one seemed concerned by the size, even the ones that were as big as snowshoes.

The biggest and baddest of them all.

The drone revved up again and soared above the trees. Corey watched it with his mouth open. Mom was talking to Oscar in the middle of the clearing. They were staring at the tower. Oscar was pointing, explaining. Something was gathered around the footings. Tin couldn't make out what it was at first; then a chill swept through her.

The toys.

Hundreds of them were lined up like a photo opportunity. Pip skipped and spun in front of them like she was performing.

Still and inanimate, they watched.

"The weirdness never ends." Corey wandered over.

He was watching the monitor on his control pad. The drone hovered near the tower. The door at the top was open. There wasn't much inside, just a post with a lever.

It had been pulled down.

"You left Clyde," Tin said.

"Who?"

She unzipped her coat. Piggy and Clyde were tucked inside. He frowned in confusion. Why would he drag that outside? It was a stuffed bear. He went back to steering the drone around the tower, his tongue between his teeth, and swung the view over the crowd of toys.

"Can I ask you a question?" she said. "It might sound weird."

"Weird is the new normal."

"Did they ever move?"

"Who?"

She gestured to the toys. He did a double take. "You're weird. Watch this."

He did something with the drone, but she didn't care. Mom was calling and waving her arm. Tin went to meet her. Pip was singing a song. The words weren't familiar, but the tune was. It was the song that was in her dreams, the one that kept them asleep. The one Awnty Awnie used to hum. Pip just couldn't remember the words.

Tin would never forget.

"Did you bring them out here last night?" Mom pointed at the toys.

Tin shrugged. "Maybe."

"You are a good sister. No wonder you were tired, putting Monkeybrain back together and then this. Don't think I forgot you went outside at night when everyone was sleeping, though. This is the wilderness, hon. Strange things can happen."

Tin smiled. "Yeah."

"Momma, momma." Pip came bouncing toward them. "Can we do a picture and put it on the wall like Uncle Wallace?"

Tin's smile grew wider. She liked the sound of that. From now on, she would call him that too. Awnty Awnie kept a journal about him. She never forgot the man she fell in love with. And he still loved her.

Uncle Wallace.

The stairs had been dragged back to the trees. The tower was safe from an easy climb. The toys watched them approach with empty eyes. Tiny patches of white stuffing were snagged on the ground, but no one seemed to notice. The gorilla and the elephant, the lion and the zebra and hippo and snake and all the rest of them were there. None of them moved, but Tin still silently whispered.

Thank you.

Mom and Oscar stood in the middle. Tin leaned against her mom, and Pip stood next to her. Corey was next to his dad, tongue out and steering the drone. It hovered above them, the camera pointing down.

"You know," Tin said, "we can stay here as long as you want."

Mom put her arm around her. This was the weirdest Christmas anyone could ever have. And unforgettable.

"Look up," Corey said. "Say Tinsley's a kook."

They looked up and said Merry Christmas. Then Pip did another dance. Later they would bring all the toys inside and put them around the lobby. They would leave them there when they went home so that when they returned, they would have someone to welcome them.

Piggy and Clyde, however, came home.

Sometimes, at night, Tin would hear Corey talking to him when he thought no one was around, confessing or talking about Brenda. He even called him Clyde. Tin never said anything.

Piggy slept with her. She would be her companion until she went to college. But when she came home for the summer, she would be waiting for her on the pillow. She never hugged her back, not like before, but the world always felt a little safer when she was around.

Sometimes she just needed to be reminded.

In time, Tin started to doubt what had happened. After a while, she reasoned that the entire thing was most likely a dream. No one else remembered it, either. She was feverish that Christmas, and maybe had a touch of something wild and wonderful. Just the dream of Awnty Awnie was worth it.

But she never saw the drone photo.

Her mom printed it. They returned to Toyland every Christmas and sometimes for the summer for years to come, but Mom never put it on the wall with the other photos.

If she did, Tin would've remembered.

They were at the tower, the five of them looking up and the toys all around. Maybe her mom knew Awnty Awnie's secrets all along, or she believed her stories. That was why she didn't put it up.

It was always a little strange how her mom accepted that Christmas so easily. Even if she didn't have the imagination to see it except in the photo where Pip, Tin, Corey, Oscar and Mom were looking up and waving at the drone.

And the toys were, too.

EPILOGUE

I hear a song that I know.

It's the one about the reindeer. Or is it the one about the sleigh? It's been so long since I've heard a song. It has that feeling, though. And there's no mistaking the evergreen smell and bubbling laughter, the ripping of wrapping paper and shuffling of boxes. Even in the dark, I know what this is.

My favorite time of year.

A child's joy, the merriment, the goodwill... it never gets old. I live for these moments. I was made for them.

You're probably wondering what happened to Pando. Rumor has it, he's on the North Pole. Toys talk, you know. Word spreads. And the legend of Wallace Noel is and always has been one of the biggest stories told throughout toys in the last century.

He found the toymaker's hat and used it.

Pando, it's told, took the metal ball that was now Wallace Noel up to the North Pole. It's hard to believe, I'm sure. But you don't wear an authentic elven hat like that without some permanent effects to your biochemistry. He created quite a mess and a bit of trouble, but nothing that a toy couldn't fix.

Wallace wasn't the toymaker. No, the toymaker is still a mystery, the last I heard. Pando was right about one thing, though: the hat will find the toymaker when it's time.

How did Wallace get a free pass to live with the elven and ride in a sleigh pulled by flying reindeer? I wouldn't exactly call it free. He paid a price. He lost his body, for one. Living in a metal ball has its advantages, I guess, but, from the toy scuttlebutt I hear, he'd rather be in flesh and bone. He is human, after all. But now he's a snowman. There's a bunch of them up there.

He'll figure it out.

But let's be honest, he knew too much. I mean, the hat told him everything—the secrets of the North Pole, the technology of the elven. He had already made a mess. Santa wasn't going to let him stay at Toyland. It's not exactly a happily ever after for him, but it could've been worse.

Much, much.

Pando's search for the toymaker wasn't fruitless. He never found him, of course, but he was something more than a toy. I don't know exactly what he is, but he's the best toy that ever lived.

As far as I'm concerned.

Pando visits Toyland every year. The fat man drops him off and picks him up. What a toy, right? Makes me proud.

Oh, and Gingerman? That's a story for another time.

Right now, my favorite morning has arrived. I can feel the box jostle and hear the paper ripping. The voices out there. I don't recognize them. This is exciting. Then comes the slice of light; the box is pulled open. Colored lights blink.

"What is it, Annabelle?" someone says.

That's when the face looks down at me. Her eyes are big and brown. There's a cute barrette holding her hair back. Her pacifier looks like a candy cane. It's darling, really.

Big, adult hands reach for me and then the world is all around—the Christmas tree, wrapping paper and plates of half-eaten cookies.

"Look how long his arms are," someone says. "And look, his hands stick together."

I don't recognize the adult. I'd remember her even if it was a long time ago. She slaps my Velcro hands together and loops me around Annabelle's neck. She bounces and smiles. The pacifier falls out when she giggles and then—I swear, this is my favorite part—she hugs me.

That's right.

Our true purpose is not to entertain or distract. We're not meant to give a child social status or fill emotional holes. It's to be there when the nights are darkest, when the days are rainy. When you need a friend. We're here to remind you that you matter.

We're the true meaning of Christmas.

"Do you know who gave him to you?" Annabelle's mom says.

And then someone picks us up and hikes Annabelle in the crook of her arm. It's not the mom, but her I recognize. She's older. Much, much older. Her hair is short and gray. Her glasses are giant circles. There's a chain around her neck and a pendant dangling from it.

"His name is Monkeybrain," Annabelle's mom says. "Isn't that funny? Can you say thank you?"

Annabelle pulls out the pacifier. "Thank you, Awnty Tinny."

And then, yes, my favorite part again, the hug. And then Great-aunt Tinny with her big round glasses and short gray hair puts us down, but not before she picks me up, just me, and gives me one last hug.

"Take care of her," she whispers.

LAST PART

NORTH POLE – Pharis Targeenis, 43, guided his 100th expedition to the North Pole. An expert adventurer, Targeenis is known for guiding trekkers into the great white north for the past decade. This past trip, however, was like no other.

He was separated from his party.

"The weather was unexpected," Targeenis said. "Visibility was zero."

Targeenis fell through an open lead and nearly drowned in the icy water of the Arctic Ocean. He shouldn't have survived.

"Someone grabbed me," Targeenis said. "Plain and simple. I thought maybe it was a polar bear. I was wet and, in those conditions, really only had a couple of minutes left."

But it wasn't a bear that pulled him out. Targeenis is reluctant to tell his story. He's aware that hallucinations are quite common in near-death situations. However, he's certain what he saw.

"It was a man," Targeenis said. "He was short and fat, with a very long and bushy beard. I mean, he wasn't wearing a red coat or anything like that, but he was unusual. The whole thing was."

Targeenis's party found him the next day cocooned in an insulated wrap. It wasn't part of the gear anyone had packed, but it saved his life.

No evidence supports his claims. And Targeenis is the first to exclaim how strange it all sounds.

"He was wearing a T-shirt with suspenders," he said. "With two moles over his eye."

Any information regarding someone who matches this description, contact the local authorities.

GINGERMAN: IN SEARCH OF THE TOYMAKER (BOOK 8)

Get the Claus Universe at:
BERTAUSKI.COM/CLAUS

❄

Gingerman: In Search of the Toymaker (Book 8)

CHAPTER 1

"You didn't fix it?"

"It's fine." Dad pointed at the dashboard like there was a gauge pointing to *fine*.

"It's not fine, Henry," Mom said. "What if it breaks down? Here. No reception, no directions." She shook her phone. "What are we going to do?"

Chris watched the trees. The window was icy on his forehead, soothing the nausea that had been stirred up by the never-ending curves in the road. The smell of Mom's cold coffee wasn't helping. He was glad he hadn't eaten breakfast. Or lunch.

"What's this?" Mom said.

The road slanted toward a tunnel. A gate blocked the entrance, steel bars that were once bright yellow now a dull mustard with patches of blue-green lichen. They stopped short. The parking brake wrenched into place.

"Do we have a pass or a code or something?" Mom said.

"We don't have a pass."

"How are we supposed to get through? Is there a guard?"

"There's no one."

"We can't just stop in the middle of the road, Henry."

Mom sounded like an animal in distress. Chris knew what she looked like when she made that sound—lines across her forehead and lips creasing a sharp line above her chin. Yu called it muppet lips.

Dad rolled the window down. Autumn snuck inside the car. Yu tapped Chris's leg.

What's happening? she signed.

We're lost.

She looked through the rear window and quickly spoke with her hands.

"Yu says we missed it," Chris said.

"Missed what?" Mom said.

"There was a guy back there."

It was eerie when his sister did that. She'd slept the entire way, impervious to the asphalt roller coaster. But somehow she saw a guy.

Mom took her seatbelt off. "Honey," she said, signing her words, "what did the guy—what're you doing? We can't back up."

"We can't turn around." Dad threw his arm across the seat. His glasses slid down his nose. Chris couldn't watch.

"How far do we have to—oh!" Mom snapped the seatbelt in place. "Ask your sister how far."

Chris half-opened his eyes. Yu's hands made soft sounds in thick cotton gloves. Chris didn't bother telling his dad what she said. He was already cruising. Mom dug into the vinyl seat like a cat. They coasted back a quarter mile. There was a guy.

"Could use a sign," his dad muttered. "Or a light or an arrow or a—"

"That's enough," Mom said.

The Visitors' Center was built into the side of a mountain. The windows were as black as swamp water. The car's reflection pulled into the empty lot. One of the headlights was out. The guy pointed at an empty parking slot. They were all empty.

The car died into silence. They sat quietly for a moment; then Dad climbed out. He unloaded two duffel bags from the trunk.

This is it? Yu signed.

Chris nodded.

Mom looked over the seat. Her smile was brave. "You ready?"

No. He wasn't. But when did that matter?

"Hello!" Mom turned on her happy voice reserved for strangers and phone calls. "We almost missed you."

Her laugh was shrill and embarrassing. She was nervous—she was always nervous—but this trip was an anxiety thrill ride. Her pills kept her from falling through what she called thin ice. When it cracked, there were dark days below. Sometimes weeks. Chris didn't want that to happen. Not now.

You getting out? Yu signed.

Chris didn't have the strength to pull the handle, even when Dad pointed. As dad-looks went, it wasn't scary. But it was serious. *We drove all this way. Because of you.*

His sister crawled out. Chris was frozen. *Fear is like jumping into a spring-fed stream,* his grandma used to say. *Cold at first. Then fun.*

Sometimes, though, it was just cold.

"There he is." The guy held out his hand. "I'm Kogen. You're Chris." He looked at a clipboard. "Christmas White Blizzard. I don't think I've ever met someone named Christmas before."

"It's a family name," Mom said.

No. It wasn't. She lied when she was nervous. Exaggerations, she called it. Words came out to fill the empty spaces. Christmas was what you named your kid when you were a seventeen-year-old mom who gave birth on Christmas Day. Yuletide was what you named the twin sister.

"Let's go inside. A little brisk for September, yeah?" Kogen pretended to shiver, even though he was wearing a black jacket. The slacks were sharply pressed. Too thin for the weather. Maybe he was cold.

He held the glass door open. A small sculpture watched them from the corner. It was a fat man with a round face and small eyes. The arms were strangely short. It was carved from granite. The belly had been worn smooth for luck. Long locks of hair cascaded over the shoulders, the details finely chiseled.

It was staring at them.

Dad gave a duffel bag to Chris. His dad was tall and skinny, not made for cold. Chris was short, thick and doughy. Built to play offensive line. If he cared about sports. His face was long and his nose a skinny slope that turned pink in the cold.

Someone dressed like Kogen took the duffel bags—the thin black slacks and dark jacket. She threw them on a gold-plated cart, the kind at expensive hotels where tips were expected. Dad didn't reach into his pocket. She didn't seem to care.

Mom announced how warm it was inside. And how lovely the drive was. And how tall Kogen was. And good looking. He smelled good, too. Did he see them drive by? Was he hungry?

It was dim and open inside. Clean. And empty, really. Just a large circular platform behind Kogen and his beautiful teeth. The place felt expensive, like the minimalist décor at an art gallery. There were rooms around the perimeter, little glass library cubicles. A girl about his age was talking to a computer.

"Welcome." Kogen clapped his hands. "This is the Visitors' Center for the—"

"Did you hurt yourself?" Mom said.

"I'm sorry?"

"You look sore. I don't mean it that way, just—" she laughed nervously "—we can sit down if that's better for you."

Kogen stalled. His introduction was thrown off the tracks. Mom could do that. Her mouth was a shotgun loaded with words; her mind a hair trigger. Then he clapped his hip.

"This? No, no. It's fine. Skiing accident." He had a short hitch when he walked. "Gets a little stiff when the weather changes."

"Have you tried ice?"

Yu tugged Mom's sleeve. Dad put his arm around her and nodded. Kogen's introductory smile returned.

"This is the Visitors' Center for the Institute of Creative Mind. You, sir, are the recipient of prestigious acceptance. Congratulations."

Chris looked at his shoes. The rubber was peeling off the toes.

"We're so proud." Mom started again. How the letter came late, they were so excited, they were so sure he didn't get in when the deadline passed, but they still submitted the application because you never know.

Kogen kept eye contact with Chris. It was strange. Not that he was looking at him. It was just Chris was accustomed to his mom taking over conversations, like going to the doctor and her explaining how he felt and the doctor sort of forgetting he was there.

"What's your passion?" Kogen said.

"Cooking," Mom said. "He's a master chef. You should see how he—"

"Cooking? Well, well." He didn't consult the clipboard. "This school has a rich history of some of the most creative minds in the world. For over two hundred years, the Pelznickel family has selected only those with the most potential. You are one of them, Chris."

What family? Yu signed.

"The Pelznickel family." Kogen's sign language was fluid.

Mom covered her chest. "You know how to sign?"

"A little. This is your sister, yeah? Yule Logan Blizzard. Pleasure to meet you." He continued signing.

Yu was often left out of conversations. She was good at reading lips, but when people started talking loudly, it made her uncomfortable. She usually waited for Chris to fill her in.

"The institute is family owned. It was started in 1805 by Lord Kris Pelznickel."

"Did you hear that, hon?" Mom said. "A lord."

"Yes." Kogen chuckled. "He saw the intrinsic value of the creative process, how it is the very backbone of the arts and sciences, the fabric that creates the world around us. Graduates have won Nobel Prizes and Pulitzers. I can attest to the school's brilliance." His smile grew impossibly brighter.

"You went here?" Mom said. "Did you hear that, hon? Kogen went to school here, too."

"And there have been multiple failures," Dad said. "I mean, the dropout rate is, you know." He tipped his head back. "High."

Kogen was ready for it. He said to Chris, "We'll challenge you to discover your true nature." Then he turned his attention to his dad, his tone softer. "But failure is part of the creative process. That said, it is a tough curriculum. And not everyone makes it. You know what they say about omelets."

"You have to break the eggs," Mom said, too cheerfully.

Kogen was strangely comfortable and flawlessly hospitable. But Chris sensed discomfort beneath the veneer. Like old wood with a new coat of paint. He hobbled up three wide steps that led to the circular table. Warm light illuminated his approach.

"Whoa. You see that, hon?"

It was a model of inconceivable detail. Gravel paths crisscrossed a glittering white ground like snowflakes after a cold night. Figurines with painted shoelaces had bookbags as large as rucksacks. The buildings were castles made of chipped rocks with mortar pasted into the seams.

Kogen pointed out the dormitory where Chris would live, the halls where he would take classes, and the cafeteria where he would eat. Of course, there were classes in nutrition and organic gardening, all the tools an aspiring culinary artisan could want.

Each one of the buildings was unique in their blocky style, the walls varying slightly in tones of granite, sandstone and limestone. They were arranged around the tallest building—a castle with toothy steeples that, perhaps in mythology, would keep giants from stepping on them.

"It started there." Kogen saw Chris looking at the castle. "The family's home. They were wealthy, of course, but chose not to spend their lives in the solitude of comfort. They wanted to contribute. To educate. The path to human freedom is paved with other."

"Other?" Dad said.

"Creativity." Kogen smiled. "So they built this campus and for the past two hundred years have operated as one of the most esteemed schools in the world."

"Why is there a wall?" Dad said.

"Privacy, hon," Mom said, shaking her head. The parade was just beginning. Don't call for rain.

The wall, however, was daunting. Even in miniature scale. It looked hand-built, as if each stone had been laboriously lugged into place, and circled the campus, the light casting dark shadows around it.

"The family owns the mountain, Mr. Blizzard. The wall, however, remains from the early days when walls were necessary."

Given how many times he'd given this speech, the answer was lame. Chris could see the symbolism. It was dark outside. But on campus, the light of creativity was bright. But that wouldn't satisfy his dad. Kogen probably knew nothing would. The hard truth about walls was that they were built to keep things out. Or in.

"And it gets cold," Kogen said. "The wall helps break the wind. But you don't mind the cold."

He winked at Chris. Like he knew. He was right. Chris slept with his window cracked in December. His dad kept the house so warm that guests fell asleep. The air conditioner had broken three summers ago, and he refused to fix it. Fans were good enough.

What's wrong with her? Yu pointed.

The girl in the library cubicle had her face in her hands. Her shoulders were quaking. It was soundproof, but Chris imagined her sobbing sounded like wet hiccups.

"It's an adjustment for some." Kogen observed her with what seemed like real compassion. He turned to Chris. "You can write as many letters as you want. But once a month, you can come here to virtually visit your family if you choose to."

If I choose to?

Kogen didn't consult the clipboard. Like he knew Chris might not. Chris spent summers at his grandparents' farm, where he built forts in the trees and stacked stones in the streams. At night, he made supper, and in the morning he'd have breakfast ready with eggs taken from the chickens and greens from the garden.

He hadn't called his parents once during those visits.

"Of course, you'll come to visit." Kogen flashed polished whites at Mom and Dad. "Parents' Day is the week after Christmas. The Visitors' Center will be staged with all of the semester's accomplishments. You'll see how much your little genius has grown."

"Visitors' Center?" Dad said. "You mean here?"

"Hon, the campus is exclusive. But that's all right. Right, honey?" Mom rubbed Chris's shoulder. "You can send pictures."

"I'm sorry. He won't be able to take pictures. Our facilities are proprietary. It was all in the application guidelines. Did you read them?"

"Of course we did. Of course. I just meant, well, the..." Her words trailed off a cliff. She twisted her fingers into a nautical knot. "It'll be nice."

"Parents' Day is a celebration," Kogen said, then signed for Yu, "And there will be presents."

"Presents?" Mom beamed. "Did you hear that, hon? There'll be presents."

Yu deadpanned a nod. It sounded dreadful, coming here over break. Presents might work for a five-year-old. It wouldn't matter. The family cruiser wasn't making it up the mountain in winter.

"There's always presents," Kogen said. "So, questions?"

Of course not. All the questions had been answered in the detailed packets Mom had showed her friends. She just didn't think Chris wouldn't be able to take pictures. It sounded absurd.

"In that case, hand it over." Kogen put out his hand.

Chris knew the deal. It had been explicitly laid out in the guidelines. No electronics of any kind. He could write all the letters he wanted, but no texts. No pictures. *We value the mind uncluttered.*

Chris gave up his phone.

"It'll be stored in the Visitors' Center. Any other electronics? Laptops? Tablets?"

The bags were probably searched. Maybe Kogen was giving him a chance to lie.

"It was wonderful to meet you." Kogen extended his hand. Mom hugged him instead. He laughed, patting her back. Probably wasn't the first time a parent clung to him.

I don't like him, Yu signed quickly.

"I didn't catch that," Kogen said.

"Don't do that." Mom grabbed Yu's hands, her friendly façade crumbling. *Don't embarrass me.* "They just sometimes… never mind. It's very nice to meet you, Kogen."

He paused, thinking, then said, "We'll take good care of him, rest assured. I'm proof good things happen here. Take your time saying goodbye. I'll wait here."

A cubicle lit up on the opposite side of the room from the sobbing girl. Dad had a last few words with Kogen. He tried to sound stern, but he could never find the words or tone to pull it off. It was bad acting, but he tried. He always tried. They'd driven up a mountain in a car that struggled on flat road. No turning back now.

The cubicle smelled like cleaning supplies. There was a table with a monitor. One chair. Mom was shaking. Her hands felt like knobby sticks on his cheek.

"We're so proud of you." She meant it. She would tell everyone at church about him, insert it into conversations at the checkout aisle, post on social media. If there was a gift shop, she would buy one of every item. But she really meant it.

"Do us proud, son." Dad's hug was stiff. A quiver melted the crusty exterior he tried to maintain. A man who pretended he didn't cry at movies thumped his back. "Okay?"

"Okay."

Chris hadn't hugged Yu since they were eight years old when Mom wanted a Christmas picture of them in matching pajamas. Their haircuts were similar back then. Now his hair was long and Yu's head shaved. Who was going to eat all her cereal before she woke up? Who was going to fix his computer?

I know, he signed, answering what Yu had said earlier.

They left him in the cubicle. He was alone with a blank monitor. In that moment, he figured, yeah, he'd come back to call.

Kogen waited.

He had his back turned, in case Chris needed to dry his eyes. It was a kind gesture, but he didn't need to. Chris was nervous, yeah. No, he was scared. The kind of scared that accompanied the unknown, the stranger waiting at the end of a dark tunnel, the ice melt in his legs.

The model of campus was dark again. An electric golf cart was behind it. The seats were buffed to a slick shine. The grainy floorboards clean. A double set of doors opened at the back of the room like mandibles. A dank, musty breeze exhaled.

"Ready to grow?" Kogen said.

Click here to get Gingerman: In Search of the Toymaker (Book 8)

YOU DONATED TO A WORTHY CAUSE!

By purchasing this book, you have donated 10% of the profits is annually donated to Toys for Tots, a non-profit organization is to deliver, through a new toy at Christmas, a message of hope to less fortunate youngsters.

ABOUT THE AUTHOR

My grandpa never graduated high school. He retired from a steel mill in the mid-70s. He was uneducated, but a voracious reader. As a kid, I'd go through his bookshelves of musty paperback novels, pulling Piers Anthony and Isaac Asimov off the shelf and promising to bring them back. I was fascinated by robots that could think and act like people. What happened when they died?

Writing is sort of a thought experiment to explore human nature and possibilities. What makes us human? What is true nature?

I'm also a big fan of plot twists.